CAMPION
Campion, Alexander.
Crime fraiche /

CRIME
FRAÎCHE

Also by Alexander Campion:

THE GRAVE GOURMET

CRIME FRAÎCHE

ALEXANDER CAMPION

KENSINGTON BOOKS
www.kensingtonbooks.com

KENSINGTON BOOKS are published by

Kensington Publishing Corp.
119 West 40th Street
New York, NY 10018

All Kensington titles, imprints and distributed lines are available at special quantity discounts for bulk purchases for sales promotion, premiums, fund-raising, educational or institutional use.

Special book excerpts or customized printings can also be created to fit specific needs. For details, write or phone the office of the Kensington Special Sales Manager: Attn. Special Sales Department. Kensington Publishing Corp., 119 West 40th Street, New York, NY 10018. Phone: 1-800-221-2647.

Kensington and the K logo Reg. U.S. Pat. & TM Off.

Library of Congress Card Catalogue Number: 2011922120

ISBN-13: 978-0-7582-4671-4
ISBN-10: 0-7582-4671-4

First Hardcover Printing: July 2011

10 9 8 7 6 5 4 3 2 1

Printed in the United States of America

Évidemment, encore une fois, pour T.

Acknowledgments

Chantal Croizette Desnoyers—who had the indulgence to put up with me as a husband for twenty-six years—dipped into her reserve of patience once again to share her extensive expertise on mushrooms.

Thanks also to my daughter Charlotte—now a registered nurse—for her tireless patience in answering my endless medical questions just as she was trying to get to sleep after a long night on the ICU floor.

And of course, I owe an enormous debt of gratitude to Sharon Bowers, my ninja agent who, in addition to being a gifted negotiator and invaluable co-conspirator, is without peer at applying the old oil when the machine starts to squeak alarmingly.

CRIME FRAÎCHE

PROLOGUE

*G*oddamn *it. There are too many of them. Way too many.* They had grouped into a tight pack and were heading straight at him. *I'm dead meat,* he said to himself.

Waiting tensely, he teased the edge of the trigger with the tip of his finger, hating himself for the nervous tic, which all by itself could spell disaster. But he couldn't help it. Too much was at stake.

When there were that many, you wanted to blast right into the middle of the flock with both barrels, but you'd miss them all if you did that. What you had to do was get a grip, focus on a single bird, and swing through on it all calm and relaxed.

But he couldn't concentrate. He kept thinking about what a glorious day it had started out to be. His first really fashionable shoot. Driven partridge, the hardest birds to hit. Something most guys never even get to see.

The *comte* himself had poured his coffee when they'd gathered. And a few minutes later he had sloshed some Calvados from his own private reserve into the dregs. To get his juices going, the *comte* had said, slapping him on the back as if he was an old friend. Even his boss, normally so standoffish, had been all over him. Wouldn't be doing that if the sad clown knew even the half of it.

He'd been in seventh heaven, and now he was going to miss them all and be a laughingstock. Being laughed at was the one thing he really couldn't stand.

Far off in the distance the beaters had begun walking slowly across the field. He had seen them tapping the ground with their long sticks. After a few long minutes, the partridge, who had been scurrying invisibly through the stubble, had taken to wing in a dark cloud a hundred yards in front of the beaters, skimming along almost at ground level. When they had reached the base of the hill, they had lifted and gained altitude, closing into a dense formation.

Shots began hesitantly, like the first kernels of corn popping loudly in a metal pot. Then the cadence picked up and birds started falling out of the sky, wings hanging down like little broken toys. But there were still too many for him to find just one to aim at. He jerked his gun right and left, each bird a better target than the last.

He made up his mind and raised his gun resolutely, stepping forward to take his first shot. Inexplicably he was brought up short, as if he had walked into a wall. A wall made of grass. He marveled at the perfection of the individual blades and the iridescence of the green. The color paled. Then he saw nothing.

CHAPTER 1

"So she wants people to think she's what? Dead? Raped? I don't get it," *Brigadier* David Martineau said, lazily twisting a silky auburn lock around his index finger with far more insouciance than was normal for *Police Judiciaire* brigadiers.

Brigadier Isabelle Lemercier rose to the bait and rolled her eyeballs skyward, shaking her head, her rough cropped hair swaying angrily like wheat in a summer storm. "Look, numnuts, wake the fuck up. It's a scam. She's hoping some patsy will get all mushy and take her home and nurse her back to health, right, *Commissaire?*"

"That's the way she works it, Isabelle," Commissaire Capucine Le Tellier said. "She's—"

"In this town people go out of their way to ignore someone lying on the sidewalk. She's gotta be doing something special," David said, glaring at Isabelle.

"She does seem to have a gift," Capucine said with just enough steel in her voice to let her rank be felt. Both the brigadiers sensed they were at the threshold of going too far and straightened up in their chairs. "Apparently, she exudes a defenselessness that attracts people. She's done it three times so far. Once in the Sixth Arrondissement, where two American tourists took her in, then in Neuilly, where a retired senior civil servant befriended her, and now in the Twentieth, where two women, magazine illustrators, cared for her in their apartment."

"And there's bling in this?" David asked.

"Oh, very definitely," Capucine said, unclipping a lethal-looking black Sig service pistol from the small of her back, reclining in her government-issue swivel chair, putting her feet on the scarred top of her desk, and dropping the inch-thick file on her lap. She caught Isabelle admiring her legs and David her shoes, a brand-new pair of Christian Louboutin sling pumps that probably weren't really appropriate for police work, at least not in the Twentieth Arrondissement.

She was well aware this wasn't the tone commissaires were supposed to take with their brigadiers, but they were all on the same side of thirty and these were two of the three street-savvy *flics* who steered her through her first murder case a year before, when she was still a rookie in the *Crim'*, the Police Judiciaire's criminal brigade. In fact, if it weren't for them, she'd probably be back watching the clock as a *lieutenant* in the fiscal fraud squad instead of running her own commissariat.

Beyond the glass wall of her office Capucine could see the third brigadier, Momo Benarouche—Momo to everyone—at his desk in the squad room, glowering at a pile of official forms as blue uniformed officers and unshaven, bejeaned, sneakered plainclothes detectives gave him as wide a birth as they could.

She snapped herself back to the present and tapped the file. "She's doing very well indeed with her con. By the way, our perp has been given a name. With their usual love of high culture, headquarters seems to think she's the archetypal Disney character and is calling her *La Belle au Marché Dormant*—the Sleeping Beauty of the Market."

David and Isabelle snorted derisively. Headquarters, the

Direction Centrale de la Police Judiciaire, was well known for its tragicomic bureaucracy.

"The Americans were both professors of French philology at someplace called Valparaiso University, which, oddly enough, is in Indiana. They'd done an apartment swap for a month and—"

"Why the fuck would anyone who lived in the Sixth Arrondissement of the City of Light want to spend a month in Indiana?" David asked. "Man, things just keep getting weirder and weirder around here."

Capucine smiled at him with the tolerance of a parent for a wayward child. "After three days of tender loving care from these Indiana philologists, the Belle walked off with an illuminated page from a medieval langue d'oïl manuscript they had bought the week before. Apparently, the thing was rare enough for the Bureau of Antiquities to question if they would allow it to be taken out of the country."

Both Isabelle and David pursed their lips in respect. "It's nice their little problem was solved for them," Isabelle said.

"In Neuilly," continued Capucine, reading from the file, "she walked off with a Daumier caricature. The civil servant in question collects them. But this was the only one in his collection that was an original drawing and not a print. It's also worth thousands."

David and Isabelle nodded appreciatively.

"The two magazine illustrators, a couple, apparently"—Capucine paused for a beat while Isabelle looked up sharply—"were robbed of a small Marie Laurencin watercolor portrait of someone called Natalie Clifford Barney. It was the single picture stolen from among at least fifty in their apartment."

"Barney was a great person," Isabelle said, "an American writer who expatriated herself to Paris to become one of the pathfinders of the lesbian movement. I'm sure a portrait of her by Laurencin is worth a bundle."

"*Voilà!*" said David with a broad smile from which any trace of sarcasm had been scrupulously scrubbed. "Finally, the ideal case for our dear Isabelle."

Isabelle's pupils contracted and her face darkened. She punched David in the arm, putting her whole upper body behind the blow, visibly causing him considerable pain.

"In fact, David, I *am* putting Isabelle in charge. This inquiry is just what I'm going to need to support her application for promotion to *brigadier-chef*. And you're going to back her up—without any lip, understood?" Isabelle put her thumb to her nose and wiggled her fingers at David as he massaged his arm. "Here's the file," Capucine said, thumping the dossier on the desk in front of Isabelle. "I'm off for a week's vacation. You can tell me all about your dazzling progress when I get back."

"Where are you going, Commissaire?" Isabelle asked. "Some fabulous island in the Antilles?"

"No such luck. Just to my uncle's house in the country. I'm not sure how it's going to work out. It's the first time I've been down there since I joined the force. He was pretty upset at the time."

"Yeah, I got that, too," David said. "My mother was devastated."

"She had her heart set on you becoming a hairdresser, right?" Isabelle asked.

"My uncle tells everyone I'm a civil servant with the Ministry of the Interior," Capucine said. "I don't know how he's going to react to seeing me as a flic in the flesh."

"Why don't you wear your uniform?" Isabelle asked. "You look fabulous in blue, and all that silver braid would set off your hair."

From the look Capucine gave her, Isabelle knew for sure she had gone too far.

CHAPTER 2

When Capucine arrived at her apartment in the Marais, she found her husband, Alexandre, in his study, sprawled in a decrepit leather club chair, frenetically typing with two fingers on a laptop nestled against the gentle protuberance of his stomach, the stubby remnant of a Havana Partagas Robusto clenched between his teeth, an empty on-the-rocks glass perched precariously on the arm of the chair, and piles of newspapers and magazines heaped in a sloppy bulwark on the floor. As she walked in, he continued to stare fixedly at the screen and lifted one hand, index finger raised, wagging it slowly from left to right in supplication to be allowed to finish his sentence. Alexandre was the senior food critic for *Le Monde,* the grande dame of Paris journalism, and Capucine was well versed in the tensions of deadlines. He typed energetically.

"Voilà," he said, raising his cigar stub high over his head for histrionic effect. " 'Chef Jacques Legras' sole aim appears to be to astonish the bourgeois with vulgar pyrotechnics so far removed from the actual taste of food that what Marcel Pagnol said of aioli—if nothing else, it has the virtue of keeping flies at a distance—can be said of Legras' entire oeuvre.' What do you think of that? One

more enemy of beauty and truth dealt the bloody nose he
so richly deserves."

"What amazes me is that you say these things and these
chefs are still delighted when you go back to their restaurants. If I were Chef Legras, I'd pee in your soup," Capucine said.

"In Legras' case it would be an improvement. Anyway,
he's desperate for his third star and mistakenly feels he'll
never get it unless I bestow my toothy smile on him. So
he'll keep on trying until he goes to the great kitchen in the
sky or learns to cook properly. Think of me as the great
protector of French gastronomy soldiering cheek by jowl
with the great defender of French deontology."

Refusing to be goaded, Capucine rocked the unstable
pile of newspapers on the floor with an elegant toe. "Are
you erecting fortifications as a defense against being carted
off to the country?"

"*Pas du tout.* I'm officially on vacation as of right *now!*"
Alexandre said, tapping the "ENTER" button with élan,
closing the laptop with a snap, and dropping it on top of
the pile of newspapers, which threatened to topple. "Copy
submitted. Pastoral rustification about to begin. A whole
week of communion with the spirits of wood and wind
and you and most especially you!" Alexandre said, standing up and bending his wife backward in a thirties Hollywood kiss.

Gasping for breath, Capucine said, "Don't get any ideas.
We have to pack. You promised. Oncle Aymerie is expecting us for lunch tomorrow. Remember, a quick lunch just
with the family, then dinner with some guests, and then a
pheasant shoot on Sunday. He said it would be his first
time out in a week. I can't imagine why. Normally he shoots
every day in season."

Alexandre said something, but since he was nibbling her
neck, Capucine missed the gist. As she was about to reply,
he swept an arm under her legs and picked her up. Ca-

pucine's mood played a vigorous volley between irritation and attraction. For a half second her muscles prepared a blow that had probably been used by the police since the long-gone days when street savate was the accepted means of dealing with the vicious apaches. But at love-forty she relaxed and melted into Alexandre's arms. Her friends could never believe that her relationship with a husband almost twice her age could be so physical, but it really was.

The next morning Capucine woke at a respectable hour and, not finding her satin robe, went to the kitchen as she was. She deftly made coffee with the Pasquini, a professional machine she had given Alexandre for Christmas years before, which, somehow, he was unable to master, his only failing as a consummate chef. Certain that Alexandre would not rise before eleven, she racked her brains for an excuse to offer Oncle Aymerie for missing his welcoming lunch. She was fully aware that if Alexandre walked in while she was in her current *déshabillé,* they would probably miss dinner as well, but she brooded on, tranquil in the knowledge that it would take an earthquake to rouse him.

This visit to the country had been like a canker in her mouth that she could not resist exploring with her tongue no matter how much the probing hurt. Of the family, Oncle Aymerie, her mother's elder brother—the paterfamilias who had inherited the title, the sixteenth-century château, and the fortune to keep it up—had been the most dismayed at her decision to join the police and the least sympathetic to her explanation that intimate contact with the grit of Paris's streets was essential to her blossoming as a person. As a result, she had not been back to Maulévrier in three years, even though she deeply missed the surrogate childhood home her parents had consigned her to as they departed on their frequent world travels. When Oncle Aymerie had called a few weeks before, she had suddenly felt he might be, maybe, finally ready to attempt a reconciliation. But as she sipped her coffee, her confidence evaporated and she toyed with the idea of picking up the phone and booking tickets for Guadeloupe before it was too late.

Two coffees later her resolve had returned and she heard Alexandre grunting and thumping his way into the bathroom. She beat a hasty retreat, slipped on a pair of jeans and an oversized Breton fisherman's sweater, returned to the kitchen, and had the Pasquini whistling away cheerfully by the time he came in.

"You won the battle but not the war," Capucine said. "We've missed lunch but are going to leave as soon as we've packed. We'll eat on the road."

"Lunch on the road?" Alexandre grimaced. "Poisoned by fast food on the autoroute? Never. That's no way to start a holiday. But don't despair. The good news is that it just so happens that I've been invited to the opening of a new little bistro only a few streets away. We can dart in, have a little something *sur le pouce*—on our thumbs, as they say—before we zip off to Normandy."

Capucine ground her teeth. She knew all about whisking in and out of restaurant openings. Her irises darkened from their normal cerulean to the purple of a stormy sea in midwinter. These physiological changes were not lost on Alexandre, who, with as much dignity as he could muster, trotted off to the bedroom to pack, coffee cup in hand, Capucine close in his wake.

As Alexandre started filling his suitcase, Capucine was again reminded that she had been married to Alexandre little more than two years and that, even though she knew he had extended family vaguely in the country, she had no experience of him *extra-muros*—beyond the walls of Paris. As he made neat piles of his country togs on the bed, she found it hard to imagine he had ever left Paris at all. He unfolded and admired a pair of extraordinarily baggy knickers that she thought might possibly match a disreputable tweed jacket she refused to allow him to wear out-side the apartment.

"What *is* that thing?" she asked.

"The knickers to my shooting suit. Plus fours. They were my father's. He was an excellent shot. Quite famous, really."

"Dear, it's true people do wear knickers shooting, but they haven't worn them as baggy as that for more than fifty years. You're going to look like Tintin. All you'll need is a little white dog."

Alexandre scowled and pulled a battered leather gun case from the back of the closet. He opened it lovingly and fit together an elegantly engraved, if diminutive, shotgun. It might have been made for a child.

"That looks a bit insubstantial," Capucine said.

"It was my mother's," Alexandre said. "Sixteen-gauge, that's what women shot in those days. More ladylike and the shells were cheaper. I had the stock reworked so it would fit me."

"I would have thought it was difficult to bring anything down with something as lightweight as a sixteen-gauge."

"It is. That's why I like it. I'm a terrible shot, and this way I can blame the gun. In any case I avoid shooting reli-giously. It's just as boring as golf, and the noise gives you splitting headaches. Mind you, every now and then you do get a half-decent lunch."

"Oh please, you know you love eating game."

"Up to a point. Unless properly hung and exceptionally well cooked, pheasant is as boring as battery-bred chicken. Mind you, there is an interesting element of Russian rou-lette involved. If you chew too vigorously, you stand a good chance of breaking a tooth on a pellet of shot. Still, there's no point to suffering through all that cold and damp. All you need, as you well know, is a handful of ac-quaintances who are shooting enthusiasts. By the middle of October they blanch at the thought of eating another pheasant and will go to any lengths to get you to accept cartloads of their wretched birds."

The facetious vein was one of Alexandre's favorites, and, once started, he was capable of amusing himself with it for hours on end. Capucine let him run on and packed her own two bags. That done, she eyed her Police Judiciaire issue Sig in its quick-draw holster that fit so neatly into the small of her back and decided there would be no need for it. She took a diminutive Beretta Px4 Storm Type F Subcompact—the official off-duty sidearm—out of the drawer of her night table, eased the slide back to peek into the chamber to make sure there was a cartridge inside, and dropped the toy-sized pistol into the silk compartment in the side of her suitcase. She added in two extra clips and decided that forty rounds of 9-millimeter ammunition was more than enough for anything she was likely to encounter during the next week.

"You're not planning on ridding the region of poachers with all that, I hope."

Capucine was not amused. She elbowed Alexandre painfully in the ribs and said, "If we're going to lunch, let's do it now. Missing dinner as well would be unforgivable."

The "bistro" turned out to be the latest venture of a chef who had already amassed sixteen Michelin stars. He had acquired a venerable restaurant that had existed in the guise of a Lyonnais *bouchon* since the late 1870s, only languishing into oblivion in recent years. The décor had been scrubbed and buffed but apparently left intact. Black-and-white squares in a convoluted mosaic on the floor, white ceramic tiles with hand-painted red-rose friezes on the wall, clusters of bright globe lights descending from the ceiling all contributed to the sensation that Toulouse-Lautrec might hobble in at any moment.

Like all Paris openings, the restaurant was packed with food critics, pals of the chef, and a sprinkling of celebrities. Capucine was amazed when she was presented to

Chef Legras, who had certainly already read Alexandre's scathing review in the morning Internet edition, but who still embraced him warmly and thumped him loudly on the back as if they were close family.

As she knew would happen, they found themselves at a table of honor populated by the cream of the culinary critics. Their group was so much the center of attention that Capucine half thought that she was morally required to scarf up every dish put in front of her with orgasmic grins and groans. The menu seemed to be as unchanged as the décor, an endless list of classic Lyonnais dishes, many unknown to Capucine.

"What on earth is a *tablier de sapeur?* It sounds like the last thing you'd want to eat," Capucine said to Alexandre.

A man across the table, sporting enormous handlebar moustaches, laughed uproariously. "You have to think of those *sapeurs* from the Foreign Legion. You know, the ones with the enormous beards, shiny axes over their shoulders, and long, thick leather aprons. The dish is the *gras-double*—"

"Exactly," the man sitting next to him interrupted. "It's the cow's *panse,* the cheapest and thickest of its four stomachs. That's why it's named after the legionnaire's apron. By far the best tripe of all. Interestingly, the Lyonnais also call it a *bonnet de nid d'abeille*—a bees' nest cap. I've always found the etymology of that term exceedingly curious. . . ."

As the conversation slid off into the subtleties of the culinary linguistics of the Rhône Valley, Capucine shuddered at the idea of eating any tripe, much less the toughest part, then glanced at Alexandre, half suspecting her leg was being pulled. He pursed his lips and raised his eyebrows in confirmation. "There are a number of things on the menu that you'd like a good deal better. Why don't you start with the *Lyonnais Pot de la Cuisinière?* It's a pig and foie gras *confit* that you'll like. Then I'd go for the *pi-*

geonneau en cocotte—you like pigeon. I'm going to start with the Lyonnais charcuterie and then have the truffled *boudin blanc*."

After its brief foray into etymology, the conversation reverted to a subject that was dear to Alexandre's heart: the underlying motivation behind the current trend for well-starred über-chefs to open traditional, relatively inexpensive bistros. Was it a desire to demonstrate their close ties to authenticity, or was it that they could double their margins because of their prestige and add yet another healthy trickle to their immense cash flows?

"The fast food of haute cuisine," one of the wags quipped.

"Don't even say that in jest," Alexandre said with mock seriousness. "We French have created our own infernal version of that particular scourge. At least with American fast food you know you're being poisoned and can act accordingly. It's an honest and straightforward frontal attack—it's appalling, yes, but it's dirt cheap.

"We French are apparently incapable of such forthrightness. We masquerade our fast food as something edible. The pictures on the menu look like the sort of thing you might actually want to put in your mouth. But when it arrives, *mon Dieu!* Take this ghastly Charolais Allô chain, where," Alexandre said, winking broadly at his audience, "save for the infinite indulgence of my peerless wife, I would be suffering perdition at this very moment. You all know what I'm talking about. You see one of them every fifty feet up and down the autoroute. Cheered by the solace of your bladder after your stop, you are deluded into thinking you might be in the presence of something that approximates a traditional steak house, but when their entrecôte arrives, it turns out to be a dog's rawhide bone that's been flavored with Viandox beef extract."

The wag raised his glass. "Here's to the eternal battle between the voluptuary and the vulgarian. May gastronomy prevail over the euro!"

Just as the debate was about to rage, the über-chef in question smilingly approached the table, brandishing a bottle of a liqueur of a rarity the targeted patrons of his bistro could only dream of.

"You're all talking about me, I hope," he said with a wry smile.

Capucine knew full well that a lively session of the group's pastime of choice—fencing with polemics—was about to begin and would last until they all got hungry again and trooped off to dinner at a competitor's restaurant. The point of no return was at hand. Capucine kicked Alexandre under the table with more force than was really required—hard enough to alarm him in any case. She jerked her head toward the door and started to walk out. He followed meekly, limping slightly. Behind her she could hear the level of hilarity rising like an incoming tide.

CHAPTER 3

Even though Maulévrier was the darling of cocktail-table architecture books—apparently it was a perfect bijou example of châteaux of the late feudal period—Capucine always found it embarrassingly scruffy, in the same way twelve-year-olds invariably find their parents mortifying.

She skidded her little Clio to a stop at the end of the long driveway bound by ancient, tall-trunked poplars to allow Alexandre a view of the structure, a disparate jumble of styles running from a brick tower that over half a millennium had mellowed to the precise shade of a lightly roasted partridge—all that remained of the fifteenth-century feudal keep—to a bright salmon and white façade dripping with Victorian prettification. The building looked out on the remains of the ward, now a neglected graveled yard bordered by a stone parapet that kept out the waters of the algae-filled canal that had once served as the moat. This architectural anomaly was the work of an earlier generation who had decided that the risk of the Saracen invasion was finally sufficiently remote to allow tearing down the fortified walls, thus enabling the inhabitants to eat lunch without the aid of candles. Behind sprawled the extensive commons, historically used to house whole herds of livestock but now useless labyrinthine structures with no purpose other than to satisfy their voracious appetites for new roofing and to provide the family children a vast theater for their illicit adventures. As testimony to their financial gluttony, a long blue tarpaulin stretched out over one of the numerous roofs.

"This is exactly the sort of place no man should be without, always assuming, of course, that he doesn't have to pay the bills," Alexandre said.

"My father's sentiments exactly."

Capucine abandoned the car in front of the main entrance, a capital offense in her uncle's canon, rushed up the steps, and pushed open the carved oak portal. "Hurry up. We're fifteen minutes late already."

"Tush. You'd be lost without a dramatic entrance," Alexandre said, his comment drowned in the turbulence of Capucine's rush.

She dragged him across a large marble hall replete with the inevitable stern-faced ancestors receding into gilt-framed dun mists and burst into a cheerful library entirely appropriate for the set of an English cozy mystery film.

"Capucine, *enfin*—at last!" said a venerable, rosy-cheeked gentleman in particularly well-patinated tweeds. An awkward pause lasted two slow beats, until he took her in his arms and said, "*Bienvenue, ma chérie*. Welcome home."

"Alexandre!" Oncle Aymerie said, grasping Alexandre's hand in a warm two-handed clasp. "The last time I saw you was at your wedding."

"And hasn't he grown so?" said an aquiline young man—superbly dressed in a blue blazer with a patterned pink Hermès silk square drooping with studied negligence from its breast pocket—while patting Alexandre on the tummy. He had a catlike look, superciliously facetious yet somehow all-knowing.

Oncle Aymerie was horrified. "*Fils,* you promised to be on your best behavior."

"*Mon oncle,* he's just teasing. They've become close friends," Capucine said. "Ever since Jacques helped me out on a case a year ago, he's been an inseparable member of our little household."

Oncle Aymerie was clearly upset at the mention of cases, and in the silence Capucine thought she could hear Alexandre's teeth grinding. A perfect left and right in the tact department, Capucine sighed to herself. A bird down with each barrel. She simply could not understand why Alexandre was so jealous of Jacques, the most favorite of her cousins. They had grown up as brother and sister, and now that he was some sort of mover and shaker in the DGSE—France's secret service—they even shared a professional bond of sorts. So he liked to grope her a little; he always had; that was just his style; it didn't mean anything; certainly nothing anyone could resent.

In a heroically chivalrous attempt to restore the evening to an even keel, Oncle Aymerie led Capucine and Alexandre around the room, introducing the other dinner guests.

"We're just picnicking tonight. Now that your *Tante* Aymone is gone, I have no appetite for these endless elaborate dinners," he whispered conspiratorially to Capucine. "I do hope dear Alexandre won't be too disappointed." He patted the back of Capucine's hand, as if it were she who was doddering.

"Now, this is my great friend Loïc Vienneau," he said to Alexandre. "His family has lived in the village since *le roi* Guillaume had the curious idea of leaving Normandy to conquer England. And, of course, he is the *propriétaire* of the *élevage* that produces the best beef in France."

With cocktail party bonhomie Alexandre shook Vienneau's hand and said, "I believe we met once a few years back at the Salon Agricole in Paris. You had demonstrated your expertise with an extremely convincing presentation of the superiority of Charolais beef over Limousin."

Vienneau smiled modestly. "You're too kind. I can't tell you how nervous I was that day. I absolutely hate speaking in public."

Oncle Aymerie forged on valiantly. "And this is Monsieur Henri Bellanger, a Parisian investment banker, who is spending a week with the Vienneaus for the shooting and who came along with them to dinner." Capucine sensed that Oncle Aymerie was less than thrilled at the idea of Bellanger's presence at his dinner table. While Jacques came across as being endearingly foppish, Bellanger was irritatingly overdressed. His clothes were too perfect for the occasion, too new, too costly. On top of it all, he exuded a miasma of new-moneyed self-assurance.

"Are you as keen on *la chasse* as everyone else in the village?" Capucine asked. At the mention of the word *chasse* the temperature of the room seemed to drop a few degrees.

"I don't shoot as much as I'd like to, just enough to keep my marksmanship up to my standard," he replied with a slick smile. Capucine could understand her uncle's reaction. He had a quality that strongly invited a bitch slap.

"And this," continued Oncle Aymerie hastily, "is Marie-Christine Vienneau." Alexandre was visibly moved by the charms of a woman who even in her forties was still a classic French beauty with a warm, broad smile, dense, dark blond hair framing her pale face, and cobalt blue eyes of infinite depth. He bowed deeply and lifted her hand for a *baisemain,* a hand kiss of a subtlety that now existed only in cape and sword movies and deep in the French countryside. Her husband scowled.

At that instant, Gauvin, Oncle Aymerie's aged *majordome,* shuffled into the room in a high-collared white jacket so severely starched, his wattles drooped over the rigid neckband, and droned in a stentorian voice, "*Madame la Comtesse est servie.*"

Capucine started, wild-eyed. For half an instant she thought her aunt might have been somehow miraculously resurrected or that inexplicably she might have missed Oncle Aymerie's remarriage. Alexandre took her by the elbow and whispered in her ear, "It's you, you ninny. You may think of yourself as only hard-nosed Commissaire Le Tellier, but you're also aristocratic Comtesse Capucine de Huguelet, wife of the charming and urbane Comte Alexandre Edouard d'Arbaumont de Huguelet, aka me. This title stuff only gets a snicker in Paris, but it's obviously quite dear to your uncle's man." Capucine repressed the knowledge of her title, which in any case she viewed as only a technicality. Her nightmare was to be nicknamed *Madame la Comtesse* by her officers. That one she would never live down.

The guests rose and Jacques sidled up to Capucine. "May I have the pleasure of escorting Madame la Comtesse to the table?" he asked. As the procession started toward the dining room, his fingers nervously scuttled up and down her back. At first she thought he was feeling around for her weapon, and then, too late, she remembered their childhood. In a very well-practiced gesture he pinched open the clasp of her brassiere, letting her heavy breasts fall free. She kicked herself mentally. Jacques had been doing this ever since she had been given her first training bra. She should know he was never going to grow up.

"It's the animal lover in me," he whispered in her ear. "I hate to see such lovely bouncy bunnies caged up." Jacques's fatuous smirk was punctuated by his other trademark, a high-pitched, extremely loud, braying laugh, which brought all conversation in the room to a halt. This time it wasn't her imagination; she really could hear teeth grinding, but she wasn't sure if it was Alexandre, who followed behind with Marie-Christine on his arm, or Vienneau, who had taken up the rearguard.

The dinner began uneventfully. Gauvin staggered in and

out of the sad old room with its damp-stained, ancient, hand-painted wallpaper, bearing and removing chipped Limoges bowls sloshing with indifferent root vegetable soup and crystal decanters of rare Bordeaux so old it was brick colored and watery tasting.

Finally Gauvin teetered in with an enormous chased silver platter.

"I'm a little embarrassed," said Oncle Aymerie with a laugh. "We're having pheasant. I know those of us from the country already can't stand the sight of them, even though we're only five weeks into the season, but I think we owe it to our Parisians, who are not as fortunate as we are and expect pheasant when they come to us." There was a titter of polite laughter, followed by an awkward silence.

Oncle Aymerie carried on valiantly. "Odile has made her famous *faisan à la Normande*. She braises it in cider and adds apples at the end. The secret, of course, is the sauce she makes with the juice of the pheasant, a dash of crème fraîche, and a few good tots of Calvados."

"The real secret," Jacques said in a stage whisper that carried the length of the table, "is the Petit Suisse suppository she applies to the poor bird just before plunking it in the oven."

Oncle Aymerie fired an angry look at his son, but it passed unnoticed.

"When you get right down to it," Jacques continued, "le Petit Suisse is Normandy's most glorious cheese, even if it's made for children and you can only buy it in supermarkets."

Oncle Aymerie glared as if firing a cannonade.

Alexandre, who had been very well trained by his parents, jumped into the breach. "Pheasant is a great luxury for Parisians," he said, sincerely admiring the platter of plump birds laid out on a bed of rich sauce. "Shooting is one of the great benefits of country living. What a blessing to have one's bag filled with every known species," he said with a clubman's comfortable chuckle.

Stunned that his anodyne comment was greeted with glacial silence, he queried Capucine with a brow-wrinkled glance, but she answered back in tacit husband-wife telegraphy that she had no clue either.

"I'm guessing that it's a standard technique for food critics to establish a baseline by putting their foot in their mouths before eating," Jacques said with his piercing falsetto laugh. "It must be one of these tricks of the métier, you know, like film directors looking at things through that odd little rectangle they make with their fingers," he said, illustrating the gesture.

Vienneau attempted to come to the rescue. "There was a tragic accident last weekend and—" He stopped, completely at a loss for words.

"Yes," Oncle Aymerie said. "On the first drive. Chap called Philippe Gerlier. Poor man died. Actually, he worked for Vienneau. Important job, apparently. These things happen, of course, but it was still a catastrophe." He made a brusque gesture at Gauvin to fill his wineglass. A sense of embarrassment settled over the table like a damp fog. Oncle Aymerie downed the wine in a single go. Alexandre winced. With some difficulty he had just identified it as a 1966 Clos des Jacobins.

"Good Lord," he said. It was not clear to Capucine if the comment was directed at the desecration of a noble wine or the tragic death.

"It was a partridge drive," Oncle Aymerie said. "The guns were stationed at the top of a hill in a semicircle and the birds started up the incline a bit low but they quickly gained altitude. Somehow—it's really not clear to me exactly what happened—this man Gerlier was hit in the chest. I suppose someone must have fired very carelessly from one of the ends of the line. He died instantly."

Gauvin, at the ready, anticipated Oncle Aymerie's authoritarian finger wave and filled his glass unprompted. It was drained instantly.

"Of course, one can only blame oneself," Oncle Aymerie said.

"Capucine," Marie-Christine asked as if she were addressing an expert, "aren't hunting accidents very common?"

Capucine beamed inwardly at having her vocation so openly acknowledged, nodded sagely, and tactfully refrained from adding that the police believed a good number of hunting accidents were actually intentional. After all, it took some doing to kill someone with a shotgun without forethought.

"You see, Monsieur le Comte! Capucine has just confirmed that these accidents happen all the time. There's no need to blame yourself," Marie-Christine said.

To Alexandre's visible horror, Oncle Aymerie downed yet another glass of wine, looking particularly morose. Capucine wondered if his gloom was due to the accident or the fact that her status as a police officer was now taken as a given.

"Gerlier was my general manager and a great friend," Vienneau said. "It's a huge loss, not only personal but also professional. He was brilliant at looking after the day-to-day management of the élevage."

There was another awkward silence.

"That must put quite a burden on you," Alexandre said. "You have quite a responsibility. No Paris establishment that aspires to haute cuisine would serve anything other than Charolais Vienneau. You've established the benchmark. Is it due to your proprietary breed?"

The prospect of a boring exegesis on the raising of steers burst the oppressive lid of tension, and the table fractured into individual conversations. No one other than Alexandre listened to Vienneau's answer.

"Oh, it's nothing as sophisticated at that," Vienneau

said with a disarming smile. "I simply apply know-how that's been in the family for generations. And, of course, there's a lot of perspiration involved," he said with a self-deprecating laugh.

"You can say what you will," said Bellanger, "but the élevage could be far better developed by a global concern with access to substantial capital. As Alexandre says, if he will permit me to call him by his first name, this is a world-class brand and you're wasting its franchise with so little flow-through. You have to think of your business potential, your patrimony, your family."

Vienneau's face hardened. "*Mon cher* Bellanger," he said almost rudely, "when we met in Paris, I made it quite clear to you that I would never sell my élevage. You told me you wanted to have a look at the ranch to use it as a comparison for some deal or other you were cooking up, and I was happy to have you down here for that and to invite you for a little shooting. But don't even try to tempt me to sell out, because that will never happen. Have I made that perfectly clear?"

With more diplomatic skill than Capucine would have ever thought she possessed, Marie-Christine calmed the crisis. She smiled a slightly bored, wifely smile at her husband. "Darling, why don't you invite Alexandre—and Capucine, too, of course—to visit the élevage? If they could come on Monday, the day after tomorrow's shoot, I could be there, too, and we could make a party of it. Wouldn't that be fun?" As an afterthought she added, "Monsieur Bellanger would come along as well, naturally. We wouldn't want to leave him out, now would we?"

They stayed at the table happily for two more hours. In the end, the only one who didn't enjoy himself was Oncle Aymerie, who played with his food and excused himself the moment the guests moved to the salon for coffee and liqueurs.

CHAPTER 4

Capucine hung on for dear life. The back of the ancient Renault Estafette van had been stripped to a bare minimum decades before; all that was left were homemade wooden benches screwed in to either side of the back and three handrails welded into the roof. In the front seat, Emilien, Oncle Aymerie's gamekeeper, a thick Gauloises Caporal glued to the corner of his mouth, drove erratically over the bumpy dirt road with the firm conviction that the pedals functioned only when fully depressed.

"So, mon oncle," Capucine shouted over the rattling din, "tell me about today's shoot."

"He can't hear you, *mam'selle*," Emilien said, turning around stiffly to address her, his face made cheerfully rosy by a latticework of bright red capillaries, the product of an abiding love of Calvados. "We're doing the Sinner's Wood, you know, the big wood in the southeast. We haven't been there since opening day. Bound to be full of birds. Your shoulder's going to be aching tonight," he said, laughing the gurgling chuckle of an inveterate smoker of *tabac brun*.

When the van shuddered to a stop, Oncle Aymerie jumped down, clipboard under his arm, with the energy of a Montgomery about to deploy his troops at the battle of El Alamein, and took sight of his terrain. He stared bleakly at Alexandre in his enormous plus fours, contemplated Capucine in her trim khaki corduroy hunting suit and loden cape draped over her shoulders, and consulted his clipboard. "I'm posting you and Alexandre together. That way he can keep you company and you can let him take the occasional shot if he gets bored," he said with command briskness and strode briskly off.

Alexandre sighed audibly with relief.

Within half an hour, Capucine and Alexandre were at their station on the line, which ran down the length of a hundred-foot-wide swath cut into the wood. Alexandre was precariously perched on a shooting stick, one of those diabolical English devices that start out looking like canes but whose handles unfold into skimpy leather seats. A small pile of distressed shooting luggage—cartridge case, gun covers, ill-defined leather bags—staked their territorial claim. A hundred feet to their left the Vienneaus formed a similar tableau, Marie-Christine sitting primly on her shooting stick while Vienneau jangled tensely. A hundred feet to their left Henri Bellanger stared lustfully at the forest with the intensity of a pig expecting a feed of potato peels. He was weighed down by an exceptionally heavy-looking skeet gun with superimposed barrels.

"I wonder if he got that cannon at a pawnshop," Alexandre said under his breath. "You know, there's something really not quite right about that citizen. Seems more like a used car salesman than an investment banker."

"Do you think he's even half the shot he would have us believe?" Capucine asked absently, fingering the shotgun shells in the leather bag that hung from her shoulder.

The sound of the beaters' gentle tapping on the trees became audible. The idea was to dose the noise level carefully to encourage the birds to run away from the beaters but not to panic them into flying off in all directions prematurely. That way when they reached the edge of the wood, they would have no alternative but to fly up over the line of guns. Capucine lifted her gun to port position across her chest.

There was a metallic whir like a small electrical appliance. A pheasant lifted almost straight up from the wood, rising steeply over Bellanger's position. As mechanically as an automaton, he raised his heavy gun, fired once, and lowered it instantly. The action was so rapid it looked like a circus trick. The bird retracted into a small ball and fell like a stone, hitting the ground with a slight bounce.

"Does that answer your question?" Alexandre asked.

The wood erupted with pheasants. Capucine fired incessantly until the barrel of her gun became too hot to touch and her shoulder began to throb. She cursed herself. She had spent so much time holding her breath, pointing, and squeezing on the pistol range that she had lost the bird shooters' golf-stroke rhythm. All at once, it was over. The beaters emerged from the wood, smiling, most with motley mongrels held by frayed bits of old rope. They walked straight through the line of guns and began the search for fallen birds in the wood behind.

Capucine seemed crestfallen. "I think I only got two. Three at the most. But, *bon sang,* it felt good."

The next two drives were repetitions of the first. Bellanger became a whispered cause célèbre. He showed no enthusiasm, nor even any real interest for shooting, yet every time his gun went up, a bird fell out of the sky. He made no friends that morning.

Alexandre's level of boredom grew exponentially. As Capucine's rhythm returned, she became an increasingly effective shot, totally absorbed, and relegated Alexandre to the role of a fixture propped up on his stick, a character she well knew he was not likely to play for long.

Just when Capucine thought Alexandre might be on the verge of something rash, the ancient Estafette puttered up with lunch. Folding tables were laid end to end and decked out with plates of charcuterie and cheese, bottles of red wine, carafes of ubiquitous Calvados. Beaters and guns congregated at opposite ends of the long counter, leaving an empty no-man's-land in the middle. As narrow-necked bottles of Touraine circulated, the jubilation of both groups escalated measurably to the background theme music of the pack of dogs running back and forth under the table with happy abandon, wrestling joyously while foraging for table scraps.

Alexandre smiled beatifically at a monstrously thick sandwich spilling over with cooked country ham and Livarot cheese pungent with the odor of the barnyard. "When all is said and done," he said, "haute cuisine is nothing more than an imitation of moments like this."

Faithful to the habits of her childhood, Capucine gravitated to the beater end of the table. Even though she recognized none, she was recognized by all and greeted warmly with a *ma p'tite 'demoiselle Capucine,* as if she were still a child. An old man braced an enormous loaf of *pain de campagne* against his chest and cut slices with his pocketknife. More powerful than even Proust's tasteless madeleines, the sight of the knife brought back the *paysans* of her childhood, who would announce the start of the family meal by clacking their knives open and placing them by their bowls and who would order the return to work by snapping them shut. She felt an irresistible tug to return to her childhood and walk a drive with the beaters.

Abandoning Alexandre to join the Vienneaus, Capucine climbed into the Estafette, hoping that Alexandre's flirting with Marie-Christine would not overly put Vienneau off his rhythm. Above the rattling of the van the beaters gossiped excitedly in an all but impenetrable country patois, apparently oblivious to Capucine's presence. The gist seemed to be that death was very much the subject of the day. It would appear that the House of Maulévrier was jinxed and a long string of fatalities was just beginning.

A venerable old man with a long white beard and a poncho made from a sheet of oilskin with a hole cut for the head and held to his waist with a piece of old rope caressed his dog, a highly mongrelized little black-and-white spaniel. "You lads don' know nuthin'. Don't got nuthin' to do with Monsieur le Comte. It's the élevage what's jinxed. Things just ain't right there. Everyone knows that. Those steers are cattle of the devil himself. An' the punishment's just a-comin' on now. An' it's going to get worse, much worse."

The van jerked to a stop and the beaters clattered out, followed by Capucine. The head beater organized them in a line and said to Capucine, "'Demoiselle Capucine, you stay next to me, right here in the middle. That way you'll be there to shoot any birds that go off the wrong way." In a minute they heard the distant triple note of Oncle Aymerie's horn and set off, dogs whining and straining but held fast on their rope leashes, sticks tapping, quiet imprecations of "*Allez là-dedans. Allez.*"

Twenty uneventful minutes later, still several hundred feet from the line of guns, they heard the popping of shots as the first birds took off. The beaters changed their rhythm, speeding up, yelling loudly, and flailing energetically with their sticks, seeking to create an even greater irritant for the birds than the din of the guns.

The beater next to Capucine—the oracular old man with the tarpaulin poncho—clutched his face and let out a cry. Blood flowed freely through his fingers and down his chest. She held him by the arm as the other beaters went on. His spaniel yanked on his rope once or twice but then realized his master's distress and sat down in front of him, looking worried and keening almost inaudibly. Capucine pulled the man's fingers away from his face and mopped up as much blood as she could with her handkerchief. In a few minutes the blood flow dwindled but his face began to swell alarmingly. The man muttered over and over, "I told them, but they didn't listen. I told them . . ."

The policewoman in Capucine took over. She led the beater out into the clearing, entrusted the dog to one of his pals, commandeered Vienneau's top-of-the-line Peugeot 607, and designated Alexandre as driver. At the car she cajoled her ward—intimidated by the luxury of the leather seats—into the back and instructed Alexandre to drive to town.

The *pharmacie* was the only option as there was no doctor in the village. The pharmacist, Monsieur Homais, a grimly serious-looking man in his early sixties, examined the beater's wounds with theatrical concentration.

"If this keeps up, I'm going to ask Monsieur le Comte for a season contract."

Capucine smiled at the joke but couldn't help remembering Oncle Aymerie's dismay at yet another bloody accident on the heels of a fatality.

"You treated Philippe Gerlier?" Capucine asked.

"Madame, even I cannot treat the deceased. He was indeed brought to me, but I could do no more than pronounce his condition." He produced an oversized magnifying glass and continued his examination, holding the tip of the man's chin with two fingers to rotate his face left and right as was needed.

"These cases are usually a waste of my time. The shot is invariably in the epidermis, where it will work its way out. Even if a pellet made its way under the skin, that would only be dangerous if it found its way into an artery, and there's nothing I could do about that." He laughed virtuously, daubing a vile-looking yellow antiseptic on the wounds. "Anyhow, Monsieur Henri here only has eleven pellets in his epidermis. They'll hurt like blazes for a week or two and then start to pop out when he shaves. It's not the first time it's happened to you, eh, Henri?" he said, addressing the beater in the familiar *tu*.

Capucine was always horrified at the callousness of country life. Two of the pellets were less than an inch from the man's eyes. She wondered if Homais would have been so cheerful if he had been blinded.

Even Henri agreed that he was too woozy to return to the shoot and reluctantly accepted to be driven home to be entrusted to his wife.

"I wonder," Alexandre mused, "if that pharmacist worries about the risk of practicing medicine without a license. Particularly in front of a flic. One reads that that sort of thing is the nemesis of his breed."

"What an odd thing for you to be thinking about," Capucine said.

"You know, of course," said Alexandre, "that it was none other than the good Monsieur Bellanger who did the damage."

"How can you be so sure?"

"We were posted next to him. As I was knocking birds out of the sky right and left, I noticed that a pheasant had walked out of the wood. Poor thing seemed to think that hoofing it was the safest course of action. But when he reached the clearing and saw all the hullabaloo, he changed his mind and took to wing. Bellanger, apparently, is not one to look a gift horse in the mouth and fired when the bird was barely at head height. I heard the beater's shout just after Bellanger's shot went off. Vienneau explained to me that in sporting circles shooting birds that are not really flying is not the done thing at all, but in Bellanger's defense the bird actually had both feet off the ground."

CHAPTER 5

The next day, well aware that she had exhausted Alexandre's patience with Nimrod's pursuits, Capucine asked Odile to prepare a picnic basket, put it in the back of the Clio, and drove Alexandre to the forest for a day of mushrooming. Capucine had never quite believed it, but according to him, Alexandre was a rabid mycologist, apparently happiest when rooting for rare mushrooms in dense cover. Many was the time she had seen him in paroxysms of delight over some fungal treasure he had uncovered in a Paris market, but she had yet to observe him *à l'œuvre* in the great outdoors. She had consulted Emilien, the gamekeeper, about the most promising spots in the forest. Clearly a mushroomer himself, he had hemmed and hawed and defended his secrets, but eventually his feudal spirit won out and he admitted he might reveal one or two of his pet locations if Capucine swore her eternal silence.

The morning was an idyll. It was a perfect autumn day, almost too warm once the sun toasted off the chilly snap. Alexandre grubbed in the ground cover on his hands and knees as happily as a little boy. It turned out he really was as familiar with the inhabitants of the undergrowth as she was with the denizens above ground. Normally chronically impatient, he seemed delighted to poke around endlessly. Within an hour Alexandre's irritation at being deprived of his beloved Paris was long gone and he had reverted to his former self, telling stories that she had never heard, as bubbly as if he had been sitting in a Paris café.

All of a sudden he exclaimed, "*Langue de bœuf!*" and held up a disgusting fungus that did look exactly like a cow's oxblood-red tongue. A few minutes later it was "*tricholome de la Saint-Georges*" and then "*pleurottes,*" followed by "*pieds de mouton.*" The basket was nearly full. They walked down a lane, swinging their clasped hands. Capucine felt a surge of romantic ecstasy as saccharine as a greeting card. They arrived at a large clearing bathed in sunlight. Capucine began looking for a spot for their picnic.

"*Arrête!*" cried Alexandre. Capucine froze. "You're about to crush a whole bunch of *agarics des jachères.* I don't think I've ever seen so many in one spot." Lunch waited as each mushroom was separated from its base with surgical care.

Eventually Capucine managed to spread the blanket and remove the napkin that had been secured to the top of the luncheon basket with kitchen twine. It contained a huge hunk of *pain de campagne,* an abundance of pâté and rillettes, and an exceptionally creamy Camembert, each wrapped in crinkly waxed paper. There were two bottles of cider that were opened by twisting off the wire and popping the cork, just like champagne. For dessert, Odile had provided two tablets of chocolate—one with nuts, the other without—to be followed by a thermos of strong coffee and, inevitably, a small decanter of Calvados.

Capucine snuggled into Alexandre's side and relaxed so completely she felt her shoulders fall away from her neck. It was appalling how tense Paris made her. Alexandre's arm draped over her shoulder as comfortably as a well-loved cashmere shawl. He kissed her gently; she responded; he kissed her more ardently; she moved her body even closer to his; he responded even more passionately. She knew full well where they were headed. And why not? They were a million miles from anywhere. There was certainly no one to see.

The situation progressed apace. And continued to progress. A young deer, a buck with small antlers culminating in two little points like serving forks, bounded across the clearing with broad leaping strides. Alexandre nuzzled Capucine's neck. "I was just thinking that with your luscious breasts and dainty feet you look like you've come straight out of one of Fragonard's rustio-erotic scenes, and that joyous little deer completes the picture."

Capucine put her index against his lips.

"Shhhh. He's not joyous. He's trying to escape."

The sound of hounds baying angrily rose in a crescendo, and thirty or so large black, tan, and white dogs loped across the clearing, howling a deafening caterwaul.

They were followed by a troop of splendidly tailored horsemen in bright green seventeenth-century outfits, complete with short swords and boots rising over their knees, looking for all the world like escapees from some Hollywood film set. One of the riders smiled at Capucine and bowed deeply from his saddle. Capucine felt her cheeks burning in a deep blush. She tried to hide her open blouse and undone bra by dropping behind the ferns but succeeded only in falling backward into a depression and waving a shapely foot at the passing hunt.

"Good Lord, what a spectacle!" Alexandre said, getting up.

Capucine, still flustered and red cheeked, pulled Alexandre back and dug as deeply as she could into the undergrowth. "Get down. There's more to come."

As promised, a procession of bent heads could be seen traversing spectrally over the ferns, moving forward, ghost-like and soundless, with no bobbing motion at all.

"It's the bicycle followers. As soon as they've gone by, we'll get out of here," Capucine said.

As they escaped down the lane, Capucine somehow felt she was being driven out of the forest by a hostile dinosaur released from the distant past. The hunt had been her passion as a child, but now it felt alien, an anachronistic ogre with a thousand eyes searching for her secrets, probing out her faults. As she plodded down the path, she sought Alexandre's hand, unsure if they were lost orphans or Adam and Eve cast out of Paradise. She told herself she really should avoid Calvados at lunch.

A burst of horns warbled through the wood. Alexandre looked at her inquiringly.

"They tell each other what's happening with the horns. That's the *hourvari*. It means the deer has pulled one of its tricks to confuse the hunt and they're stuck. Usually, they take the hounds back to the point where the scent was strong and see if they can figure it out from there. For everyone not on a horse, it's a time-out."

Farther down the lane they came across a lively alfresco cocktail party. Cars were pulled up haphazardly with trunks open, while people in dark green loden or Barbours milled around with glasses, gesticulating with long sandwiches made from baguettes and the riches of the *terroir*. The atmosphere was even more aggressively jovial than an art gallery opening.

Capucine was far less than pleased at the idea of running the gauntlet between the parked cars. The bubble of her bucolic contentment had already been rudely popped, and now she was going to be subjected to one of those horrible country moments when people she had no memory of would know all there was to know about her. Perfect strangers would tell her how much she had grown and what a pretty little woman she had become. She felt like screaming. Miraculously, Alexandre saved the day.

"You old dog!" a voice rang out. Alexandre replied with the exuberant whoop he reserved for his best cronies. His interlocutor was dressed in the standard getup of hunt followers, loden overcoat, corduroy britches buckled just below the knee, and muddy green Wellington boots. What set him apart was an entirely incongruous flowing white beard and a brightly colored silk kerchief tied around his neck. The general effect was of a wild man of the mountain in borrowed clothes.

The two embraced warmly with loud back thumping. The newfound friend held Alexandre at arm's length and exclaimed, "You, here of all places! Drink this immediately. It's something I'll bet you don't get every day. A true Domfrontais Calvados, one-third pear brandy and two-thirds Calvados."

Appreciatively sipping his Domfrontais, Alexandre introduced his long-lost friend to Capucine. He was an artist who specialized in etchings and oils of hunt scenes.

"I'd heard you'd married, but I didn't believe it. But now that I am confronted by the plenitude of madame's pulchritude, the scales fall from my eyes," the artist said, bowing from the waist and performing a perfectly executed *baisemain.*

After three tiny silver *timbales* of the Domfrontais—which struck Capucine as packing even more of a punch than regular Calvados—they heard the warble of the horns again.

The *"bien aller!"* An excited ripple went through the crowd. This time it was the artist who explained to Alexandre, "They're off. The hounds have found again. Time to get going." Cars were started, baskets were thrown pell-mell into trunks, and the crowd moved off in an excited procession, leaving a faint gray haze of exhaust fumes.

For the second day in a row, the afternoon ended at the Pharmacie Homais. This time it was for another sacred duty of every French pharmacist: supreme arbiter of mushrooms. Homais carefully spread Alexandre's harvest on a table and picked through them one by one until he finally wrinkled his nose, put one aside, and studiously washed his hands with great thoroughness.

"*Amanite vireuse,*" he said as solemnly as an oncologist announcing a particularly pernicious form of cancer. "Not quite as lethal as its cousin, *Amanite phalloïd,* but it will definitely do the job. Mind you, it looks almost exactly like an *Agaricus silvicola,* which is what all of these are," he said, pushing a number of mushrooms into a pile. "Even a very experienced collector could easily have been fooled. Everything else in your basket is guaranteed to be perfectly healthy."

Capucine looked very closely at the poisonous mushroom isolated at the edge of the desk and could see no difference whatsoever from its "guaranteed" brethren.

"I wrote an article about this particular killer just last year," Homais continued, puffing out his chest. "Even though I live in the remote countryside, I'm the official correspondent on mushrooms for the biggest newspaper in Rouen."

"The *Fanal?*" Alexandre asked with a wry smile.

Homais looked puzzled. "The *Paris-Normandie,* of course," he said. "I've never even heard of a paper called the *Fanal.*"

CHAPTER 6

Capucine hadn't been to the Elevage Vienneau since she was a child. At first she thought she might have taken a wrong turn, but as apple orchards turned into fields filled with chubby white steers as well groomed as if they had been children's ponies, she knew she was on the right road. A few minutes later they came to a tall stone archway supporting an ornate wrought-iron gate. At the apex of the arch, foot-high flowing italic letters announced ELE-VAGE VIENNEAU and smaller letters below boasted ETAB. 1821.

Capucine shot the Clio through the gate, spitting gravel, and announced happily, "It all comes back to me now. You'll see. It's a fabulous place."

She turned hard left into a road lined with towering poplars standing as stiffly as soldiers on parade and emerged into the courtyard of a striking two-story, timber-faced manor house with a steeply-sloped thatch roof. The building had clearly started out life as the home of some modest Norman lord.

Inside, the original great hall had been left intact. Despite an attempt on the part of the current occupants to create some coziness by cordoning off the area in front of the looming stone fireplace with sofas and chairs, the barnlike proportions of the room demanded exhausting loudness. In addition to the Vienneaus, only Bellanger was present, kitted out in another outfit so new looking Capucine half expected to see a price tag fluttering from the back of his jacket.

As they walked in, the topic of conversation was Marie-Christine's desire to take lessons on a shooting range in order to become an active participant at hunts.

"It's so humiliating sitting there on a stick like some sort of ornament," she said.

"But what a charming ornament," Bellanger said with dripping unctuousness.

"I myself am quite proud of the way my manly air embellishes Capucine's station," Alexandre said, rooting around on a long table behind the sofa so laden with cattle memorabilia it would have been at home in the Paul Bert flea market in Paris.

"Marie-Christine, don't listen to him. You really should learn to shoot," Capucine said. "Women have a natural gift for it. It's because we have a better sense of rhythm and we're more supple than men."

"Shooting is very dangerous," Vienneau said. "Just look at what happened to poor Philippe."

"That was so strange," Marie-Christine said, tears welling in her eyes. "How could he have been shot accidentally? The whole thing just seems so crazy."

Capucine noticed that Bellanger darted a particularly venomous look at her and seemed about to say something, but the cook, round and rosy as a turnip, opened the door to the kitchen and popped her head out, a tacit invitation to the luncheon table.

Inevitably, it was steak. But it was nonetheless extraordinary: flawless tournedos wrapped in French bacon, perfect *pommes soufflés,* an impeccable béarnaise. Alexandre's beatific smile was of a depth seen only in churches and in three-star restaurants. He breathed a deep sigh of contentment. "Loïc," he said. "This is quite possibly the best fillet I've ever eaten. How on earth do you do it?"

Vienneau laughed. "Well, you know we've been at it since the nineteenth century. My great-great-grandfather was a colonel in Napoleon's Grand Armée. His leg was shot off at Waterloo. He was only twenty-seven at the time, can you imagine? He recuperated right here in this house, which had been in the family for generations, and he fell in love with Charolais cattle and my great-great-grandmother.

"Our herd's been refined for nearly two centuries, which is why it's so well marbled. And, of course, we've learned a thing or two about the care and feeding of the little devils over the generations. That's all there is to it, really."

"It's such a waste," Bellanger said. "The Vienneau name is a completely underexploited brand on the French fast-moving-consumer-goods scene. With the proper backing you could transform your franchise into a significant family heritage. You could expand your volume, become a known name in supermarkets, even diversify into prepared dishes. Your business has huge potential."

"Henri," Vienneau said, "I've made it perfectly clear I have no intention whatsoever of selling out. Our discussions are to be confined to the possibility of raising a small amount of capital to make some needed improvements to the élevage, nothing more. The idea of linking my family name to the 'fast-moving-consumer-goods scene' is utterly repugnant."

Before Alexandre had the chance to spread his diplomatic oil on waters troubled yet again, there was a discreet knock at the dining room door.

"*Ah, oui,*" Vienneau said. "I've asked one of my foremen to come by to show you around the élevage. I have a conference call coming up, but I'll catch up to you on your tour."

The door opened to admit a heavyset man in his early forties with muscles as lumpy as a Charolais steer. Capucine wondered if it was in his genes or a mimetic imitation of his wards. Vienneau introduced him as Pierre Martel, foreman in charge of final phases of the breeding cycle. He touched his forelock with his knuckle, bobbed his head, and muttered, "*M'sieu'dame,*" the age-old salutation of the working classes. A bright-faced young man peeped out from behind Martel's broad shoulder.

"Oh yes, of course," said Vienneau. "This is Clément Devere. He's an intern from the agricultural college at Rouen who's here to spend his last semester with us."

Once lunch was over, Martel led them off at a brisk pace. "Monsieur Bellanger, you know the place backward and forward by now," he said. "You should be giving the tour, not me." He led them toward a complex of cinder-block structures glowing with white paint.

"This is where we feed the cattle when they come off grass and are put on grain," Martel said.

"They don't eat grass?" Capucine asked in a surprised tone.

"They do when they're very young. But they're put on grain feed very quickly," Martel snapped, impatient with Capucine's surprise. "We need these steers to grow from eighty pounds to twelve hundred in fourteen months. That's not going to happen on a diet of grass, the same way you're not going to get a rugby player up to weight by feeding him salad." Martel snorted in pleasure at the veracity of his truism.

"The other thing," Martel continued, "is that they need their vitamins and antibiotics. We administer those in the feed. We couldn't just sprinkle it on the grass, now could we?" He paused to think over what he had just said. "Of course, we could inject them, but that would mean running them through the chute once a week. It's enough of a pain in the ass to do that for the inoculations."

Capucine was going to ask a question but realized that, for some reason, Martel was on the defensive about the artificial feeding of the cattle. Did she really look like one of those Green hippies? It must be all these clothes she was borrowing from the cloakroom.

After an uninteresting trudge through a labyrinth of galvanized pens and stainless-steel feeding troughs while they dutifully mouthed the inane questions required on guided tours of industrial installations, they arrived at the next attraction, the abattoir.

This sinister-sounding feature turned out to be no more than a long, unpleasantly chilly room with low-hanging overhead steel tracks. A group of men wearing long white coats hosed the floor down and vigorously swept the bloody water into channels cut into the perimeter. They all smiled at Martel and the guests with an air of forced enthusiasm.

"Sorry, but there's nothing to see in here right now. The abattoir starts early in the morning and shuts down around noon, and then they clean up until two or three," Martel said. "Anyway, the interesting part is through here." He led them through a curtain made of long strips of loose-hanging plastic.

"The butchery atelier," he announced. An army of beef carcasses hung in neat rows from four ceiling tracks. The room was just above freezing. Workers, made rotund by thermal vests under their bloodstained white coats, split the carcasses in two with rasping electric knives, buzzing like angry bees. "These guys produce what we call 'sides.' That's what we sell to butchers, our bread-and-butter product," he said, leading them through another plastic curtain.

"Next, the sides are parked in this room here for a couple of weeks." The temperature had dropped to close to freezing. "I'll get you guys out of here in a sec," Martel laughed. "The temperature can't go above thirty-three degrees. See, one of the reasons the Elevage Vienneau is so famous is that we age our beef twenty-four days, a whole week longer than our competitors. It costs money and the meat loses a lot of weight, but it's worth it in tenderness and flavor, believe you me!"

Alexandre nodded his agreement with an encouraging grunt and hugged Capucine, who was beginning to tremble.

"Of course, not all our meat is sold to butchers," Martel went on. "Some of it goes to fancy restaurants, in what they call 'retail cuts.' To make those, the sides go back to the butcher and are cut up into sections the size restaurants will buy. The sections come back in here and sit for still another two weeks before they can go out the door." Endless rows of nearly black slabs of beef were stored on stainless-steel racks behind a long glass wall.

"*M'sieu'dame*, right here you're looking at our family jewels. This is the best beef in the world. But let's get the hell out'a here before we turn into steaks ourselves," he said with a ritual laugh.

They emerged in a parking lot filled with dozens of meticulously aligned white refrigerated trucks marked with the Vienneau logo of a stylized Charolais bull. They climbed into the last vehicle in the lot, a white Renault Espace van decked out with the same logo, Alexandre in back with Devere and Capucine, while Bellanger, as if he were in charge, commandeered the front seat next to Martel.

Martel drove slowly down a well-tended dirt road lined with more white wood fencing and commented on the contents of each field: brood cows, steers, isolated bulls. The estate seemed endless.

In an effort to be polite Capucine asked Devere if he was finding his internship useful.

"Oh, yes, madame," he replied. "The Elevage Vienneau is at the state of the art. Why, we have growth rates equaled only in the United States, where they use hormones that are not allowed by the European Community. I'm learning all sorts of things."

Capucine smiled sweetly at Clément. "Have you figured out the secrets to the legendary quality of the Elevage Vienneau yet?"

"Madame, I really don't think there are any secrets. It's all about attention to detail and, of course, love of the animals. For example, I learned that the growth rate has fallen off a bit since the passing of Monsieur Gerlier, you know, the general manager who died in a shooting accident about a week ago. It seems he was so attentive to the cattle that they are mourning him. Isn't that amazing!"

Martel barked a cynical laugh and shot Clément a look. "Clément is like a pig in *choucroute* here. That guy Jean Bouvard is coming to town tomorrow for another one of his damn demonstrations. He always manages to pull off a real show. You know, lots of police, a big crowd, TV cameras all over the place. It's going to be like a holiday fairway. I gave Clément the day off so he won't miss a thing." Martel smiled at Clément indulgently.

At the mention of Bouvard, Alexandre pricked up his ears. "Bouvard? I did a piece on him last year. He's a press whore, that's for sure, but his heart's in the right place. What's he protesting now?"

Clément turned to Alexandre with adolescent eagerness. "It's that awful steak chain, Charolais Allô. They're planning on opening a restaurant right in the middle of Saint-Nicolas. Bouvard says their steaks are made from beef imported from the United States that has been laced with growth hormones, despite EC regulations. We just can't have that! I think Jean Bouvard is the Jeanne d'Arc of the

French culinary tradition," he said with an adolescent's depth of feeling.

"I rather agree with you," said Alexandre. "But don't quote me. I might go tomorrow myself if I can get my better half to give me the day off. *Aux barricades!*" he said with an eye on Capucine while raising a clenched fist and laughing happily.

CHAPTER 7

The next day Capucine and Alexandre arrived in the village punctually at nine. The château's below-stairs rumor mill had it that Jean Bouvard's demonstration was going to begin at ten, and Alexandre did not want to miss a minute of it. They squeezed into the last available seats on the packed terrace of the only café on the village square and ordered coffee, which arrived promptly in clunky dark-green demitasses.

With one glaring exception the village square was a marvel of unsullied authenticity. A single round window— a Cyclops eye in the broad, flat face of an ancient, lichen-covered Romanesque church—benignly supervised the timeworn wooden storefronts that supplied the village its necessities: butcher, baker, *épicerie,* and, of course, the café. The scene was so familiar to Capucine that she didn't take it in, except for one shocking addition: a garish white and red structure that had been erected directly opposite the church in an empty lot formerly used for an open-air farmers' market. Lurid red letters nearly six feet tall proclaimed it the infamous Charolais Allô.

Even though it was a workday, a sizable throng—mainly

paysans in mud-spattered blue overalls—milled in the square, as keyed up and happily boisterous as if waiting for the Bastille Day fireworks. Vans marked with the logos of France's three national television networks were parked in front of the church, and a small troupe of reporters and camera technicians smoked and gibed loudly with each other. Capucine's trained eye caught two dark blue gendarmerie vans, packed with uniformed officers, tucked discreetly up the street next to the church.

A waiter stood by Capucine and Alexandre's table, angrily flicking his side towel. "Look at that *belle merde*. You should see it at night. The letters light up and flash. It's as bad as Pigalle."

Just then they heard the throaty roar of a heavy-duty diesel motor. The crowd cheered as if greeting a beloved movie star. A large yellow bulldozer rumbled cheerfully down a side street toward the restaurant. As it crossed the square, the driver lowered the blade and waved enthusiastically. The drooping russet walrus mustache and the paysan's work clothes had been made famous by repeated TV news coverage. Jean Bouvard raised his hands high over his head, fists joined side by side at the thumbs, his famous victory sign, usually seen with him in handcuffs as he was led off to a short prison sentence following one of his highly mediatized protests.

"I'd give a month's tips to see him pull this off," the waiter said.

When the bulldozer approached the restaurant, Bouvard threw it into low gear. The tread clanked noisily and the engine growled menacingly. The news teams, who had already pushed through the crowd to take up position in front of the restaurant, went into action, three talking heads speaking animatedly and gesticulating into their cameras with the blow-by-blow of what was happening.

Less noticeable, a dozen gendarmes were disgorged by

the vans and hovered, hesitating, behind the crowd, clearly unsure of what to do. Capucine frowned.

The bulldozer reached the building. The motor rose in pitch, the cap on the exhaust pipe blowing straight up. Bouvard was clearly handy with the thing. In a clean sweep he ripped off a corner of the building with the blade. With visible élan he plunged one steering lever forward and the other into reverse, and the bulldozer made an elegant pirouette to advance on the other corner, which was amputated with the same economy of motion.

The waiter tapped Alexandre's shoulder. "I love to see a man at work who really knows what he's doing," he said with a broad grin.

The gendarmes seemed to finally make up their minds and attempted to push through the crowd, who resisted them vigorously, resulting in a confused mêlée. Bouvard stood on the seat of the bulldozer and shouted, "Down with the enemies of La France and her traditions!" heard clearly even above the din.

A third gendarmerie van arrived with flashing lights, emitting a loud *pan-pom, pan-pom,* and spewed a handful of men in full black riot gear complete with Plexiglas shields, shotguns, and tear gas launchers. There were yells and taunts from the crowd. Shots were heard. The police charged en masse with the riot squad at the vanguard. More shots crackled as the crowd retreated slowly in the direction of the bulldozer and the restaurant. Bouvard waved them back imperiously.

"The courage that man has," the waiter said. "He refuses to surrender."

"I think he's trying to warn them that the building is about to collapse," Capucine said.

As if on cue, there was a loud groaning and the sound of breaking glass; the façade of the building buckled slowly and the roof fell in violently with a loud crash, dragging the elevated sign down with it. The letters were strewn in front of the crowd, with one of them landing only a few feet away from Bouvard and the gendarmes. The crowd erupted in wild cheering. This was definitely far better than Bastille Day. Amid the rubble the letters now seemed to be attempting to spell out OH, CALORIES.

Two of the helmeted gendarmes leapt up on the bull-dozer's tread and handcuffed Bouvard, who raised his hands, thumbs hooked together, in his customary victory gesture. It was a marvelous photo op: the valiant artisan in shabby work clothes defending his country's traditional heritage as he is manhandled by vicious police thugs in menacingly futuristic outfits. The crowd chanted, "Set him free! Freedom for Bouvard!" But as soon as Bouvard was driven off, they began to wander slowly back to their fields and orchards in groups of two or three.

Alexandre laughed heartily. After a few seconds of shaking her head at the inefficiency of the local gen-darmerie, Capucine reluctantly joined him. "That alone was worth the trip," Alexandre said. "I know it wasn't the police's finest hour, but I do think it would still be in order to celebrate with a small Calva."

"It'll be on the house and I think I'll join you," said the waiter.

As they drank and discussed the merits of Jean Bouvard, Capucine noticed that a group of people seemed to be col-lecting at the edge of the square, in front of the demolished restaurant, peering down intently at something. There were no gendarmes near. She jumped up, pushed through the crowd, and she closed in on the epicenter. Two gen-darmes appeared and blocked her way. She produced her police ID wallet from her handbag. The gendarmes fell back at attention, saluting. The villagers in the vicinity looked at her with suspicion.

A young man lay on his back on the paving stones of the

square—unquestionably dead—his sweater soaked in blood, a large black hole in the exact middle of his chest. Capucine turned his head to feel for a pulse in his neck and was horrified to recognize Clément Devere, his expression of youthful enthusiasm—even though now tempered with a hint of surprise—unchanged even in death.

CHAPTER 8

"So this insufferable policeman," Vienneau said as he continued his story relentlessly while Gauvin waited patiently to serve him, bracing his back like a mule against the weight of the heavy silver platter of pheasants. "*Oh, pardon*, Capucine, I always forget you're with the Police Judiciaire, but that's hardly the same thing as the gendarmerie, is it?"

"A flic is just a flic, but I understand this particular one may be in a class apart," Capucine said.

"Anyhow," Vienneau continued, finally serving himself, "this Capitaine Dallemagne had the temerity to come to the élevage and insist on seeing me without an appointment. All he wanted was a few administrative details of that poor intern, but he saw no reason not to barge in on the Président-Directeur Général of the company to get it."

"Did the capitaine have any ideas about how the man died?" Oncle Aymerie asked.

"Oh yes, he had no doubts about that at all," Vienneau said. "The police surgeon dug out a Brenneke shotgun slug that had hit the poor boy right in the heart, killing him instantly."

"Solid bullets that can be used in a shotgun instead of

pellets if you want to shoot big game," Capucine said parenthetically for Alexandre's benefit.

"So," continued Vienneau, "this excellent police capitaine concluded that since most of the paysans use them, that was proof positive that a villager had fired off a shot in the excitement of Bouvard's demonstration and hit Devere accidentally. Case closed as far as he was concerned."

"That's all he said?" Capucine asked.

"*Pas du tout,*" Vienneau said. "He went on at length to explain that this was the sort of thing that was bound to happen with this country's lax gun controls and that the police really had their hands tied and the backwardness in the countryside was not going to change unless the legislative climate improved and so on and on until I really had to ask him to leave. Is this the way you work in Paris, Capucine?"

Capucine was saved from agreeing with Vienneau's dim view of the provincial gendarmerie by Gauvin, who bent over to whisper excitedly in her ear, "Telephone, Madame la Comtesse. Pardon me for interrupting, but it's the police!"

As Capucine made her way to the study, Gauvin, who had followed her out of the dining room, again whispered, "Madame la Comtesse might be more at her ease on the cloakroom telephone. It is much more private." He led her through a large walk-in closet next to the front door where coats and boots and the accoutrements of country life were kept. At the very end was an alcove with a table used by the servants to clean boots and oil guns. An ancient rotary telephone had sat on a corner of the table for as long as Capucine could remember. Conspiratorially, the majordome handed her the receiver. "Madame la Comtesse is not to worry," he said. "I shall go to the study and ensure no one picks up that extension."

"Commissaire, I sure hope you'll be back here tomorrow. All hell's breaking loose." Despite the tinniness of the ancient receiver, Isabelle's sharp voice was like a bracing icy draft of winter air when a window was opened in an overheated room. Capucine felt a burst of longing as compelling as sexual desire to be back in her office at the commissariat.

"What's up, Isabelle? Why are you calling on a Sunday?" Capucine asked.

"La Belle's been at it again. This time she was rescued by two male ballet dancers from the Opéra de Paris, a couple, of course. She walked off with a small bronze statue of a deer. They claim it's worth a bundle."

"Some of those things can be valuable. Call the two dancers and find out when we can see them tomorrow. You can tell me all the rest over coffee first thing in the morning. I'll bring the croissants."

Capucine returned to the table, part of her happier than she had been in a week, another part a bit crestfallen.

Back at the table Oncle Aymerie was fighting a rearguard skirmish. "Alexandre, it's not that hard to understand. Five years ago there was a brief and very unpleasant interlude when the village elected an outsider as mayor. This man proved to be unscrupulous in his administration. The villagers came to their senses very quickly and voted him out, but he had succeeded in taking a great number of liberties without anyone noticing. One of those was the lease he signed with the company that owns this Charolais Allô for the marketplace lot opposite the church. They paid the rent quietly for years, and everyone at the *mairie* forgot about the lease until six months ago, when they announced their plan to build that infernal restaurant. There was nothing anyone could do to stop them."

"So what happens now?" Alexandre asked.

"Oh, we won't be seeing any fast-food restaurants in this village again," Oncle Aymerie said with a smug smirk. "The current mayor has ordered the damaged building to be completely demolished because it's unsafe. He also thinks that an early version of the town's zoning regulations prohibit any commercial structures on that specific site, which has been an open-air marketplace since time immemorial. He's forming an ad hoc committee to study the question, and, of course, there can be no question of rebuilding the restaurant while the committee deliberates. I happen to have had a small Calva with the mayor this morning after breakfast, and he asked me to sit on that committee. *Cela va sans dire* that we will not come to any conclusions until well after the Charolais Allô lease has expired."

"Another bloody nose well delivered in exactly the right place," exclaimed Alexandre. "I'll drink a toast to that!"

"But what I don't know is what happened to Jean Bouvard? Does anyone have any idea?" Oncle Aymerie asked.

"The most worthy capitaine was very forthcoming about that," Vienneau said. "Since he was apprehended in *flagrant délit,* as the lawyers like to say—red-handed—he fell under the special provision for instant justice. They hustled him off to a court in Rouen, where he was sentenced to three months on the spot and taken directly to jail. The capitaine was there as the arresting officer. He said there was a big contingent of press and Bouvard did his famous victory salute, you know, with his fists raised in handcuffs as he was led off to prison. The capitaine was quite put out that it was Bouvard and not him at the center of the press's attention."

Just then Gauvin returned with a magnum of champagne, which he opened with a theatrical pop that made Alexandre wince. But when he saw it was a Krug 1988, his wrinkled forehead relaxed and he broke into one of his beatific smiles.

"I hope this is not to celebrate our departure," Capucine said.

"Au contraire," said Oncle Aymerie. "It's to thank you

and Alexandre for your visit. You both have made an old man extremely happy."

The rest of the evening was perfection. Capucine felt the deep warm glow of the prodigal child reincorporated into the bosom of her family. Of course, she told herself, serving her community as a police officer for a pittance hardly constituted prodigality. Even Alexandre's enthusiasm seemed sincere when he promised their speedy return.

Later, hand in hand with Alexandre on their way up the stairs to their last night in the canopied bed, Capucine could not help but wonder why the capitaine had been so insistent that the Brenneke slug proved death by an accidental shot from a paysan's shotgun. Not only did it seem hard to believe that a shot fired in the air could wind up in someone's chest, but also every riot squad in the country carried at least one short-barreled shotgun and a good supply of Brennekes in case things got really out of hand.

CHAPTER 9

Capucine squirmed in what she guessed was an original Breuer Wassily chair. The hard black leather straps were as slippery as an over-waxed hardwood floor and bit painfully into the backs of her knees. The day, she thought to herself, the Paris police received the same budgets as those designer cops on American TV, she would be sure to buy a whole set of Bauhaus furniture for her interrogation rooms.

David perched perfectly comfortably in the chair's twin, lazily twirling a feathery lock around his index finger, preening for the two victims, who sat decorously draped on a Le Corbusier sofa in poses that left no doubt of their vocations as dancers. The two men had eyes only for him. For the hundredth time Capucine wondered if the entirety of David's sensual life didn't consist of sparking erotic attraction. Isabelle glowered at the scene, awkwardly balanced on a Gerrit Rietveld Z chair that looked like it would collapse into kindling at her first brusque movement.

"She knew we absolutely loathed the damn thing," said one of the dancers.

"It was a bronze statuette of a deer. A deer, of all things, can you imagine? The only thing my horrible father left me," added the other dancer. "He was a career army officer. Saint-Cyr and all that. Besides the army, the only thing that interested him was wearing ridiculous outfits and massacring deer with hounds. He certainly didn't give a damn about his children. The day I told him I was gay, he disinherited me and never spoke to me again. When he died, he left me that fucking statuette as a pointed reminder of the virtuous life I should have led."

"So you encouraged her to take it?" Isabelle asked.

"Now, wait a minute," the first dancer said. "That piece is very valuable. It's an original Pierre-Jules Mene. His work sells for quite a lot. We had it appraised at over ten thousand euros."

"Bertrand, don't be silly. You know perfectly well that we both detested the ghastly thing. You only kept it on the Saarinen table so you could stick your bills on the antlers and laugh at it. And what's stolen is stolen whether you cry over it or not, isn't that right, Officer?" The latter directed exclusively at David.

"Oh, you'll get the insurance money, no doubt about that," Capucine said. "I'm more interested in your relationship with the perp."

"What a vulgar term," the dancer called Claude said. "Her name is Célestine. We found her collapsed at the Marché de Grenelle last Sunday. She's a poet. She had run away from a lover who was abusive and did horrible things to her. She's so noble she stayed with that terrible man out of a sense of duty until finally she could stand it no longer and then she bolted. She spent the whole night wandering around and found herself in the market in the morning. She had fainted just the instant before we arrived. Isn't that right, Bertrand?"

"A beautiful and moving story. We brought her home

with us, of course," Bertrand said. "She needed to be nursed back to health. After a day it was as if we had known her all our lives. She fit right in. She became happy. She made us happy. It was a wonderful moment for all of us." He paused, as crestfallen as a children's cartoon character. "Then one day Claude and I came home from rehearsal and she had gone. Poof." He waved his fingers limply but gracefully in the air. "Just like that."

"And she stole the Mene. We didn't give it to her. Let's be perfectly clear," Claude said.

"Oh, how can you talk like that?" Bertrand said.

"Look, no one's going to question your goddamn insurance claim," Isabelle said irritably. "You'll get every centime of the appraisal value, even though the perp is sure to have sold it for less than a third of that."

Isabelle paused and consulted a piece of paper. "Did this woman have a long, melancholy face, which she usually carried slightly tilted to the right, an exceptionally long neck, and flowing, shoulder-length dark blond hair"—Isabelle held up the paper and quoted—" 'just like a spurned Modigliani model'?"

"Wait a minute!" Claude said. "Do you mean she's done this before? We were taken in by a scam? I find that impossible to believe. She's our friend."

Bertrand stared into space, searching his memory, and breathed a sigh of relief. "Actually, she did look a teeny bit like a Modigliani sometimes, but her hair wasn't blond. It was very dark brown, almost black," he said triumphantly.

"Hair coloring," Claude said. "Now that I think about it, it was one of those horrid home-dyes. That's our Célestine. No doubt about it."

"Good," Capucine said, standing up. "At your convenience you need to call Brigadier Lemercier to make an appointment to give your deposition. Bring a copy of your appraisal. She'll give you the affidavit for your insurance claim."

The dancer called Claude looked like he would burst into tears.

Bertrand staved off the crisis by putting a hand on his partner's thigh. "It all worked out for the best. We're going to get cash for that eyesore, and Célestine, sweet creature whoever she may really be, will have enough to get by on for a month or so. What more could you ask for?" he asked with an only slightly cynical laugh.

CHAPTER 10

That afternoon Capucine indulged in a session of self-recrimination, a luxury she had only begun to permit herself once that she had established her authority over the commissariat and their arrest statistics had become the envy of the Paris force. The irritant was the interview of the two dancers. Isabelle had not lived up to expectations, clear proof that she was not being properly managed. David had stolen the focal point from her. Yes, the participants' sexual orientation was a factor, but was that really all that was at work?

As she danced between the Scylla and Charybdis of under- and over-managing Isabelle, she began to nibble away at the pile of files on her desk that seemed once again to have risen in the night like a bowlful of bread dough. Just as she was immersing herself in the peccadilloes of a gang of pickpockets who were doing quite well off the American tourists at the Père-Lachaise Cemetery, the phone rang. She picked it up, still swimming in the file.

"*Allô! Allô! Ma nièce?*" asked Oncle Aymerie in the overloud voice of those who mistrust technology of any sort. "Are you there? It's your uncle."

"Mon oncle," Capucine said, turning a page, "how

good to hear your voice. I was just going to call you to tell you how much Alexandre and I enjoyed our week at Maulévrier. So foolish of me to have stayed away."

"*Formidable.* I'm delighted you feel that way because I want you to come back. Would this weekend be too soon?"

"Alexandre enjoyed himself immensely. He was particularly impressed with Odile's cooking." She turned another page. "And I was so happy to see you again. We must come down again soon. Maybe after Christmas."

"Perfect! We're going to walk up Saint Agnès' field on Saturday. It's in stubble and there will be excellent partridge. The weather will be perfect. Not too sunny. Not too cold. Alexandre needs to get out more. He has definite potential as a gun. I'm going to put him in the center of the line."

Capucine turned another page. The lieutenant in charge of the investigation seemed to think there was a gang of at least twenty adolescents involved. She was going to have to adjust the duty roster and add more personnel to the case.

"No point in arriving too early on Friday. It will just be family. Jacques will be here, of course. That will please Alexandre. And we can eat whenever you shake off the dust of the trip."

Capucine closed the file with a snap. "Mon oncle, we can't possibly come this weekend." A tiny furrow appeared in her forehead. "Is something the matter?"

"In a way. I've been thinking. I believe this tragic death last week is linked to the mishap at our shoot. I'm sure neither one was an accident and both were connected to Vienneau's élevage somehow. So I said to myself, since you are a commissaire in the Police Judiciaire, you would be the best person to investigate."

Capucine's heart leapt like a little robin flying off into the sun at Oncle Aymerie's acknowledgment of her chosen career, but she succeeded in marshaling the gravitas of a senior police officer. "Mon oncle, these are very serious accusations. If you feel this way, you should alert the local police."

Oncle Aymerie snorted. "But *you* are the police. Besides, you've met this *plaisantin,* the local capitaine of the gendarmerie. Be serious, ma nièce. I need you to come back and conduct a proper investigation. Don't forget this is *our* village. Has been for centuries. We have a responsibility to the villagers. Noblesse oblige is not to be taken lightly. I need you to be here."

Capucine smiled. It was ridiculous. She'd had her little vacation and now it was time to get back to work. What nagged her was that she half suspected Oncle Aymerie was right. There was no doubt that the death at Bouvard's demonstration had been foul play of some sort, and it did seem unlikely that both victims having the same employer was mere coincidence.

"Mon oncle, look, it really is going to be next to impossible to leave Paris right now, but I will talk it over with Alexandre tonight. Odile's *faisan au choux* made a great impression on him. Why don't I call you in the morning. We'll make a decision then."

Late that night Capucine arrived at her apartment, as she so often did, simultaneously fulfilled, drained, and frustrated. Alexandre, as he so often did, stormed around the kitchen, humming loudly, moving a great deal of air in preparing dinner. Alexandre had owned the rambling apartment in the Marais since his antediluvian university days. He had bought it for a song well before the Marais even thought of becoming fashionable. The third story had housed a cheap brothel, and, day and night, the stairwell had been packed with a long line of illegal Maghrebian day laborers waiting for a quick ten minutes with a fat elderly prostitute. Of course, all that was long gone and the area was now prime Paris real estate. Needless to say, Alexandre would not even entertain theoretical discussions about selling, and Capucine agreed, feeling that its twenty-five hundred square feet would be perfect for rearing a squabbling brood when the time came.

As she liked to tell her friends, Capucine had managed to housebreak almost the entire apartment, replacing Alexandre's bachelor clutter with carefully chosen antiques from her family and setting them off with bright pastel colors on the walls and drapes. But two rooms remained unquestionably Alexandre's, his study and the kitchen. From Alexandre's point of view, the kitchen was even more inviolate than the study. It was the largest room in the house, filled with hanging garlic and sausages, shelves crammed with odd-shaped bottles of spices and culinary effluvia, long rows of copper pots dangling from rails on the wall. An immense brass and black enamel La Cornue stove enjoyed center stage against the far wall.

Capucine rejoiced in dinner at home. Alexandre's cooking was a solace and had the same salubrious effect as snuggling up to him on the sofa and rubbing the endearing gibbosity of his stomach. But as she walked in, her face fell. Beef! There was the unmistakable odor of beef cooking. A delicious enough odor for sure, but it was still beef, and she had told Alexandre that very morning that beef or game of any sort would not pass her lips for the rest of the month.

Alexandre fully understood her frown. Catching her moods was one of his talents. "Yes, princess, it *is* beef," he said, handing her a flute of champagne. "But it's no dish your dear Odile would ever cook." He swept Capucine in his arms. "This is a recipe that embraces the very essence of modern Paris." He tightened his hug, lifted her, and spun with the lack of grace of a trained bear. Capucine let out a little yell. Alexandre dropped her. "What's the matter?" he asked.

"You're crushing my Sig into my spine," she said, laughing and reaching to the back of her waist to unclip the holster and gun, which she clunked on the long table as she kicked off her shoes. "There, that's better. So what is this dish?"

"It's an *onglet*—a hanger steak—that marinated all afternoon in a bath of wine, onions, and carrots, and was then rolled tightly around a horseradish paste, and is now happily cooking in the oven, waiting for you. It will be served with a sauce made from a reduction of the marinade and lovingly presented over a bed of the chopped leaves of celery and parsley. Can't get farther away from Maulévrier than that, can you?"

Capucine kissed Alexandre. "Only you understand me."

It took some time for Alexandre to finish cooking. The sauce seemed a great deal more complicated than he had described, involving egg yolks and furious whipping with a whisk. Completed, the dish was delicious, if a bit bizarre, with a sharp bite that was more Japanese than French. Imagining Oncle Aymerie wrinkling his nose in disapproval reminded Capucine of his call.

"Oncle Aymerie called me this morning. He wants me—us, really—to go back to Maulévrier this weekend. He's got it in his head that neither of the deaths were accidents and that they have something to do with the élevage."

"Back to Maulévrier, *quelle idée!*" Alexandre paused, looking closely into Capucine's face. "Good God. You're tempted, aren't you?"

"Maybe. A little. I don't know. I shouldn't even think of taking more time off, of course, but Oncle Aymerie seemed so distraught. If I'm going to discover anything, I'd have to leave before the weekend."

"Follow your heart and all that good stuff, but think twice about encouraging your uncle in the delusions of an old man. That gendarme capitaine seemed completely convinced the deaths were accidents, and it's hardly surprising that both the victims worked at the élevage since it's virtually the only business in town."

"The provincial gendarmerie is hardly expert in criminal investigation. It's not their function. That's why the Police Judiciaire has authority throughout France."

"Maybe," said Alexandre with just the hint of an edge in his voice, "but don't forget that the Elevage Vienneau is one of the pillars of French gastronomy. Even the slightest hint that it's involved in a crime in any way would sully its reputation, and that would be a blow to the national glory. You know how fickle the world of haute cuisine is. Not to mention the fact that rooting around the village like a Périgord pig after truffles isn't going to make you any friends either."

Capucine's brow wrinkled as she contemplated his response.

In a flash she brightened. "There's also the matter of my accrued vacation time," she said. "I have four weeks left to take. If I don't use them before the end of the year it will send the wrong message to the troops. I want them to be fulfilled and well adjusted, not mindless slaves to their jobs."

"Well, do what you want," Alexandre said. "I won't be able to go with you. I'm in the middle of writing a piece. It's going to be called 'Critics Who Hurt—Critics Who Kill,' all about the damage some restaurant critics have done to haute cuisine."

"It doesn't sound like the piece is going to make you any friends either."

"Well, you know my policy, bloody the noses that deserve to be bloodied." Alexandre paused and looked at his wife fondly. "Actually, if you were to go, I think I could come down for the weekend and finish the piece there. I could take the train on Friday. I still have four more interviews to finish, not to mention a restaurant to review on Thursday." Alexandre smiled and kissed her on the forehead. "Besides, a few nights out with the *copains*—my dear old buddies—would do me a world of good."

The fact that Alexandre had been so quick to let her go off by herself tipped the scale back away from another week in the country. But as she remembered the glow of affection for her family that the week at Maulévrier had rekindled, it teetered back the other way. It was going to take more than irritation with Alexandre to get her to renege on familial duty, particularly as that piece of the puzzle of her life seemed to be fitting itself so nicely back into its slot.

"You deserve some time off with your playmates," she said. "I'll go, but you have to promise to come on Friday evening and to behave while I'm gone." When Alexandre kissed her forehead again, she felt her face flush.

CHAPTER 11

"It's very unwise not to bring me mushrooms before taking them home. Very. Everyone in the village should know that," Homais said as he methodically probed the basket with a surgical forceps. "You say you found these in the kitchen. That poor Odile has lost all her good sense." He dumped the mushrooms on his worktable and began examining them one by one.

Capucine felt a twinge of embarrassment at the primitiveness of her investigative technique, but this was *les provinces* after all. "Yes," she said, "Odile was going to do something with them for dinner, but I thought it would be prudent to ask someone of your expertise to look them over first."

"*Someone* of my expertise? Please. There's no one with anything close to my knowledge of mycology between here and Rouen," Homais said with utter seriousness. "Well, so far so good," he said, continuing his examination. "These are all oyster *pleurottes*. A bit early for the season but sure to be very tasty."

"While I'm here, Monsieur Homais, I thought I'd ask you about that poor man who was killed accidentally at my uncle's shoot. They brought the body here, didn't they?"

"Yes, they did. As you know, we don't have a doctor in Saint-Nicolas, so I am often the resource of last resort, as it were. In fact, as you have seen, even though I don't have a medical degree, I'm probably more skilled at dealing with bird-shot wounds than most doctors. But in that particular case there was nothing I could do. The poor man was dead long before he made it to this table." Homais picked up a mushroom and held it high between index and thumb with the reverence of the *curé* elevating the host at mass.

"Now, this one is what we scholars call a *Cortinarius praestens*," Homais said in what he imagined was the dusty tone of the university lecture hall. "What the *paysans* call the *cortinaire remarquable*. You have only a handful of them, but they are quite rare and exceptionally tasty. They're already beginning to dry out, so I'd suggest you get the good Odile to make an omelet with them for your breakfast tomorrow morning."

To Capucine the *cortinaire* in question looked more shriveled and nasty than remarkable. No matter how rare it was, it certainly was not going to be gracing her breakfast table in the morning.

"So the poor man was DOA," Capucine said, fanning the embers of Homais' description of the body.

"Dead a good deal before OA," Homais said with a dry laugh. "He took almost the full charge of shot in the chest. Now, you might not know this, but the physiological effect of shotgun shot is entirely different from solid bullets. Imagine we are shooting a pheasant. No single pellet is lethal, and, in fact, the pellets rarely go into vital organs, but once you reach the critical mass of four pellets, the bird is rendered unconscious. Six pellets and it's dead. It's what we medical men call 'shock.'"

"So you think the victim died instantly?"

"Or within seconds. There were at least thirty pellets lodged in the reticular layer of the dermis of his chest. None of them were very deep since the penetration was transversal." He looked at Capucine and decided she was not up to the word. "By that I mean he had been shot from the left and the pellets entered diagonally and did not penetrate the chest very deeply. It was the shock that did him in, all the more since it was number six shot and not the smaller number eight one normally uses for partridge. The heavier pellets create that much more trauma, you see."

"Isn't using heavy shot on partridge unusual?"

"Remember we're in the Pays d'Auge here, madame, not the Ile-de-France, close to Paris. Obviously, shooting small birds like partridge with number six is heresy, but here they throw anything that comes to hand into their cartridge bags. I've even seen pheasants fall out of the sky cut in half by Brenneke solids. To prove my point, these pellets were lead, which—as I'm sure you know—has been illegal in France for fifteen years. In the civilized world everyone threw out his lead shot when the law went into effect and bought cartridges with steel shot. But not here. Even fifteen years after they stopped selling it, people still have lead shot cartridges in the bottom of their bags."

"And you're convinced it really was an accident?"

"Madame, as long as people persist in downing three or four Calvas before going out in the hot sun and blazing away at anything that moves, there will be accidents like this. Trust me on that."

CHAPTER 12

The next morning Capucine joined Oncle Aymerie for breakfast in what he liked to call the *petit salon,* a bright circular room at the bottom of the old turret. Several French windows cut through the thick wall looked out over the old moat and the fields beyond and made the room dance with dappling light reflected from the surface of the water. It was Oncle Aymerie's refuge, where he spent most of his day and took his meals when he was alone.

After café au lait and a blotting-paper-dry croissant—one of the many impenetrable gastronomic mysteries of France being the striking inferiority of country bakers compared to their Paris brethren—Oncle Aymerie asked her how her discussion with Homais had gone.

"We talked about mushrooms mostly. But he is definitely certain that Gerlier's death was accidental. He says that sort of thing happens all the time."

"He's quite correct, of course. Shooting accidents are very frequent. But this was no accident." He poured a quarter of a cup of coffee from a delicate silver *cafetière* and stirred in a lump of sugar. "But what I haven't told you, *ma chère petite nièce,* is that I think I can prove it was a murder."

"You actually have proof?"

"An ocular witness, as I believe you say in the police."

"Can you be more specific?"

"More specific? I'm taking you to lunch with him today. Is that specific enough?"

Colonel Hubert de Blignières lived in a square two-story house that had been built in the reign of Louis XV as a hunting lodge. Capucine had met him often; since the death of Tante Aymone he had become her uncle's inseparable companion. A widower himself and not overburdened with intelligence, since his retirement he had become devoted to Phébus—his Brittany spaniel—shooting, and gardening, in that order.

Lunch was served by a prodigiously rotund woman who not only cooked but also "did" for Blignières. As they sat down at the table, he strictured the housekeeper, Euphémie, sharply. "There can be no wineglasses on the table when we serve eggs. It creates anxiety. The guests wait for wine, which will not come, because it is unthinkable to drink wine with eggs. I'm sure your husband does precisely the same," he said, addressing Capucine.

The housekeeper removed the offending glasses with an exasperated shake of her head and retreated to the kitchen to return with a porcelain tureen of creamy scrambled eggs slowly cooked in a *bain-marie*. It was the way Alexandre loved making eggs on Sundays. Alexandre, of course, got around the no-wine-with-eggs rule by insisting that champagne was a legitimate exception. He also served his eggs with finely chopped black truffles. Still, Capucine admitted to herself that the orange-yoked country eggs, unobtainable in Paris, elevated the dish to its acme.

After the eggs came a *blanquette de veau*. Even though this one was well enough prepared and the wineglasses were back for an exceptional Côtes du Rhône, Capucine had never been able to find it in her heart to love *blan-*

quettes. The runny white milk sauce always seemed particularly ill-assorted to the veal. Still, it was one of the great classics, and she lavished compliments on Blignières, who beamed.

As the meal progressed, Oncle Aymerie became progressively more and more agitated. Finally he could contain himself no longer.

"Hubert, you must share your thoughts with Capucine."

"Aymerie, we've discussed this. It is not appropriate that I make allegations to the police, and Capucine is not only a police officer but a very senior one."

Reflexively, Capucine put a soothing hand on Blignières' arm. As she did so, she cringed inwardly. It was one of the basic gestures taught in interrogation courses, in the part about dealing with a reluctant witness—"confidence building: use a physical gesture that develops camaraderie and demonstrates the interviewer's concern." So she was now using police techniques on her uncle's friends? Had it come to that?

"I'm hardly here as a police officer," she said with what she hoped was her little-girl smile. "Oncle Aymerie tells me you're troubled about the death at his shoot."

"*Troubled* is precisely the right word. You see, everyone thinks I'm the one who fired the fatal shot. It's a terrible thing to live with. But I'm quite certain it wasn't me. I think I can demonstrate that beyond the shadow of a doubt."

"You seem very sure," said Capucine.

"I am. Let me show you." He went to the sideboard and returned with two fistfuls of silver knives, which he arranged on the table in a curve. "This is the way the line was set up, a shallow semicircle close to the crest of a steep hill. The victim, Gerlier, was two positions to the left of center. By left I mean from the birds' point of view, of course." He put a silver saltcellar slightly to the left of the middle of the line of cutlery. "And I was all the way down here on the right, on point, at the bottom of the hill. Aymerie always puts people on point there in case the birds veer off at the last minute. Maxime Boisson-Brideau, one of our good friends, had the point position opposite me on the left side." He removed the crystal vessels of oil and vinegar from a silver cruet set and put them perpendicular to the ends of the line to indicate their positions.

As the battle map was being sketched out in tableware, Capucine heard a barely audible keening and glanced down to find Phébus looking up at her in wide-eyed expectation. She divined correctly that the dog had learned the precise volume that would slip by unnoticed beneath the radar of his master's diminished hearing. Surreptitiously, she slipped him a large piece of veal.

"As the birds came in, I fired toward the field."

"And got a very elegant double," Oncle Aymerie said, giving him a playful punch in the arm.

Another piece of veal descended Phébus's gullet soundlessly.

"But," Blignières continued doggedly, "when the birds started up the hill, they were so low over the ground, it would not have been sporting to fire. It wasn't until they reached the crest that they gained enough altitude for anyone to be able to begin shooting. Do you understand?" he asked Capucine anxiously.

"Absolutely. Go on."

"Obviously, once they rose, I started shooting for all I was worth. But Maxime—remember he was opposite me at the bottom of the hill—couldn't shoot because his gun jammed. He still uses his father's old Callens et Modé, and he hasn't had it gone over by a gunsmith in twenty years, so the ejectors are very prone to freeze up, which is exactly what they did. He was dancing quite a merry little jig when the birds flew in, believe me."

Capucine nodded her understanding and surreptitiously slipped Phébus some more of her veal.

"So you see, the only person who could possibly have shot Gerlier accidentally was me, since the people next to him were shooting high in the air at birds well over their heads. And I am absolutely positive it wasn't me. I saw him jerk when he was hit. A military man knows all too well what that looks like. And at that moment my gun was broken open and I was reloading."

"Voilà!" Oncle Aymerie said, banging his fist on the table. "What more proof do you want?"

"Mon oncle, that's certainly a very convincing argument, but, unfortunately, courts only consider tangible facts as proof. Let me ask you a question, Colonel. What size shot were you shooting that day? Do you remember?"

"Do I remember? What kind of question is that? I was shooting number eights, of course. What else would I be shooting?"

"And there's no chance that you had the odd number six cartridge in your bag?"

"There are certain things a gentleman does when he returns home from the field," Blignières said rigidly. "He cleans and lightly oils his gun, he brushes the mud off his shoes and puts trees in them, and he takes whatever cartridges are left in his bag and puts them back in their boxes. And only then, and not one second before, does he allow himself a whiskey."

"And, of course, you use steel shot, not lead."

"Madame, I have devoted my life to serving my country and its laws. Lead shot has been prohibited for fifteen years. I would no more use it than powder my garden with DDT, even though I deeply regret the loss of both."

"I wouldn't have thought any less of you, Colonel. It will interest you to learn that the shot in Monsieur Gerlier's wound was number six lead shot."

"Voilà! What a relief. I knew I hadn't fired that shot, but I still lost a good deal of sleep over it. Ah, that calls for a celebration. Euphémie! Bring us some Calva! No, no, no, not that! The good stuff in the crystal decanter."

As they left, Phébus wagged his little stub of a tail vigorously at Capucine. If nothing else, she had made a new friend. Walking home to the château, Oncle Aymerie gave tongue to the two pertinent questions she had been juggling silently. "Well, if it wasn't Hubert, it had to be intentional. But who? And why?"

CHAPTER 13

"You want me to pedal a bicycle all day long? In this freezing weather? *Quelle idée!* Have you completely taken leave of your senses?" Alexandre asked, outraged. "Capucine, this country living has definitely addled your brain." It was the first time in their relationship Capucine had seen Alexandre genuinely flabbergasted.

"You have to come," Capucine said with almost schoolgirlish enthusiasm. "Jacques and I used to do it all the time when we were kids." She took a deep breath, realizing this was precisely the wrong thing to have said. "It'll be great fun. We follow the *chasse à courre* on bicycles and have one of Odile's marvelous picnic lunches. We'll get lots of exercise and fresh air. Just what you need after all your excesses of the past few days." She poked him playfully in the stomach. Alexandre's eyes darkened.

Alexandre had been out of sorts since he had arrived the day before. He had driven down with Jacques, who, it appeared, had regaled him for the hour-and-a-half ride with stories of his and Capucine's youth at the château. Capucine could easily imagine Jacques lacing the tales of rainy afternoons spent playing hide-and-go-seek in the labyrinthine commons with sexual innuendo and then delighting in Alexandre's struggle to control his jealousy.

Of course, Alexandre's mood had improved conspicuously when Jacques had insisted on taking them and his father to dinner at a nearby two-star restaurant. Later, as they prepared for bed, Alexandre had gone into paeans of delight over the country version of haute cuisine. The marinated boar with chestnuts he had eaten was apparently in a class apart from what could be found in Paris. Capucine could at least attest to the boar's aphrodisiac qualities.

But now his mood had fallen back to its nadir. Alexandre, as was his wont, had come down to breakfast rather late, only to discover the plan of following the hunt had been elevated to canonic status by Capucine's insatiable desire to relive her childhood pursuits. He clung grimly to his opposition until Capucine flicked her trump card on the table: it would be of inestimable value to her investigation since she would pick up all sorts of invaluable gossip from the villagers. A principal bylaw of their marriage was that matters relating to Capucine's vocation were inviolate. Oncle Aymerie, who had only been half listening, seized on the word investigation and, with the enthusiasm of those who do not have to participate, expounded a series of well-worn chestnuts of the sort that involve wild oats, teams of horses, and ten years of regained youth. Capucine was almost sad to see the light of obstinacy fade in her husband's eyes.

In the garage they unearthed three ancient bicycles that would have been all the rage in Saint-Germain if pedaled by pretty young *minettes* in stiletto heels but in their native habitat were just cumbersome and squeaky. In the cloakroom they found well-worn Barbours, faded knitted scarves, and ancient rubber Wellingtons and proceeded to waver off down a tree-lined lane, picturesque enough to serve as a screen saver, to the hunt's "rendezvous."

Either the rendezvous had become a much more elaborate affair than it had been in her youth or her childhood memories had been filtered by the years. Well over a hundred people from all walks of life milled enthusiastically. Some were holding bicycles, many had come by car, but all were in some form of olive drab hunting garb. They circulated, shook hands, air-kissed, pounded backs, and wished each other well with the forced gaiety of an office Christmas party. The crowning emotion was an almost palpable sense of anticipation that something of major import was about to happen. At the epicenter, the two dozen members of the hunt in their bright emerald green coats fretted nervously with their grooms over bored-looking horses decked out in elegant blankets with crested monograms.

Despite the chill, Jacques had opened his Barbour to reveal ostentatiously a magnificent crushed red velvet waistcoat with gold piping and elaborate filigree buttons identifying him as a junior member of the hunt. Capucine told herself she should have known Jacques could not have contented himself with anonymous olive drab for an entire day.

"Has your dear husband become an adept of the *chasse à courre,* or is it just his hound's nose for food and booze?" Jacques asked, indicating a distant Alexandre with his chin. Alexandre had wandered off with his new-found painter friend and was deep in animated conversation with a small group of people.

"Oh, very definitely the latter," Capucine said as Alexandre and his crony cheerfully set out on a broad lap among the hunt followers.

Fifteen minutes later a distinguished gray-haired man, who could easily have been employed as an actor in German luxury car advertisements, separated himself from his horses and called for order. With perfect timing Alexandre sidled up, looking particularly pleased with himself, and insinuated himself between Jacques and Capucine.

"Ah, the dictum from on high," Jacques—who had appointed himself Alexandre's Virgil for the day—whispered in Alexandre's ear. "The master in all his glory. He's going to bore us comatose before he gets around to telling us where we're going."

The augury proved painfully accurate. It was only after an eternal and seemingly pointless preamble about wind speed and direction, a snap freeze in the night that had been intense enough to ice the lake, and an endless enumeration of the name, gender, and age of each hound who would be running, that the master announced that at six that morning they had seen the tracks of a good-sized stag accompanied by a herd of at least ten other deer leading into a thicket. In the hopes the deer were still there, that was where the hunt would start.

At long last, the horsemen took off down a lane, leading a pack of forty or so exuberant hounds, followed at a respectful distance by the crowd on bicycles. A far larger group in cars took to the paved road they hoped would keep them close to the hunt.

Ten minutes later everyone stopped; the hounds were checked by riders cracking their long, snakelike whips; and a lone horseman disappeared into the wood with a single hound. Nothing happened for several minutes. Capucine could see Alexandre getting bored.

Several antlerless deer crashed out of the wood and ran down the lane. The pack of hounds bayed excitedly but were held in check by more whip cracking and the judicious use of menacing expletives.

Jacques leaned toward Alexandre with a smirk. "That's the poor stag's harem driven out into the cold."

Four larger deer with small antlers followed the does. "Now the squires. The stag collects them to amuse the harem while he plays the voyeur and broods, smoking Gauloises *bruns* and thinking dark existential thoughts. When they're exhausted, it's his turn. Curiously, it's the last time around that puts the bun in the oven. Mr. Big is like a Mexican *jefe.* All the kids in the village have to look like him."

"The perfect phallocrat, eh?" Capucine said. "Too bad Simone de Beauvoir never wrote about it."

Finally, there was a tremendous crashing and an enormous stag with the sort of antlers usually seen on whiskey bottles erupted from the wood and tore off with the hounds in close pursuit, baying hysterically, followed by galloping horsemen blaring equally hysterically on their horns.

"*Le débuché!* Off we go," said Jacques, hopping on his bicycle. Jacques and Capucine pedaled away energetically enough but were bridled by Alexandre, whose initially sluggish pace quickly slowed to a squeaky meander. Within a few minutes the hunt was as gone as if it had never existed and the forest filled again with its delicate sounds. Alexandre exhaled an audible sigh of relief.

After ten more minutes of labored pedaling, he stopped with the air of a man who has accomplished something worthwhile and looked ostentatiously at his watch. "Past noon," he said. "Wouldn't this be a good time to have an *apéro* and then start thinking about lunch?"

To Capucine's intense irritation, Jacques agreed enthusiastically. They found a small clearing covered with drooping ferns, spread a blanket in a ray of sunshine, and ceremoniously laid down Odile's picnic basket. Alexandre raised his hand. "I came prepared." He reached into the pocket of his Barbour and produced an ancient and well-dented silver flask of substantial proportions. "It's a nineteen-eighty-eight Yoichi single malt," he said, pouring a measure into the cap and handing it to Jacques, who raised it in a toast to his cousin-in-law with an appreciative smile. Capucine shook her head in dismay.

A good hour and a half later they were well satiated with Odile's hams and cheeses and bubbling over with the effects of her cider. But despite the steaming espresso from thermoses and the rest of the Yoichi from Alexandre's flask, they felt the autumn chill.

"Well," said Alexandre with the sort of smile Capucine supposed Napoleon had worn at Austerlitz, "I guess there's nothing else to do but pedal back to the château. You were quite right, my dear. All this exercise has done me a world of good."

The road home was Capucine's favorite part of the forest. Half a mile before the village, the road narrowed into a lane which fed into a wooden trestle bridge over a long and narrow lake. The seventeenth-century architects who had dug the lake had shortened the bridge by building long embankments jutting out from either bank and preserved them from erosion by planting rows of beeches. Over the years the branches had reached across the track to intertwine in a dense canopy, effectively blotting out all the light, save for the occasional dramatic primrose shaft. For Capucine the moment when the cavernous track suddenly debouched onto the brilliance of the lake had always been magical.

But that afternoon the narrow lane was jammed with cars and thronged with olive-clad followers rushing back and forth with the purposefulness of ants or witnesses at a road crash. But this was no accident. The entire hunt in its green-coated glory had taken up position on the pencil-thin bridge.

Capucine, Alexandre, and Jacques pushed their bicycles through the crowd out to the center of the bridge, where a small van with a dinghy strapped to its top seemed to mark the command post. The master grandly sat on his horse next to the van and surveyed the lake, which was covered with dark, dangerous-looking, thin black ice sloshing with puddles of icy water. The center of attention was the stag, which made pained progress across the ice, slipping constantly, falling to its knees every now and then, only to get up and continue on, playing out its last few cards. It was a wrenching sight even for the hardest of hearts.

"*Bon,*" said the master decisively to the rider next to him, the senior hunt servant, mysteriously called a *piqueux* since medieval times. "*A toi*—it's your move."

The piqueux dismounted and unsheathed a rifle from under his saddle flap, a lever-action .30-30 Winchester, the rifle that Hollywood Westerns made famous.

"Not exactly the weapon I'd choose for a long shot like that," Jacques said to Capucine in the tone one professional uses to another. Their intimacy was not lost on Alexandre.

As the piqueux went down on one knee and used the bridge's railing as a rest for the rifle's barrel, two paysans began to remove the boat from the roof of the van and prepared to put it on the ice. Their plan was obvious— push the boat across the ice to the deer and use it as a life raft in case the ice gave way.

Jacques resumed his Virgil's mantle and commented on the scene to Alexandre. "The master's made a complete balls-up. These big stags love to swim out on the lake to get away from the hounds, but this one must have been addled by all the yummy sex he had last night and made a bad tactical error by going out on thin ice. If they don't shoot him, he'll break through, drown, and sink to the bottom. Some left-wing journalist is sure to be lurking and will make coinage of an atrocity of that order." Jacques indicated the far bank with a nod of his head. A large crowd from the village had collected on the far side.

"Nothing excites the lumpenproletariat more than a cruel death. The part that's meant to entertain the gentry is the brave chaps in the little boat. They pray the ice won't break and they can push it out there fast enough to get to the deer before it goes under. You'll see. It's going to be a sporting event. I'll bet you twenty-five euros they get the deer just in the nick of time."

The piqueux fired his first shot. The sharp crack rolled out across the ice and echoed back from the far bank. The deer took no notice and continued its desperate struggle. The piqueux drew a deep breath, worked the rifle's lever, and fired another shot. The deer jerked slightly and scrabbled wildly in the icy slush until its forelegs plunged through a breach, imprisoning its body.

"What a buffoon," Jacques said to Alexandre. "He hit him in the abdomen. That's not going to do anyone any good."

The piqueux fired a third shot, another clear miss. Jacques snorted, loud enough to turn some heads.

The men with the boat made good progress, scuttling along on their knees, one hand on the gunwale of the boat, the other on the ice. The ice crackled under their weight but held.

At the fourth shot the deer collapsed and fell over at a forty-five-degree angle, supported by his legs trapped in the hole. Capucine fervently hoped he was dead and not just stunned. At the same moment the ice around the boat gave way and the two men jumped in, soaking wet. A pair of oars appeared and one man began rowing. The ice was so thin that it broke easily at each stroke of the oars. The second paysan sat primly in the stern, his weight raising the bow out of the water, creating a perfect icebreaker.

As the dinghy approached the deer, the surrounding ice fractured and the animal began to sink. The men just managed to secure a loop of rope around its antlers, hauled the deer fast against the stern of the dinghy, and began to row back. The emotions on the bridge were ambivalent, the relief of success tainted by the pathos of the scene.

On the town side of the lake the crowd had grown considerably and seemed to have split around two distinct focal points. Even though they were a good five hundred yards away, it was clear that while most of the spectators seemed riveted on the boat towing the dead deer, a smaller group seemed interested in something on the ground. Capucine saw two gendarmes approach at a run.

She nudged Jacques, who understood immediately. The two cousins jumped on their bicycles and pedaled off at speed. Alexandre, who had missed the exchange, hesitated and then followed at his sedate pace, his bicycle squeaking loudly.

Capucine's worst fears were confirmed. The crowd was huddled around the supine body of a man. Three gendarmes had given up the effort to keep them at a distance. This time they recognized Capucine as she pushed through, and they straightened up, saluting smartly.

A man was lying on the gravel at the edge of the lake, his sweater soaked in blood, an all-too-familiar black hole gaping in the middle of his chest.

CHAPTER 14

A dank gloom weighed heavily over the dinner table that night. The dining room seemed damper; the Réveillon wallpaper seemed to peel more severely; the root vegetable soup seemed more bland. Even Jacques was despondent.

It turned out that the man who had been shot had worked at the élevage. Oncle Aymerie had learned from Vienneau that he was a native of the village who had been a hand at the élevage for close to fifteen years. Even though the latest death supported Oncle Aymerie's suspicions, he seemed more depressed than vindicated. Capucine suspected he felt he was letting "his" village down since he was unable to stay the malignant tide.

The minute they rose from the table, Oncle Aymerie shuffled off to his room and Alexandre, Capucine, and Jacques made for the library to seek what solace the château's *cave* could provide.

Capucine moodily prodded the logs in the fireplace back into flame. "Three deaths in a month does seem a bit much, even at what Alexandre persists in calling the marchland of French civilization."

Jacques had his head deep in a cabinet under the book-shelves, noisily shuffling the stock of liqueurs. "Urrrmfllll!" he said, his voice muffled by the enclosure and drowned out by the loud tintinnabulation of the clinking bottles.

"Got it! This will cheer us up. Alexandre, it's going to be your saint's day." Jacques proudly held up a bleach bottle with a faded antique label.

"What I was saying, my shapely little cousin, is that I wouldn't be too hasty assuming these are murders. Don't forget that our beloved yokelry has been notoriously cavalier with firearms since our suckling days. Where else on earth but Saint-Nicolas would you see someone shooting across a frozen lake in the direction of a large crowd with absolutely no one thinking that might be a dangerous thing to do?"

"What's in that bottle? I'm hoping it's not really bleach," Alexandre asked, loyal as ever to his guiding sense of priorities.

"This, *très cher cousin,* is one of the château's great treasures. Just before the war there was a gardener here who was very fond of making *alcool de poire*—pear liqueur. He would take his pear juice to the copper alembic owned by the canton and distill pure nectar.

"This good man was clever enough to guess what those *Boche* Nazis would get up to when they reached here, so he put up all his stock of poire in bleach bottles and hid them in the commons. Decades later Capucine and I—when we were taking a short break from our childish pursuits," he said, leering and elbowing Alexandre in the ribs theatrically—"found the stash."

"You're right, of course," Capucine said. "But it's just become too much. I'm going to need to investigate."

"I thought you were already," Alexandre said. "Spirits are not supposed to age, but this stuff certainly has. There's not even a hint of pear, but there is a definite note of bleach. I wonder how scrupulous your gardener was in cleaning out his bottles."

"Sweetheart, there's a whole world of difference between a little poking around and a proper investigation. For starters, I'm going to pay a formal visit to the good capitaine de gendarmerie and find out what actual work has been done on these cases."

"You might have a hard time with that one," Alexandre said. It was no longer clear if the subject was *alcool de poire* or gendarmes.

Capucine plopped down on her husband's lap and sipped the water-clear, slightly toxic liquid from a delicately stemmed crystal liqueur glass with a chipped base. It might taste of bleach, but it was certainly effective. "I thought I saw you doing an inordinate amount of gossiping at the rendezvous. What did you find out? Come on, out with it," she said, rubbing the tumescence of her husband's stomach.

"Le Capitaine de Gendarmerie Départementale Augustin Dallemagne would appear to be a very frustrated man. It seems his ambition was to become an army officer, but he was neither smart enough nor from a good enough family to get into Saint-Cyr. He was also frustrated in his other great ambition, to marry well—an aristocrat or a *grande bourgeoise* at the very least. He settled for the gendarmerie and for a woman who is attractive enough and who has a good bit of money since her father owns a large Mercedes distributorship in Lyon."

"My dear, the things you can learn in so little time!"

"It's my training as a journalist. And there's a good deal more," Alexandre said with studied modesty. "The good capitaine tried very hard to become introduced into the society of Saint-Nicolas when he arrived two years ago. But, naturally, the harder he tried, the more he was rejected. In the end he gave up and is just counting the days until his next posting, which will be in eight and a half months."

"My heart bleeds," Jacques said, pouring everyone more *alcool de poire*.

"The irony is that the village adores Madame Dallemagne, who bakes delicious pastry and is a paragon among mothers. She's become a welcome addition to all the village teas and bridge afternoons."

"That must drive her husband wild," Capucine said.

"It does. And here's the best part. It seems that the capitaine is particularly jealous of you, not only because of your social position in the village and—I blush to even mention it—your title, but also because of the brilliant success of your career in the Police Judiciaire. I hardly think he's going to welcome you with open arms as a colleague when you start up your little investigation."

"Have you been assigned an active role in the investigation? I received no communication to that effect," Capitaine Dallemagne said crisply over the telephone.

"Good heavens, no, Capitaine. It's nothing more than occupational curiosity. Since I've been down here, three people have been shot. All three worked for the business of one of my uncle's close friends. Any flic's ears would prick up, don't you think?"

"It seems an odd way to spend one's holiday, madame, but you're welcome to stop by the gendarmerie if it pleases you. Come at eleven tomorrow. We'll have a cup of coffee, and I'll tell you the very little there is to be told."

Capucine thought that he didn't seem to be anywhere near as bad as the village made him out to be. But that was before things started to go downhill.

The coffee turned out to be more drinkable than what the Police Judiciaire usually offered, and the gendarmerie, as clean and efficient as an army facility, was poles apart from the seediness of any Paris PJ installation.

"So what precisely is it you want to know, Commissaire?" the capitaine asked as prissily as a cormorant, his lips tightly pursed and his neck muscles stretched.

"I just wanted to learn what the official view was on these deaths. Purely informally, of course."

"By these deaths, Commissaire, I assume you mean the one at the demonstration in the town square and the one at the hunt yesterday. The view of the gendarmerie is that they were both the result of accidental discharges of firearms, nothing more."

"And was that confirmed by the autopsies?"

"Madame, the gendarmerie only performs autopsies in the event of a criminal death. Obviously, for accidental deaths we do not. It intensifies the grief of the family, serves no useful purpose, and increases the burden on the taxpayer."

"So no autopsies were performed?" Capucine was astonished.

"Madame, we are not in Paris here. The gendarmerie surgeon examined the body of the victim who died at the demonstration and extracted a Brenneke solid from the wound. As I'm sure I don't have to tell you, these Brenneke solids are used commonly by paysans when they hunt big game. The fact that he was killed by one is an obvious indication that the shot was fired by one of the villagers during the commotion. This is exactly the sort of tragedy that will continue to occur until more stringent arms controls are put into effect."

"I see. And what about the death at the lake?"

"The body is still downstairs. The gendarmerie medical officer will examine it when he arrives at some point this week. But I can tell you, I have had a great deal of experience with gunshot wounds and this one is fully consistent with a thirty-thirty fired from the piqueux's Winchester."

"But the trajectory is all wrong. Since the piqueux had been aiming at the deer, the elevation would not have been sufficient for the bullet to have reached the other side of the lake."

"Ah, you see, that's exactly why it's so obviously an accident. The piqueux missed the deer. The bullet ricocheted off the ice and into the crowd. It seems impossible for it to have been otherwise."

"I see," said Capucine. "And what about the man who died three weeks ago at Maulévrier? Was an autopsy done on that one?"

The capitaine looked sincerely puzzled and shuffled through the papers in the right-hand drawer of his desk. He finally extracted a thin file and said, "Of course, the shooting accident. I'd forgotten about it. That sort of thing happens all the time. We certainly don't have the time to investigate those. Good Lord, if we did, I'd have to ask for another platoon of gendarmes."

"So what happened to the body?"

"I have no idea. I'm sure it was buried."

"Capitaine, you have a very different way of treating these incidents than we do in Paris."

"Of course we do, madame. What would be highly suspicious on the streets of Paris is nothing more than commonplace on the dirt roads of the country."

CHAPTER 15

At eight o'clock the next morning, while Capucine was at breakfast in the petit salon, Gauvin announced she had a phone call. As he accompanied her to the cloakroom, he whispered conspiratorially, "It's Capitaine Dallemagne, and he sounds very official."

"Madame," said Dallemagne, "if you would care to stop by the gendarmerie today, I have some supplemental information that will resolve our discussion of yesterday and put your mind at rest. I would be able to receive you at ten this morning." Gauvin was right. Dallemagne did seem to have risen to new heights of self-importance.

At the gendarmerie she was shown into Dallemagne's office and invited to sit across the desk from him. It was as if she were being interviewed formally in a case.

"Voilà, madame, the gendarmerie surgeon came by on his rounds yesterday and examined the body of, ahh"—he glanced down at a file on his desk—"Bellec, Lucien. The death was from a gunshot wound in the chest. He extracted the bullet and measured it. Seven-point-eight-four-nine millimeters. Exactly the diameter of the bullet from the thirty-thirty Winchester the piqueux was shooting. So you see it is irrefutable that it was an accident."

"May I see the bullet?"

"See the bullet? Whatever for?" Dallemagne recoiled as if she had proposed they take their clothes off and perform an indecent act on the desk. "I'm sure the surgeon took it with him and filed it somewhere. No need for the bullet. It's all right here in his report," he said, picking up a sheet of paper and flicking it dismissively with the backs of his fingers. He read, " 'Bullet extracted. Caliber noted. Seven-point-eight-four-nine millimeters. Resulting in wound possibly perforating aorta, resulting in death.' Voilà. Cut and dried. What else is there to say?" Dallemagne was very pleased with himself.

" 'Possibly perforating?' And you're still not tempted to perform an autopsy?"

"Of course not. You see crime everywhere. It's a deformation of the Police Judiciaire. We are in the country here, madame, not Paris. These people are simple paysans, not master criminals. As I explained yesterday, we have shooting accidents all the time. If we were to autopsy each and every one of them, we would need a whole new budget. And there would be an outcry from the families. They certainly don't want their loved ones mutilated." He laughed dryly. "No, my report is written. Bellec, Lucien, died accidentally as a result of a stray bullet fired at a deer on the lake. Lamentable, but hardly a crime."

"Does the surgeon describe the bullet at all? Does he make any mention of the slug being flattened from ricocheting off the ice?" Capucine asked.

Making a show of humoring her, Dallemagne studied the one-page report with exaggerated care. "No, madame, there is a description of the man's identifying marks and that is all." He leaned across the desk and said as sternly as if he were a high school teacher scolding a student for having failed to bring her homework, "Madame, it is highly irresponsible to attempt to create a crime where none exists."

Capucine left the commissariat in a rage. It had been pointless to explain the realities of the situation to Dallemagne. At least twenty popular cartridges fired a bullet that was 7.849 millimeters in diameter, not the least of which were a current NATO round and the very common .30-06 big-game cartridge. In the real world of crime detection one called for a thorough forensics examination and ordered a full autopsy. One didn't beg for crumbs from a pompous gendarme in an overstarched uniform who was counting the days until he could retire on his pension. She drove home twenty-five miles an hour over the speed limit, hoping a roadside gendarme would pull her over and she could give him a piece of her mind.

Back at the château, Gauvin heard her arrive and opened the door gravely. "Madame La Comtesse has had another telephone call. This time from the Police Judiciaire," he said as if they shared a deep secret. Capucine bridled. Alexandre was right. This country living was becoming too much. Gauvin incessantly calling her "Madame La Comtesse" was too much. His vicarious thrill with all these calls from the police was too much. Oncle Aymerie's conspiracy suspicions and his resultant guilt were too much. Getting interested in a case that no one under the age of seventy wanted her to solve was too much.

She picked up the telephone. "Commissaire," Isabelle said, a little more high-strung than usual, if that was possible, "I may have fucked up."

Capucine sat down on a little stool Gauvin had placed next to the telephone table in the cloakroom. What was going to be next? A little vase of flowers? A picture of Alexandre in a silver frame? She forced her larynx to produce a gentle tone. "Tell me about it, Isabelle."

"Well, two reporter types showed up at the commissariat this morning and asked for the officer in charge of the Belle au Marché case. The brigadier at the reception desk put them in the waiting area before calling me, so it was impossible to refuse to see them. Actually, it was a reporter and a photographer. The reporter was one of these guys who thinks he's totally sexy in a way that just pissed me off. So he asks all these questions about the Belle and wants to know if we agree that all three incidents had been done by the same person. He gets me so cheesed off that I blurt out that there were four incidents, not three. Then I really lose my temper and this photographer guy is snapping pictures the whole time and the flashes are getting me even more pissed off. So there I am, about to have them thrown out, and David steps up and does his little number. You know, he gets all palsy and invites these guys into an interrogation room for coffee and acts like he's having a fucking cocktail party. He says, yes, there might be a fourth case, but that we were looking into it and nothing was sure, but we'd be sure to keep them in the loop, and could he have their cards so he could call them when something happened? Anyhow, they wind up leaving, and I don't think they're going to write anything, but I sure got the impression they want to turn our Belle into some kind of folk heroine."

"So let them. No problem there," Capucine said.

"Yeah, but the other thing is that it would have been a disaster without David. You know how I get when I lose my temper."

"Isabelle, it sounds to me like you showed good leadership. You left the stage to David when his skills were needed. Knowing how and when to delegate is the hardest part of responsibility."

"Maybe," Isabelle said in a sulk. "Anyway, I really want to get going on this case. What about if I get those two faggoty dancer guys down here to look at mug books? What would be even better would be rounding up some suspects and having a lineup. What do you think, Commissaire?"

"Isabelle, if you're going to advance in the force, you're

going to have to learn patience. Mug shots and lineups are going to get you nowhere except irritating a lot of people. Sit and wait and let it happen. I'll be up there before the end of the week."

Capucine rang off, none too delicately. In the ensuing quiet, the closeness of the cloakroom weighing on her like the claustrophobic sanctity of a church confessional, she realized that she had done more harm in the last few seconds of the call than whatever good she had achieved in the rest. Why? Because Isabelle had expressed exactly the same frustration Capucine was feeling? Or did she genuinely feel she needed to smooth out Isabelle's rough spots to make her viable for the promotion? The only thing she was sure of was that her duty lay in Paris, not in the damned cloakroom.

CHAPTER 16

That night Capucine slept badly. Exceedingly badly. At two in the morning she woke with a start, fleeing a nightmare. She had been dating two boys who were identical twins. She thought neither knew she was seeing his brother but wasn't entirely sure. Even though she couldn't tell them apart physically, their personalities were entirely different: one was a spendthrift party boy and the other was serious and committed to a meaningful life. Every time she would go out with one of them, she writhed in fear that it was actually the sibling, who had been sent as a joke. But when her father opened the door to let the boy in, he immediately knew which one it was and greeted him by name without the slightest hesitation. Her father became her main anxiety. She suspected he was in on the game and it was part of his plan to control her life. She detested his obsession with appearances, good taste, and manners, but both her beaux told her she was even more obsessed with superficialities than her father. She wanted desperately to explain they were wrong but didn't dare, because she was terrified of being caught out not knowing which twin she was speaking to.

Capucine huddled up next to Alexandre and put her

hand on the roundness of his stomach. The world fell back into focus. She was on vacation. It was not as relaxing as it was supposed to be, true, but she was still on vacation. It was important that she make that vacation a success. That was an important goal. A responsibility, in fact. She decided the next day they would do something fun. Something really fun. Not necessarily fun for her but fun for Alexandre. He was the center of her life, after all. She would focus on him and stop fussing. She settled into a deep, untroubled sleep.

She came down early and breakfasted in the petit salon with Oncle Aymerie, leaving Alexandre to complete his *grasse matinée*—his lazy morning in bed. The torment of the night was long gone. Rosy flecks of early morning sun danced on the moat. Bone china and silver flatware tinkled cheerfully like oriental prayer bells. Neither spoke. Oncle Aymerie had never tolerated chatter at his breakfast table, unless, of course, he initiated it.

When he had finished his second piece of toast and was adding milk to his third cup of coffee, Oncle Aymerie looked critically at his niece.

"You don't seem to have slept well, ma nièce. Is something bothering you?"

Capucine constructed what she hoped was a radiant smile. "*Au contraire*, mon oncle, I'm delighted to be back at the château. And I'm so glad you're getting to know Alexandre. We're having a wonderful time. We really are."

Oncle Aymerie scowled at her, lips pursed and brow wrinkled. "I'm afraid it's my fault. I've turned your needed rest into a busman's holiday," he said.

Capucine put her hand on his arm. "Please don't think that, mon oncle. We really are having a wonderful time. And I had a brainstorm this morning," Capucine said, encouraging her enthusiasm into a trot with spur and whip. "I thought I'd take Alexandre on a tour of local producers of the three famous Norman cheeses and, of course, Calvados and that stuff, you know—what's it called?—when it's part Calvados and part pear *alcool*."

"Domfrontais," Alexandre said, striding into the petit salon. "Now, this is the sort of conversation that makes for a healthy breakfast."

"Bonjour, Alexandre. You've come at exactly the right moment. Capucine is planning a gastronomic tour of a Normandy that I'm sad to say no longer exists," Oncle Aymerie said.

"A tour of a Normandy that no longer exists? That sounds like something out of a science fiction novel."

Oncle Aymerie chuckled happily. He had finally tuned in to the wavelength of Alexandre's humor.

"She has a notion of taking you to see the *producteurs fermiers* of Pont l'Evêque, Camembert, and Livarot. I think she has visions of cheerful paysans and their round wives making cheese in their barns. Sadly, that ended in the fifties, when the industrial producers took over." He paused and took a reflective bite of toast.

Alexandre knew better than to interrupt.

"Look at what's happened to our Camembert, once the pride of Normandy. Now it's all made in giant factories that also make Pont l'Evêque and Lord knows what else. The artisanal producers and their beautiful cheeses are long gone." He shook his head sadly.

"I'm afraid you're all too right," Alexandre said. "I wrote a piece last year about industrial Camembert. The decisive buying factor in supermarkets is the feel of the cheese. The little boxes are made to be easy to open to encourage customers to squeeze. Of course, the cheese is adjusted chemically for perfect squeezability, same way car doors are made to sound solid when slammed in the showroom. No artisanal producer can compete with that."

Alexandre buttered a huge piece of country-bread toast and slathered it with acacia honey.

"But in France there will always be a culinary underground," he continued. "It just so happens I know a man who really does make artisanal Livarot. He made a killing in the dot-com bubble and retired when he was thirty, just before it burst. His parents had been artisanal producers before industrial production took over, and he was so sick of life in the fast lane, he moved back in with them and re-financed their little business, with him doing all the hard work, of course. Now he's making another fortune selling his cheese at fabulous prices to the Paris restaurants. I'd love to pay him a visit," he said, smiling at Capucine.

"And there's a family just outside of Domfront who have been in business for six generations, working their seven acres of orchard. They refuse to grow, even though some of their older bottles now sell for prices well into the five figures at auction. While we're down there, we could pay a call on them as well. Darling, your idea is absolutely *épatant*. You're a genius! But we need to get a move on. Domfront is a good hour and a half away, and you can never make up lost drinking time, right, Oncle Aymerie?"

CHAPTER 17

Despite his well-worn blue workers' overalls and hint of barnyard miasma, Alain Cochenet wasn't altogether convincing in the role of the last *producteur fermier* of Livarot cheese. From the neck up he remained the Paris intellectual techie with a luminous green and purple silk neckerchief, unmistakably from Turnbull & Asser in Piccadilly, and a well-scrubbed face fluorescent with recondite learning.

Overjoyed to see Alexandre, Cochenet embraced him as if he were a long-lost cousin. "No one from Paris ever comes to see me anymore," he said plaintively but cheered immediately. "Let's go over to the house. I'll introduce you to the parents, we'll have a little drop of something, and then we'll go pay a visit to my little darlings."

"You must have found it quite an adjustment to move back in with your parents," Capucine said.

Cochenet stared at her, attempting to define his new world. "Au contraire, sometimes late at night I do have a yen for slick restaurant dinners and all-night club bashes, but Paris was nothing compared to what I have here. I'm finally doing something genuinely fulfilling. And," he said, leaning toward Capucine confidentially, "I was *déboussolé* without my parents—a boat without a compass, sailing in circles."

"You all live together in this house?" Capucine asked with barely disguised incredulity.

"Of course we do. And Mama spoils us with her delicious cooking. Tonight we're having *râbles de lapin à la normande,*" he said, walking in and smiling lovingly at his parents. "You know, saddle of rabbit cooked in cider with lots and lots of onions. Nothing beats the old peasant dishes."

Capucine suppressed a grimace.

Twenty minutes later father and son steered them to an ancient barnlike outbuilding listing so conspicuously that collapse seemed imminent. "Of course," Cochenet said, "my father is the éminence grise. He knows all there is to know about Livarot and then some, don't you, Papa?" He smiled warmly at his father, who slipped his arm through his son's. With perfect complicity, the two led the way into the building.

Inside, the fruits of Cochenet *fils'* checkbook were clearly in evidence. Stainless steel gleamed; electric motors hummed; a handful of workers in white coats strode around purposefully.

"It all starts in these big vats. The *caillage*—curdling—is done with enzymes from something called *rénette,* a product made from calves' stomachs. Ours comes from Charolais calves bred in a small élevage just up the road and is made using a few secrets that only my father knows."

The father blessed his son with a paternal smile.

"Next comes the *rompage.*" They moved into a room that was almost uncomfortably warm. "The curd is cut so it matures more quickly." The air was pungent with wood smoke. "We hang on to our leaky old stove. The smoke is a component of our cheese's complexity.

"Then comes the *égouttage*—where the curds are drained before they go into the *moulage* and are put up in molds.

That happens down here," he said, leading the way down a precipitous, rickety staircase into a chilly cellar.

"We still use the wooden molds that have been in the family for generations. Industrial manufacturers use steel ones. One more element of our distinctive flavor.

"The cheese matures in here for four months and acquires its orange *robe* from natural bacteria. The industrial producers can't control the process, so they use something called 'annatto,' which comes from Latin America."

"*Oui, c'est vrai. L'Amérique latine!*" said Cochenet *père,* widening his eyes at this substantiation of the insanity of the modern age.

"It's evil stuff. Gives the cheese a nasty artificial tint and has a distinct peppery flavor." He shook his head in distaste.

"When the cheeses are finally ready, we tie them up with five bands of bulrush, pop them in their little boxes, stick our label on top, and ship them out. That's all there is to it!"

"Except for the fact that you've taken one of the oldest cheeses in France to new heights. Livarot Cochenet has pride of place on more than one three-star cheese tray," Alexandre said.

Both father and son beamed.

When Capucine and Alexandre finally made it back to the Clio, they discovered that a small crate of twenty-five cheeses had been put in the baggage area behind the rear seat. Protestations and offers of money were useless.

"Put it in the cellar of the château and dip into it slowly. Another three months of *affinage* will make it even better," Cochenet said.

The Clio didn't have a trunk, just an empty area behind the rear seat. As they drove off, the car filled pleasantly with the earthy pungency of Livarot.

"You know, when you get right down to it, this is turning into the best day we've had on this trip," Capucine said. "It's because we're far away from those killings and all that fuss. I made a great mistake getting involved, didn't I? We should probably just forget all about it and go right back to Paris, don't you think?"

"Don't be silly," Alexandre said. "You know perfectly well we're not going back to Paris. You've started your hare and now you have to run him to ground." He scrunched up his nose in distaste. "But I have a sneaking suspicion it's going to be more difficult than you think."

"Is that what you're wrinkling your nose at? Don't be silly. I'll have this thing solved in no time."

"Actually, it's the cheese. It's getting decidedly whiffy in here. Do you think you could roll down your window?"

The open windows had no effect at all. Mercifully, they made it to the Lemonnot domain in seventeen minutes flat.

As they pulled up into the rock-strewn courtyard, three generations of Lemonnots ambled out to greet them: Jean, alert and wiry in his seventies; his son, Pierre, in his forties, just beginning to develop a managerial paunch; and Frédéric, a twelve-year-old clearly awestruck by Alexandre. Capucine suspected that Alexandre's influence in the culinary world had been overdramatized. All three wore jeans, sweatshirts, and brown rubber boots.

Pierre opened the car door for Capucine. "Ah, I see you've been buying cheese," he said with a histrionic grimace. "Before we start our tour, my father's going to take you over to his house for a taste of the product while I make a few calls. Then I'm all yours."

Jean led them off to an ancient stone cottage at the far end of the courtyard.

"Pierre and his family live over there," Jean said, proudly pointing to an even smaller stone cottage. Capucine tried, and failed, to imagine what it would be like having her parents living fifty feet away, peering into her living room every time they walked by.

In his house Jean opened the doors of a nondescript oak armoire. The shelves were packed with thickset bottles with a red and tan label depicting a cheerful medieval paysan in a pointed hat sitting in front of a roaring fire, smoking a churchwarden, and sipping contentedly from a tiny glass.

"This is my personal *cave,*" Jean said. "I keep a selection of our recent production alongside of some of our more notable older *millésimes*. Pierre has the reins of the domain firmly in hand, but I still have the memory. That's why we work so well together." His face softened as he looked out the window toward his son's house. "I plan to hang around until I can see young Frédéric getting involved too.

"Enough of that! Let's get to work. I'm only going to give you two grades to taste. The first is our Réserve Familiale. It's been in the cask for six years and is our mainstay. The second is the nineteen seventy *millésime,* which has been in wood for fifteen years and is the finest product we commercialize." Alexandre's tiny glasses filled, Jean began pouring for Capucine. She stopped him.

"I have to drive back," she said with an embarrassed laugh.

Jean puffed out a snort, as if to say that these Parisians really lived in an incomprehensible world all of their own.

Rapt, Alexandre ignored the exchange. "It's extraordinary," he said. "The nineteen seventy has a far more pronounced pear note in the mouth than the Réserve. And, naturally, it's much more subtle and nuanced, with hints of licorice, almond, orange, and, of course, wood, but it's the presence of the pear that makes it so exceptional. Monsieur, I congratulate you. It's truly extraordinary."

Pierre, with Frédéric in tow, walked in just as Alexandre was giving his verdict. All three looked at each other without expression, but their joy was nonetheless palpable. This was the ultimate reward.

"Let me tell you about the domain," Pierre said. "We've had the same seven acres for over a hundred and fifty years, so we're getting to know them quite well. Most Domfrontais is thirty percent pear, but that's not enough. Ours is made with seven pears to every three apples. And, of course, all of our fruit comes from right out there," he said, pointing through the window at rows of gnarled, leafless trees aligned with military precision.

"Let's go see the distillery and I'll show you how it's made."

The first stop in the ramshackle outbuilding was the head-high oak fermentation vats.

"The apples and pears are crushed in those presses over there, and the juice is left in these vats for eleven months, until it turns into nice hard cider. Then the fun starts." They moved on to the next room, filled with a gleaming copper alembic and a row of shining copper tanks.

"We only distill once. Most producers double distill, but we think our way preserves the depth of the fruit taste. You should come back when the distillation is going full steam. You get drunk just standing here, right, Frédéric?" Father and son laughed happily.

"At that point the liquor is clear as water. It's the oak barrels in the next room that give it its color. The distillate goes into the barrels at a hundred and forty proof. Years later it comes out in its distinctive golden *robe* at only eighty proof. The missing alcohol is what we call the *part des anges*—the angels' share. The longer it stays in the barrel, the more the angels get. When we die, we're going to come back as Domfrontais angels, aren't we, Frédéric? They're the ones who have all the fun." Father and son laughed uproariously at the funniest joke in the world, even though it must have been trotted out at every visit.

Before they left, Alexandre bought two bottles of the 1970 *millésime* for himself and a wooden case of six of the Réserve Familiale for Oncle Aymerie.

As the bottles were being loaded into the car, Jean came out to say good-bye. He shook Alexandre's and Capucine's hands and then wrinkled his nose. "What's that smell? Good Lord, you have a whole case of Livarot back here, cooking in the sun. Enjoy your trip home," he said with a grin. As they drove off, all three generations of Lemonnots were doubled over in laughter at the hapless Parisians.

The Livarot became too much for them even before they reached the town of Domfront, seven minutes away.

"Let's leave it at a railroad crossing. Isn't that what you're supposed to do with foundlings?" Capucine asked.

"Defeat is not in the code of the Huguelets. We'll stop in the village, procure some twine, stow the damned stuff on the roof of the car, and turn on the air-conditioning. That should do it."

The solution proved imperfect. Even with the windows closed as tightly as the twine would allow, the odor of Livarot was still very much in evidence. Capucine counted the minutes. She searched for a topic that did not involve cheese.

Alexandre came to the rescue. "You know, of course, that I don't have the slightest doubt you'll find the culprit. I just hope you won't suffer in the process."

"I'm suffering already. But if you're referring to Dallemagne, there's no problem there. The Police Judiciaire has authority throughout France. Actually, I was planning on paying a visit to a pal I have on the DCPJ." She paused at Alexandre's blank look. "I thought you knew all the ins and outs of the PJ by now. The Direction Centrale de la

Police Judiciaire. Headquarters. The loonies who make staffing decisions with a Ouija board, remember them? Sure, they'll think I'm being a bit impetuous, but I have a good pal there from the commissaire's school. No problem at all. He'll fix it all up."

"I was thinking more about the village. It would be a mistake to underestimate Dallemagne. Your success will be his failure, after all. The village knows you as a sweet little girl who blossomed into the charming Madame La Comtesse. They're not going to like it when you rip off your rubber princess mask and reveal yourself as a Police Judiciaire fiend who has come to prize open their little boxes of nasty secrets."

Capucine giggled but her eyes hardened and her mood swung.

"*Tant pis.* As Napoleon said, 'You can't make an omelet without breaking a few eggs.' It's simply beyond me to let a murderer walk away free. That's all there is to it."

"Wasn't that Robespierre? But you're sure there really *is* a murderer?"

"Of course there is, you ninny. And I even have a good idea of who it is and what it's all about. But suspicions hardly make a case I can take to a magistrate, do they?"

Just then they mercifully arrived at Maulévrier. Gauvin rushed up, checked at the odor, but bravely opened the car door for Capucine. She nearly wept in gratitude.

CHAPTER 18

"Did you cut your vacation short?" Isabelle asked hopefully when she caught sight of Capucine walking into the commissariat at ten in the morning.

"Nope. I had to come to Paris for the day to deal with something, and I thought I'd stop by and see if you guys were playing together nicely."

Capucine made a tour of the open-plan office while Isabelle hovered at a distance, making a pointed display of her patience. She reminded Capucine of a dog hoping to be taken out for a walk. There was no doubt that ambition was the most insidious of the vices.

The commissariat seemed to be carrying on quite happily in her absence. Two almost anorexic young men sat on either side of a desk, dressed identically in torn jeans and slack hoodies. Only the fact that one pecked hesitantly at a keyboard labeled him as the flic, while the waves of intense animosity radiating from the other identified him as the perp who had been apprehended in some misdemeanor or other. A few desks beyond, a detective with a shaved head and muscles that made his tight olive drab T-shirt look like an overfull bag of potatoes waited patiently with a warm smile, ready to take the deposition of a woman who quieted a crying baby with a bottle as two grubby children sat listlessly on the floor by her chair, sucking their filthy thumbs. The woman had a bright fuchsia hematoma over most of one side of her face. Capucine wondered what instrument her husband had used to produce it.

The uniformed receptionist at the front desk waved his telephone receiver in the air at Capucine, indicating that he had a call he thought she should take. She went to her office.

"*Salut,* Capu!" She didn't recognize the voice, but it had to be one of her classmates from the commissaire's course at the ENSP, where she had been stigmatized with the odious nickname. Then it hit her: Bruno Lacombe, the oldest member of the class, well into his fifties, an up-from-the-ranks cop who started out as a *gardien de la paix* directing traffic and was now the commissaire in charge of the Fourth Arrondissement East, which covered the ultra-chic Ile Saint-Louis and the fashionable part of the Marais.

"So how're you making out in my commissariat?" His laugh was rusty from cheap Cognac and exhaust fumes. The big joke when the class had received their postings was that working-class Lacombe wound up in the Fourth while Capucine was sent to Paris' tough Twentieth.

"I've been meaning to call you, but you know how it is," he said. Capucine allowed that she did indeed.

"I'm inviting you to lunch. Better late than never, right? Is twelve thirty okay?"

"Today?" Capucine was taken aback. In her world asking someone to a social function for the next day was an affront, much less for the same day.

"Of course today. Fact is, we've got a case here that I think really belongs to you. No reason not to discuss it over lunch. My treat. We'll have a good one. Seems like a legitimate enough expense account item to me."

"What's this about a case?"

"I'll tell you over lunch."

"You're on. Actually, I have to be in your neck of the woods at eleven to see our dear classmate Damien Pelletier. It would be fun to have lunch after."

"Pelletier? What are you doing at headquarters? You didn't get yourself into trouble, did you?"

Capucine laughed. "I'll tell you over lunch."

Headquarters, the Direction Centrale de la Police Judiciaire, was viewed by most PJ officers as a useless, vestigial organ good for nothing except generating an endless stream of seriocomic bureaucratic bumf and surreal staffing assignments. They also saw relevance in the fact that the DCPJ was located at number eleven rue des Saussaies, headquarters of the Paris Gestapo during the WWII occupation.

Commissaire Damien Pelletier had been an unassuming, clean-cut, well-scrubbed, considerate, zealous student, highly unpopular with his colleagues for those very virtues. He had drawn what his peers considered the worst possible posting—human resources in the DCPJ—and had rejoiced.

"So let me see if I understand this right. You want to be seconded part-time to the Normandy subdivision to work on a case in your native village? Is that it, Capu?"

That nickname again. If Alexandre ever got wind of it, it would be an unmitigated disaster.

"Not quite my native village but almost. My uncle lives there, and I pretty much grew up in his house. I know the village inside and out. There have been three violent deaths in as many weeks, and my uncle is convinced they're foul play. Actually, he's pretty much convinced me, too."

"And the local gendarmerie in all this?"

"Damien, the local capitaine is a card-carrying asshole whose only interest in life is making it to retirement age without rocking his boat. Look, if I don't focus on this, a murderer will go scot-free, thumbing his nose at the police."

Pelletier stared at the wall, massaging the wattle under his jaw, for fifteen seconds. "Capu, you were admired in our class for your pragmatism. I understand what's driving you here. I really do. But it just can't happen. It's true the PJ has national jurisdiction and ascendance over the gendarmerie, but, when the sun goes down, we all drink at the same watering hole." He looked earnestly at Capucine, verifying that the metaphorical subtlety of his nyet had registered.

"So you're turning me down?"

"I don't decide these matters on my own, of course. If you absolutely insist, I suppose I could air the idea at the next staffing committee meeting, but it would be a waste of time. There's not a hope in hell they'll approve it."

He looked at her earnestly. "Capu, you need to forget about this. But I'll tell you what. Not to let a classmate down, I'm going to send a memo to the Normandy division of the gendarmerie indicating our interest in the case. That will trickle down through channels to your capitaine, and I think you'll find it will have a decidedly salutary effect on him, letting him know he has to keep you fully abreast of his progress."

On her way out Capucine was torn between attempting to demolish the elevator door with a Louboutin ostrich flat and dissolving into giggles at the notion of the "decidedly salutary" effect a memo that would "trickle down through channels" was going to have on Dallemagne. Anyway, that was that. The bad news was that she was off the case. The good news was that she had been lifted off the horns of her dilemma and she could get back to the real world. With a groan of defeat and a sigh of relief, she walked off to lunch.

Mercifully, the restaurant where she was to meet Lacombe was only two streets away and she was no more than her customary fifteen minutes late.

Surprisingly for such an upmarket neighborhood, the bistro was an authentic period-piece *bar à vin* run by the owner and his family. As she walked in, a boisterous wave of roiling guttural diphthongs, *tabac brun* fug, and the earthy odor of robust red wine washed away most of the bad taste of the morning.

Lacombe was hunched over a glass of whiskey at the bar in earnest conversation with the owner—a shaggy man with a drooping ginger mustache who could have passed as a character in an Asterix comic—and his large Griffon Vendéen, a perfect clone of his master, save for some unfortunate technical glitch resulting in it coming out as a quadruped. Both of them reminded Capucine of Bouvard, who must be happily proselytizing in Fresnes Prison. She tapped Lacombe on the shoulder.

"Capu!" he exclaimed. "You've gotten even more beautiful, and I do believe your ass is just a tiny bit bigger and even more luscious."

"*Vieux cochon,*" Capucine said, delighted, giving him a slap that wound up as a caress. A whiskey later they were both ready to brave the tight circular staircase and be shoehorned into a table, elbow hard against elbow with their neighbors. The owner's wife flatly announced what they would be drinking—a Tavel, "the likes of which had never before come through the gates of Paris"—and left them to their deliberations over the menu.

Lacombe had gained a few pounds and lost the worry lines on his face, which had been his most salient feature during the commissaire's course.

"You seem to have prospered in the Fourth East."

"Who wouldn't? You get it all, from the *Amerloque* richies on the Ile Saint-Louis to the creepies on the boulevard Bourdon and back to the caviar leftists on the place des Vosges. You know how it is. I hear you're doing not so bad yourself. I admit that I thought the Twentieth was going to be too much for you, but I hear you've turned into quite the little star."

"You know how it is." They both laughed. "So what's this case that you think is mine?"

But the owner's wife scurried up importantly with the food and preempted center stage. A tangy dish of marinated herrings cooked with shallots, coriander leaves, *herbes de Provence*, and bay leaves, served on a bed of tiny, round *ratte* potatoes sautéed in the herrings' oily marinade for Lacombe and a duck *magret* for Capucine. Being a commissaire had its compensations, particularly when you could take two hours for lunch, followed by a long walk back for your *digestion*.

"It's a pretty weird little story, even for my commissariat. See, a couple of days ago we get this missing person's report from Hubert Lafontaine. You'd have known who he was, but I didn't have a clue this guy is the major living French composer. The sort of dude who will be known five hundred years from now."

"Lafontaine must be over ninety now."

"Ninety-two. But he's spry enough. I went to see him. He has an apartment at the end of the Ile Saint-Louis. Filled with antiques and stuff, overlooks the Seine, very nice, just what you'd expect. He told us that his niece, who is living with him, had been missing for four days."

"And you can't find her?"

"That's not it. Problem is that the niece died thirty-six years ago. At the time, she was living in Lafontaine's apartment, same place he's in now, while she was going to university. It was nineteen sixty-nine and she had just entered the Sorbonne and was staying at her uncle's because her mother—Lafontaine's sister—was worried that a simple girl from the provinces would be corrupted by Paris living." Lacombe snorted. "The girl went home for a long weekend and was killed in a car crash down there. She drove into a combine harvester coming down the wrong side of the road with no lights on."

"So it's senile dementia. Nothing exceptional about that at the age of ninety-two."

"Oh, he has dementia all right, no doubt about that, but there actually *was* someone staying with him last week. I interviewed the cleaning lady, who never really saw anyone, but she did make a bed that had been slept in and changed towels that had been used. The concierge saw Lafontaine going up the stairs the previous Sunday with a woman she described as being in her early twenties, wearing a long, flowing white dress, and having a 'face like an angel.' Anyway, one day this angel just upped and left." Lacombe filled their glasses, emptying the bottle of the Tavel. "Kinda sounds like it might be your Belle au Marché, doesn't it?"

"Is anything missing from the apartment?"

"Not that I know of. But I certainly didn't do an inventory, and I doubt Lafontaine would notice anything was gone unless it was his piano or something like that."

"It could be her. It's her style. But how is it you know so much about the Belle's MO? Have you taken to reading the PJ circulars?"

"Circulars my ass. Your Belle is the darling of the press. Have you been on vacation in Tahiti or someplace where they don't get papers? She's the queen of page one."

Back at the commissariat Capucine told Isabelle to bring David and come to her office in half an hour. There might have been a development in the Belle case. Isabelle buzzed off, humming like a high-voltage transformer.

Capucine closed the door to her office and put a call in to Jacques. Amazingly she got straight through. When she suggested dinner that night, Jacques purred, "I knew it was just a question of time before you tired of your portly old sybarite. And I know *just* the place to take you." His shrieking laugh was even more jarring when it came over the phone.

Her delight in getting a quiet moment with Jacques on such short notice, never an easy thing to do, was offset by the realization that she would have to make up some plausible excuse to Alexandre for spending the night in Paris. She was hardly going to sneak into Maulévrier at three in the morning. She had a vision of the appearance of a blinking Oncle Aymerie at the head of the stairs in his brocade dressing gown. As she giggled, wondering if he wore mustache bags in bed like Hercule Poirot in that movie, Isabelle walked in with David, frowning, sure that Capucine was laughing at her.

"I think our dear Belle's scored another victim. Hubert Lafontaine," Capucine said.

"The composer? Is he still alive? I thought he died in the seventies." Capucine was always amazed at the depths of Isabelle's knowledge. The phone in Capucine's hand came alive. She'd forgotten she'd dialed a number.

"Allô?" said a frail, elderly voice.

"*Bonjour,* monsieur. This is Commissaire Le Tellier of the Police Judiciaire. I'm calling about your niece."

The faint voice blossomed into a smile, obvious even through the tiny speaker of the earpiece. "Wonderful! Have you found her?"

"Not quite yet, but it won't be long, Monsieur Lafontaine. Actually, some more details would speed up our search. Would it inconvenience you if we came by tomorrow?"

"Of course it wouldn't. Anything to bring my poor niece back more quickly. Anything at all."

CHAPTER 19

Lafontaine lived in the quiet half of the Ile Saint-Louis, the part that still remained Aragon's island heart of the town, embraced by the languid arms of the Seine, where all was eternally tranquil—a world apart from the tourist-trap side, crammed with overpriced ice cream shops, cheap kicky clothing boutiques, and foreigners in shorts screaming at their bawling children. His apartment on the serene quai d'Anjou was in a perfectly proportioned *hôtel particulier* overlooking the gently flowing river.

Capucine tapped the brass fist-shaped knocker on the shiny green door of the flat with some trepidation. Lafontaine was far more than a mere celebrity; he really would still be known in five hundred years.

The man who opened the door was immediately recognizable as the celebrated composer, even across the chasm of the thirty years since the pictures on his CDs had been taken. But after the first rush of realization, the larger-than-life being collapsed into the frail frame of a mortal body, ancient and blinking.

Capucine smiled as reassuringly as she could. "We spoke on the telephone yesterday. We've come to help you find your niece. Do you remember?"

Like the sun coming out from behind a cloud, his face cleared. "Yes, of course!" he said in a trembling voice. "Do you have any news?"

"We'd like to ask you some questions so our search will be more effective. May we come in?" Capucine asked.

The apartment was a treasure trove. An enormous Steinway, topped with silver-framed photographs as dense and ordered as a field of corn, dominated the room. Out of the corner of her eye Capucine recognized three presidents, two popes, Sartre, Mahatma Gandhi, and a charming snap of Jacqueline Onassis bending down and kissing a seated Lafontaine on the forehead. Beyond the piano, every flat surface supported memorabilia, each item more remarkable than the other.

Forcing herself not to ogle, Capucine tuned in as Isabelle was saying, as usual in a slightly bellicose tone, "So you thought you ran across your niece at the market after she had been gone for thirty-five years. Is that correct?"

"Good Lord! It hasn't been thirty-five years. Only four days." Lafontaine smiled tolerantly.

"But your concierge told one of our officers your niece had died in nineteen sixty-nine."

"Poor Yvette. I'm afraid she's getting on in years. You know"—Lafontaine paused as if explaining to a small child—"a little gaga. She's confused. She's only kept on because the residents of the building have become attached to her. All the actual cleaning work is done by an outside service. It's a little extra cost, of course, but we don't mind. It's such a pleasure to have Yvette deliver the mail in the morning and gossip about what's going on in the building." He paused, looking puzzled. "What was it you were asking me, young lady?"

"I was saying that the concierge in the building seemed to think that your niece had died thirty-five years ago."

"That poor woman." It was not clear of whom he

spoke. "My sister did die thirty-five years ago, and that's why her daughter has been living with me ever since."

David decided it was up to him to sow some order in the interview. "And how old is your niece, then?"

"Why, the same age she's always been, of course, twenty-one." Lafontaine spoke to David as if he were dim-witted.

Capucine, who had been a great fan of the literature of pataphysics while at university, left them to it, finding the banter a perfect backdrop to her perusal of Lafontaine's memorabilia. She was sorely tempted to let it go on, but she finally found what she was looking for and meanness was not among her vices.

"Excuse me, Monsieur Lafontaine. This is absolutely re-markable. Tell me about it," she said, pointing to an odd-looking picture frame over the fireplace, deep enough to hold a book, elaborately gilded, but completely empty.

"Ah, that. It's my most prized possession. They're Berlioz's drafts for his famous letters to Harriet Smithson. I'm sure that you know the story. Berlioz was madly in love with the Irish actress for years." He picked up a silver frame from a table and handed it to Capucine. "This is a copy of her portrait. Lovely, don't you think?"

Isabelle and David trotted over to see the image, which featured a young woman whose prissy features seemed undersized on her curiously pear-shaped head. Her hard, round breasts strove valiantly to burst out of a low-cut velvet gown. Her hair had been pulled back tightly and coiffed into elaborate curly cascades at her temples and her nape. It was not the sort of beauty that would break hearts in the present age.

"Berlioz wooed her for years. He tirelessly wrote her letter after letter declaring his love, but she wanted noth-ing to do with him. His passion for her grew and grew until it finally found its outlet in the fervor and violence of the *Symphonie Fantastique*. It was only then that the gods smiled at him and, quite by accident, Harriet found herself at the premiere and somehow divined that the symphony had been written for her. She relented and later they were married."

"What a lovely story," David said.

"In his will Berlioz ordered that the drafts of his letters to Harriet be destroyed, but his family couldn't bring themselves to do it. A few years ago they were given to me. I was very moved."

Capucine peered intently at the empty frame. "Monsieur, please come help me. Here Berlioz says, 'Without you my life is nothing but an empty . . .' and a whole series of words have been crossed out. Then there is a scribble that I can't quite decipher. What does it say?"

Lafontaine examined the frame, David and Isabelle staring over his shoulder. Lafontaine squinted, shot Capucine a shrewd glance, then craned his neck to look more closely. "Madame, the word is *rêve*—dream. It explains much about the *Symphonie Fantastique*." He looked levelly at Capucine, perfectly lucid. "Do you really think you'll be able to find my niece?"

Very gently Capucine put her hand on his arm. "I'm confident, monsieur, you will be reunited with her soon."

As Lafontaine walked them to the door, he turned to David. "Yes, it is a lovely story. But you know, some historians claim that it wasn't the *Symphonie Fantastique* at all that changed Smithson's mind. When she went to that premiere, her acting career was failing, she was beginning to get fat, she had run out of money, and Berlioz had become famous and quite well-to-do. But why should that make a difference? As Liszt said, once she had inspired that monumental work, Smithson's duty was fulfilled."

In the Clio going back to the commissariat, Isabelle smoldered in a silent white rage. After a while she could contain herself no longer. "Damn it, Commissaire, you should have let me grill that old fool. At the very least I would have gotten a decent description of the girl, and I probably could have talked him into filing a complaint. It really pisses me off that this theft is not going to make it onto La Belle's charge sheet." She glared at Capucine.

"Isabelle, he made it as clear as he could that he had gladly given up his letters for the few unexpected days he had with his niece. Even in the Police Judiciaire you're not expected to be cruel enough to take that away from him."

CHAPTER 20

"Alexandre absolutely loathes this place," Capucine said with a happy smile. "When it opened, his review said they served fluorescent fluff, not food."

"I picked it because I was sure you wouldn't want to sit next to a bunch of grumpy old Cognac-marinated buffers who won't eat anything that isn't excrementally brown and flaccid from being soaked in wine for a week. You get far too much of that with your corpulent consort," Jacques said, bleating his loud cackle.

"And just when I thought you were getting to like him," Capucine said with an exaggerated moue.

The restaurant was very definitely not part of Alexandre's econiche. The white enameled room was filled with organically formless white composite marble tables, each dotted with a glaring bottom-lit plastic bauble in a brilliant primary color. Thumping techno-rock throbbed through an overly efficient sound system. It might be the perfect setting for its fauna—willowy and emaciated golden young things posing self-consciously, large eyes nervously darting, seeing and desperately hoping to be seen—but it was certainly suboptimal for what Capucine had in mind.

The evening was off to a bad start. Jacques launched into his banter, screeching his innuendo-laden gibes over the background noise. He had donned his Paris plumage: a pale gray Prince of Wales check suit over a light purple silk shirt, as crisp and perfectly ironed as if he had just put it on—a trick Capucine would love to learn—a pale yellow Hermès tie, and tan suede Weston loafers. Even though Jacques's sartorial excesses didn't seem to present the slightest detriment to his career, in the family it was often wondered if he might not be, well, just a little fey.

Jacques arched an eyebrow at a passing waiter, who stopped short as if he'd been harpooned—another trick Capucine would love to learn. After a whispered instruction, the waiter returned promptly with martini glasses filled with noxiously green cocktails that tasted mildly of mint and madly of alcohol.

"Tell me, my nubile cousin, to what do I owe the pleasure of this delightfully sudden assignation?" Jacques asked with a cartoon leer.

Capucine was spared the need to answer by the waiter, who returned with the menus. She smiled enigmatically and studied hers closely. In keeping with the birdlike eating habits of its clientele, the restaurant offered mainly appetizers and desserts with only a small handful of decidedly bizarre main dishes.

"Try the *poulet au Coca,*" Jacques suggested. "It's actually quite good. Even your tubby hubby will tell you that Coke syrup isn't all that different from balsamic vinegar."

The mandatory restaurant antiphony dragged on for long minutes, slowed by Jacques's salacious teasing of the lithe waiter. In the end Capucine wound up with a salmon tortilla and Jacques with the chicken braised in Coca-Cola.

During the interminable dialogue with the waiter, Capucine had become increasingly despondent, realizing that the dinner was a vast mistake. Jacques, acutely sensitive as usual, picked up her mood shift, instantly becoming the concerned cousin.

"You're worried about something, aren't you?"

"Well—"

"It's the family, isn't it?"

"Actually—"

"I know, I know. I remember all that brouhaha when you announced you were joining the police and how upset you were." He gave her hand a fraternal squeeze.

"No—"

"Look, you're worrying about nothing. Trust me. Of course they were all up in arms at the time, but they're over it. It's forgotten. And, hard as it is to believe, they all love Alexandre."

"Jacques—"

"No, no, listen to me. Look how they were all deferring to you last weekend about those deaths. You're the official family sleuth now. Even Father seemed to be trying to get you to investigate." Jacques hee-hawed loudly.

"Jacques, that's not it at *all*." Capucine paused for breath. "The DCPJ declined my request to be allowed to investigate the incidents in Saint-Nicolas."

"Excellent! The last thing anyone needs is you plodding around the village with your big flat feet, digging up people's secrets. Besides, you have your career to think of. Face it, Jane Marple wouldn't have made it in the PJ even if she'd had your boobs."

"Jacques, stop. You absolutely *have* to help me. I need you to pull one of your many strings. The last two deaths were clearly murders. The local gendarmerie doesn't give a damn. Somebody's got to do something about it." Capucine's lips had rounded into a pucker and her eyebrows had contracted into an angry V.

"Of course they were murders. But that's not the point."

"So what *is* the fucking point, then?"

"*Ma cousine*, the hardest thing for me to accept in my job is that it's all about compromise. Let's say I were to pull one of my moldy little strings and get the DCPJ to see things a little more your way. Do you realize how antagonistic the Normandy gendarmerie would become toward the Police Judiciaire? Do you have any idea of how many criminals would slip through the cracks because of that rancor? Not to mention that there would be a big ugly blot on your pristine little copybook that might well bar you from promotion to the senior echelons."

Her back to the wall, Capucine pulled an ace from her boot and slapped it on the table. "What about your father? It was Oncle Aymerie who got me started. He's dead set on getting to the bottom of these deaths."

"That's what you think. It's true he has a rosy vision of himself as the flower of French feudalism. He's overprotective of 'his' village and feels the murder victims were 'ill used' and it's somehow all his fault. He wants to set things to rights and sees you as his paladin. But he's sure as hell not going to be feeling that way if you start flipping over stones and the creepy crawlies come slithering out."

Jacques paused and delicately sliced off a piece of his chicken. "And I'll tell you another thing. The last time I got you out of the soup, I didn't have to pull any strings. All I did was nudge a few people in my own agency and convince them that your case was really in the national interest, which it was. I hardly think the director is going to feel that the death of a couple of ranch hands is a threat to the country's security."

Jacques took a bite of chicken. "It used to be that you just wanted to get a little street grime on your lily-white Sixteenth Arrondissement hands. That suited you. It went with the kohl you bought for your eyes on vacation in Marrakech. But galloping eternally after the grail of justice seems a bit OTT."

"Jacques, it's not about justice, not really. I don't know

what it is. It's the principle of the thing, I guess. But I know I couldn't sleep at night if I let a killer go loose because it was politically expedient."

Jacques shrieked his braying laugh. "My poor cousine, what makes you so adorable is that you aren't even slightly embarrassed saying things like that out loud. 'Couldn't sleep at night!' I know what's keeping you awake. It's trying to get your geriatric, gastronomic hedgehog pumped up. He told me all about it," Jacques said with an exceptionally loud bray of laughter.

With the petulance of adolescence, Capucine kicked Jacques's shin as hard as she could. Jacques looked into her eyes and saw what only he could have seen: beneath the iron resolve of her cobalt blue eyes, she was on the edge of tears.

As if suddenly bored by the tiff, he fell into a reverie, an elbow on the table, chin cradled in his hand, index reaching up to his cheekbone, staring unseeing into the middle distance. As it happened, at the exact center of that middle distance were the gym-hardened gluteals of a lissome blonde who was leaning over her table to ensure maximum visibility while flirting with her beau of the evening. With the radar of her breed, she noticed Jacques's stare and smiled fleetingly at him. Jacques was oblivious.

"You know, cousine, plucking you out of the ministerial bouillabaisse is going to turn into a bad habit. But I suppose someone in the family has to have exemplary ideals. There is an interministerial committee meeting in a few days that's intended to coordinate efforts of the various intelligence services and police departments, and I happen to sit on it. I'm certainly not going to put this on the agenda, but I might see my way to make an utterance at the urinals other than my usual relieved groan."

Capucine whooped like a schoolgirl and leaned far over the table to kiss her cousin on the forehead. The males at surrounding tables smiled admiringly.

"But, don't think this is a done deal. Messing outside of my own ministry is poking into a can of nasty worms that often bite."

"Jacques, thank you. I don't know what I'd do without you."

Jacques shrieked his inimitable laugh. "And to think that when you called me to have dinner on such short notice, I was sure it was all about finishing what we started that rainy afternoon in the commons—"

Jacques started as if he had been goosed. His hand darted into his jacket. Reflexively—thinking he was reaching for a gun—Capucine leaned forward, pushing her chair back, grabbing for her Sig as she searched the room for the danger. Jacques's volcanic bray was loud enough to stop conversation at all the surrounding tables. He fished a beeper from an inside pocket, inspected it, and held it up disdainfully between thumb and index. It twitched and buzzed like a captured insect.

He stood up and hiked his eyebrows in apology. "Gotta run, luscious."

Just as he started off, he turned back and whispered in Capucine's ear. "I feel guilty about leaving you in the lurch. If one of the things you had on your mind was resolving that issue I was just talking about, I can recommend that little citizen at the next table." He indicated the blonde who was following their conversation intently. "I'm sure she'd be amenable to anything you might conjure up."

CHAPTER 21

At seven thirty the next morning, just as night was reluctantly beginning to relax its grip on the dark, Capucine jerked awake. For a brief horrible instant she thought it had happened again, like that one time—that single time—she had woken up in the strange bed of a boy she had met at a party. But this was her own bed, in her own apartment. Still, it took her several minutes to find the courage to leave the warm security of her eiderdown and face the desolate flat.

She went into the kitchen, coaxed a café au lait out of the Pasquini, and stared out the window, willing the familiar kaleidoscope of the dawn reflected on the zinc rooftops of Paris to break her mood.

Two coffees later she was fully awake but still a little disoriented. She'd boiled it down to one of two possible causes: a feeling that she'd made a fool of herself by asking—hell, begging—Jacques to fight her battles for her or having fibbed to Alexandre about why she'd had to spend the night in Paris. Maybe it was both.

At nine she picked up the phone and dialed Maulévrier. Gauvin answered. His continued insistence on addressing her as "Madame La Comtesse" irritated her more than usual. Neither Alexandre nor Oncle Aymerie was reach-able—the former still in bed and the latter in conference with his gardener—but Gauvin was voluble with the day's plans: a walk-up shoot after lunch over some fields of stubble that were believed to be rich in partridge. Aston-ishingly, Alexandre had agreed to participate. She felt a rush of love for her husband, who was trying so hard to be a good consort. She rang off, announcing she would be there for dinner.

She felt an urge to manifest her appreciation and love for Alexandre with some sort of material gesture. But what? She dragged her feet through the morning er-rands—sorting through the accumulated mail, packing more clothes to take to the country, spending the hour she never had time for in the bathroom, attending to all the *petit soins* so dear to the Frenchwoman—racking her brains for the perfect gift to take him, but nothing came to mind.

Eventually, she capitulated and accepted that, *faute de mieux,* a sweater from that exorbitantly priced English store on the boulevard Saint-Germain was the best she could do. It wasn't ideal, but just maybe, if she could find the perfect color, it might get her message across.

As she walked down the boulevard, she passed a dusty umbrella store that was held to have been there since the time of Louis Philippe. Her emotional register blipped. A walking stick! It wouldn't have the passive-aggressive character of the usual woman's gift, which was no better than a thinly disguised attempt to impose her taste on her husband. No, this present was going to be something he would cherish for life.

The store lived up to its reputation, crammed with beautifully made canes and umbrellas that all looked like they had been made before the Great War, to be used promenading up and down the Champs-Elysées while it was still lined with walled town houses. Her first thought was one of those hunting sticks that open up into a flimsy little saddle, but those were really for dutiful wives to sit on daintily as they admired their husbands' shooting prowess. Completely wrong. But here it was! A robust malacca cane with a large semicircular handle. The perfect stick for a postprandial country stroll. Just the thing to whack at weeds and raise in the air to emphasize a point. But what made this cane absolutely perfect was that the handle unscrewed to reveal the cap of a slim silver flask that, the salesman assured her, would hold a third of a bottle of wine or whatever the owner chose to fill it with. Alexandre would be overjoyed.

Her next stop was at Hédiard in the place de la Madeleine, where she purchased an absurdly expensive bottle of Francis Darroze fifteen-year-old Grand Bas-Armagnac so Alexandre could provision his cane the minute she gave it to him. As an afterthought she bought an elegant two-pound tin of breakfast tea for Oncle Aymerie and headed the Clio back to Normandy.

Dinner turned out to be a very boisterous affair. The Vienneaus and Henri Bellanger, who seemed to dog Vienneau like a bad conscience, had been invited. The men were in high spirit as the four had spent the afternoon trudging through fields with the household dogs in search of partridge and had returned with nine birds, six downed by Bellanger, two by Oncle Aymerie, none by Vienneau, and, astonishingly, one by Alexandre.

"He has a natural talent, your husband," said Bellanger, who was now established as an indisputable paragon with a shotgun. "If you took him out regularly, he could become quite a useful shot."

Even though he had used the same tone as if suggesting Capucine give her dog more exercise, Alexandre couldn't have been more pleased. Her husband never ceased to amaze her.

Gauvin arrived at his usual lugubrious pace with the main dish, a grim-looking array of small parchment paper bundles securely tied with string, suggesting tiny bodies wrapped in shrouds after some massacre in a distant land. A kitchen servant, abjectly terrified, looking not a day older than thirteen, followed at Gauvin's heels with a fragrant dish of golden girolle mushrooms.

"Partridge," Oncle Aymerie announced proudly, looking at Alexandre. "Of course, not the ones we took this afternoon. These have been hung for exactly the right amount of time. In fact they're from that shoot two weeks ago, when, ah . . ."

In an effort to redeem his gaffe, he summoned Gauvin sharply to bring him the serving dish. But Marie-Christine stared at him with a rigidly polite smile that did not quite mask her horror and desperation.

"This is a recipe that's been in the family for generations," Oncle Aymerie said with forced cheerfulness, picking up one of the partridges with two forks to show it off. "The secret is that you wrap them in fat and then tie them up in a paper package so they come out nice and moist."

There was much awkward cutting of string with dull table knives and clumsy opening of the paper parcels with forks. For some mysterious reason, good manners dictated that the unwrapping, which would have been difficult enough with a sharp knife and nimble fingers, be done entirely with cumbersome tableware. Once open, the little bundles yielded appealingly moist golden partridges crammed with stuffing that smelled invitingly of onion.

"Aymerie," Alexandre said, fanning the aroma of the birds to his nostrils with an open hand in that odd gesture that high-level chefs seemed to cherish, "your family recipe is a classic that comes direct from Dumas père." He had assumed the full pompous gravitas of a celebrated food critic. "The birds are stuffed with a mixture of finely chopped fatback, shallots, parsley, and the minced heart and liver of the bird. And then they're wrapped in very thinly sliced fatback and wrapped again in baking parchment. The beauty of the recipe is that it reinforces the natural bitterness of the bird rather than struggling with it. Your Odile is a treasure."

Oncle Aymerie beamed and started to ramble on about the connection between Dumas and his family. Bellanger smirked and leaned over to make a whispered aside to Vienneau. Oncle Aymerie scowled and said, "Here! There are no low masses said at my table. What are you on about?"

"I was saying to my neighbor, monsieur," Bellanger said with a smug smile, "that I hoped you were not claiming Dumas in your ancestry." He chuckled as if he had scored a subtle debating point.

Oncle Aymerie was furious. "I take it, monsieur, that you are alluding to the fact that the immortal writer's grandfather, the Marquis de la Pailleterie, chose a black slave girl from the colonies for a wife. Could that be what you are referring to, monsieur?" Oncle Aymerie was red in the face.

It was a double-barreled gaffe: not only did Oncle Aymerie's clan have two crossings with the Pailleteries, of which they were quite proud, but Dumas' *métissage* was known to every high-school student in France and was hardly the nugget of literary erudition Bellanger seemed to think it was. Indeed, President Chirac's speech when Dumas' ashes were transferred to the Panthéon the year before attributed at least some of Dumas' greatness to the mélange of his blue and black blood.

The cold splash hastened the dinner's end, which was a shame since the partridge was exceptional. As soon as decently possible, Vienneau left, followed by Bellanger with his tail between his legs and Marie-Christine trotting obediently behind.

As Capucine escorted them out to their car, she took

Marie-Christine aside. "I was planning on a little shopping expedition to Honfleur tomorrow, but I haven't been there in years and I have no idea which are the good stores anymore. What if you came with me?"

Marie-Christine jumped at the idea.

Capucine postponed giving Alexandre his surprise gift until they were alone in their room after dinner. It turned out to be a wise decision. He was genuinely delighted with the cane and insisted on opening the Armagnac with the corkscrew of his pocketknife and sloshing it into the cigar-shaped silver flask.

"This is glorious," he said, topping up the vial with the exaggerated care of the slightly soused. "Now let's put it to the test." He screwed the components of the stick back together. "I stroll down the boulevard with the insouciance of a true *flâneur*," he said, walking around the room with exaggerated strides, "and—*hop!*—I am suddenly overcome with a desperate need of sustenance." Alexandre halted, unscrewed the stick, and took a deep draught.

"Perfect. And the Armagnac is exquisite. Your turn!"

Capucine entered into the spirit of the thing, and before long the two were marching around the room, Alexandre swinging his new cane in a parody of Charlie Chaplin, singing Maurice Chevalier tunes, pausing every now and then to refill the little flask.

Much later, Oncle Aymerie banged loudly on their door. "*Oh là là. Ça suffit comme ça, les enfants! Au lit!*" They giggled like schoolchildren and whispered happily to each other. Obeying Oncle Aymerie's dictate, they found themselves under the covers in abbreviated sleeping attire and set about the dramatic representation for which they were costumed.

Alexandre froze as if he had seen another deer leaping. He sat bolt upright in bed.

"Did I hear you say you were going to Honfleur tomorrow with Marie-Christine Vienneau? I have to spend *another* day watching the grass grow up between my toes? And I suppose you're going to tell me this is more police business."

"It is, sort of. I have a feeling, an intuition really, that there's a little more going on there than meets the eye."

"And there's a great deal that *does* meet the eye, too." He resumed his snuggling, then propped himself up on one elbow. "I thought the *cherchez-la-femme* approach to crime investigation went out of style with Dumas, that great African Frenchman." They both giggled.

Alexandre sat up again. "So where did you go to dinner with this . . . What was his name, anyway?"

"Damien Pelletier," said Capucine. "We were in the same commissaire's course at the police school. When we graduated, he was assigned to headquarters. He loves it."

"And where did you two go for dinner?"

"The Green Cow. You were right. It was really awful," she said loyally, even though in hindsight she had enjoyed the restaurant. "I had a salmon tortilla." Alexandre groaned. "Damien had the famous *poulet au Coca*. The *frites* that came with it were unbelievable."

"Of course they were. They fry them the way the Belgians do, in pure beef tallow. Your face is going to explode with pimples any second now, and your heart is going to slow down like a toilet stuffed with too much paper. Even McDonald's stopped using that stuff years ago."

Capucine hoped Alexandre's interest in the dinner had been deflected, but he looked at her with the slyness of an interrogation's bad cop. "Strange place for two flics to go to discuss business, the Green Cow," he said with a flinty look.

"It's the new police. Maigret's day is over. It's all leather jackets and two-day stubble now." Capucine slid under the covers in an attempt to reinitiate their former pursuit, delighting at the speed at which Alexandre's interest reemerged. There would be no more imaginary deer prancing through the room that night. In fact, within twenty minutes he was sound asleep, emitting just the slightest growl of a snore. Capucine nestled up against him and rubbed the slight convexity of his stomach. Men were such pushovers.

CHAPTER 22

"Is this really a police car?" Marie-Christine asked, looking around Capucine's Clio, wide-eyed.

"It most certainly is." Capucine clunked the pulsing blue beacon on the top of the dashboard and flicked a switch to emit the strident *pan-pom, pan-pom* of French police vehicles. A Peugeot a hundred yards ahead pulled over and stopped. As they passed by, they could see the driver reaching into the glove compartment for his car's papers. Both women waved, giggling.

"And do you have a big black gun like they have in the movies?"

"Actually, today it's a cute little one in my handbag, but when I'm on duty, I have to carry a service weapon. I keep it in a holster in the small of my back, and it's torture when I'm sitting down. But when you need it, you're definitely glad to have it."

"How exciting. You have no idea how much I envy you. You're so courageous to have done something so daring and . . . well . . . you know," she giggled.

Capucine laughed. "My parents certainly didn't share your point of view."

Marie-Christine's face was flushed with excitement like

a little girl's. "We're having a real outing. I never get out of Saint-Nicolas. This is such fun!" She squeezed Capucine's arm in appreciation.

They rolled through the brilliant jade-green countryside dotted with white cows, gnarled apple trees, and rustic thatched cottages with thin wisps of smoke drifting up from chimneys. Marie-Christine seemed as oblivious as Capucine was delighted. In forty-five minutes they were in Honfleur, a town that, despite the glowing hype in tourist guides, had been sucked dry by generations of day-trippers, who had left only a hollow, empty shell of quaintness. Nonetheless Marie-Christine was ecstatic and insisted on seeing even the most desiccated sites: drab, empty Saint Catherine's Church, rebuilt in the fifteenth century by shipbuilders with salvaged ships' timbers to celebrate the end of the Hundred Years' War; the commercial dock with its remaining handful of fishing boats struggling to eke out a desperate living from dwindling stocks of fish; and finally the Vieux Bassin, the square inner harbor with its anorexically thin houses and shabby sailboats.

The shopping was also a disappointment. Summer was long gone. Most of the clothing stores were closed for the winter, and the handful of knickknack shops offered nothing more exciting than garish ashtrays made from seashells or bad reproductions of the more famous of Corot's and Boudin's paintings of the region.

"We'll make up for it over lunch," Marie-Christine giggled. With some misgivings they settled on a restaurant that, even though its authenticity seemed to be the product of an interior decorator, did have a pretty view of the Vieux Bassin.

It was almost empty. After a few minutes' wait, during which a loud altercation could be heard in the kitchen, a waiter arrived, darting angry looks over his shoulder. He slapped two cracked plastic menus on the table and held them down with his open hand. "I'd recommend the oysters. They're Belons and they came in fresh about an hour ago. After, I'd recommend the red snappers, which I know for a fact the chef bought at the dock this morning. I certainly wouldn't recommend anything else unless you have a taste for antiquities." He said this loudly enough to make it perfectly clear he wanted to be overheard in the kitchen.

All that was left for the two women to do was order the inevitable bottle of Sancerre. Despite the ominous portents, the oysters were delightfully briny and alive with the fresh tang of the sea, while the yellow-green Sancerre was lemony, tooth achingly cold, and made them shiver with delight.

Marie-Christine rapidly downed two oysters, tilting her head back and letting the pulsing little globs slide down her throat. "Bliss!" she exclaimed.

"Alexandre always tries to convince me that oysters are a potent aphrodisiac," Capucine said. "He insists they work individually. He once claimed that he had had two dozen at lunch and that we were going to have an even better time than the first night of our honeymoon."

Somehow, it was the completely wrong thing to say. Marie-Christine grimaced as if she had felt a sudden twinge of pain and drained her half glass of Sancerre in one go. With an angry gesture she speared an oyster with her tiny fork and swished it around violently in a ramekin of mignonette sauce the color of blood mixed with water, sloshing the liquid on the white tablecloth. She looked up with a forced smile and prattled a rapid recitative of inanities until the waiter came to remove their dishes.

He returned with dented little metal *coupes*. "Calvados sorbet to clear your palate for the next course, our highly unique little Norman specialty," he said cynically.

Marie-Christine burst into tears. "Goddamn this fucking Normandy. I can't stand another second of it!" She smacked the table with her open palm. At the sound the waiter turned around to see if he was needed, quickly took the measure of the situation, and continued his retreat without making a sound. Even in this worn-out place being a waiter was a responsible enterprise.

"This is about Philippe Gerlier, isn't it?" Capucine asked.

With that deep, quiet tone women adopt in crises, Marie-Christine said, "How on earth could you have possibly known? You weren't even here."

"Had the relationship been going on for long?"

"Oh my God, I don't remember. A year, maybe more."

"Do you want to talk about it?" Capucine asked.

"I do. Of course I do. It's the only thing I want to do. But what is there to say? It was an addiction. In France we are brought up believing being a woman is all about entrapping our men with our bodies. We must make ourselves beautiful with our endless *petits soins,* and then we must make ourselves *artistes* in the bedroom so that we can hold on to them. We believe that's the only way we can keep the little stallions faithful, don't we?" Tears welled in her eyes.

"I suppose so."

"But with me it was the exact opposite. My husband could care less what I look like. With any luck we make love once every two months, and he falls sound asleep the second it's over for him." She shuddered.

"When I saw Philippe for the first time, it was like someone hit me on the head. I was all dizzy. It was more than lust. I needed him physically like you need a drug. Have you ever felt that?" Her eyes burned into Capucine's.

"Yes, but the feeling was never as sustained as yours."

"I know it was nothing more than an infatuation. Everything that happened between us happened in bed. But it was still wonderful."

Saying nothing, Capucine raised her eyebrows to encourage her to continue.

"Please don't get me wrong. The fact that it was so physical didn't mean that Philippe wasn't a wonderful, caring person. He bought me all sorts of presents. He had an eye for lingerie and would always bring me things from La Perla or some other place in Paris. And it wasn't just me. He was devoted to his poor mother. He was always going to America to visit her. She had some terrible disease—Alzheimer's, cancer, or something like that—and was having extensive treatment in a clinic in the Midwest. He was so sweet. He always brought back gifts for me when he went to America. Usually from a lingerie place they have there called Victoria's Secret. They have such naughty things." She giggled girlishly.

"It must have been an enormous blow when he died."

"I felt like an addict who has been deprived of her source. It was agony. It was terrifying. It was like the bottom had dropped out of my life."

"And now?"

"It's still just as bad. Worse even. The drug addict gets over it. I can't." Tears welled up in her eyes. "It gets worse and worse, every day."

"Does Loïc know?"

"Of course not! He's such a dear. I could never hurt him. Why should he know? It was just something biological. A physical urge. It had absolutely nothing to do with Loïc. Can't you understand that?" She was on the edge of hysteria.

"I might be able to understand. I'm not so sure he would."

"That's why he can never find out. Loïc is my life. He's so kind and wonderful. I admire him so much. When his father died, the élevage was not doing at all well. Loïc took it over and made it successful again. Of course, I helped a little when I invested my inheritance—which wasn't all that much, really—but it was Loïc who did it all, new marketing plans, new strains of cattle, new ideas. He made the business what it is today, and we share that."

"Does that mean you own shares in the élevage?"

"No. Loïc owns them all. My investment was in the form of a perpetual short-term loan. I wanted Loïc to feel secure in his ownership of the business, even though we are technically equal partners. Do you see how close that makes us? Philippe was just a physical need. I don't even see it as an infidelity. If I had started taking something like cocaine and got over it and never told Loïc, that wouldn't be an infidelity, would it? It would just be a sickness, right?"

"So did you get over it?"

Marie-Christine burst into sobs. "No!" She paused. "You're right. I didn't. I don't know what I should do."

As artlessly as in a TV sitcom, an idea bloomed and her face brightened with a radiant smile. She reached out and took both of Capucine's hands. "I know what! Do me another favor? Please! Come to dinner tomorrow—with Alexandre, of course. It will just be the four of us. I'll make sure that awful Bellanger person isn't there. And you can see how Loïc and I are when we're together. And then you can tell me what to do. Please, oh please, do come!"

CHAPTER 23

Alexandre was in seventh heaven. As he had explained to Capucine, the last time they were at the Vienneaus, he had been torn away from "Loïc's Ali Baba cavern of cattle kitscheries," and now he was making up for lost time. Having exhausted the pleasures of the table behind the sofa, Alexandre had now expanded his horizons to include the whole vastness of the immense sitting room. And he was well rewarded. On a side table he had come across a cow's hoof skillfully made into a silver inkwell. A little farther on he joyfully discovered a lamp that emerged from the back of a porcelain figurine of a cow. In no time at all he found that pulling the cow's tail not only turned the lamp on and off but also caused the contraption to emit a melodic mooing sound. As the three other people in the room turned their heads toward the noise, Capucine directed a warning moue at Alexandre. She had recognized the overinflated-balloon look of suppressed mirth, always a danger sign with Alexandre.

"I see the herd has followed you into the house, Loïc," Alexandre said.

Instead of the awkward silence Capucine feared, Marie-Christine giggled happily.

"This is nothing!" she said. "When we were first married, he wanted to have a prize bull that had just died stuffed and put in the foyer." She squeezed Vienneau, who beamed and looked at her with deep affection.

"I still think it's a great idea," Vienneau said. "After all, that famous American cowboy put his stuffed horse in his living room and everyone thought it was very endearing."

"And his dog as well, sitting alertly by the fireplace for all eternity," Capucine said.

Marie-Christine smiled joyfully at the exchange, but somehow her happiness had an unreal quality, as if it had been created chemically.

At that moment the Vienneaus' cook made her curious semaphore signal of opening the kitchen door to signify dinner was ready, and the quartet trooped obediently off to the dining room.

The first course was astonishing in its simplicity, a carpaccio of raw beef sliced so thin it was translucent, seasoned only with salt, pepper, a trickle of excellent olive oil, and a few drops of lemon juice. It was as rich and full tasting as only uncooked beef can be and as unctuous as a slice of poached fish. But the effect was spoiled when Vienneau announced that the meat came from "Moloch, one of the best steers we've produced in ages," and then proceeded to give a lengthy description of the Moloch-in-question's lineage and astonishing physical conformity to the Charolais standard. Capucine glanced at Alexandre and was dismayed to see he wore the highly artificial stony face that novice poker players affect when they have been dealt three of a kind. He was an inch away from uncontrollable laughter.

A little later Marie-Christine disappeared into the kitchen to return with a serving dish of tournedos Rossini, an out-of-fashion, overrich recipe involving fillets of beef topped with foie gras, crowned with truffle slices, and splashed with a thick sauce of Madeira and Cognac.

"Moloch redux?" Alexandre asked with exaggerated seriousness.

"Oh, absolutely. Can't waste a morsel of a creature like that," Vienneau said.

Capucine broke in rapidly. "So when did you two meet?" she asked with cocktail party gaiety.

"Oh, we've been sweethearts since we were students," Marie-Christine answered.

"Yes," Vienneau said, taking over the narrative. This was obviously a subject dear to his heart. "We married the summer after I graduated from HEC." Capucine had no idea he had gone to such a prestigious business school. "We moved into a much smaller house down the road—my parents lived here in those days—and I started working at the élevage."

"I didn't know the country at all, I'm a Paris girl, really, but I fell in love with it," Marie-Christine filled in with the perfect timing of a couple of talking heads spooling out the evening news on TV.

"Then came the hard years." Vienneau had the microphone again.

Capucine glanced nervously at Alexandre. He had a very low tolerance for this sort of hyperbole, but he seemed interested enough.

Capucine smiled and raised an eyebrow to encourage Vienneau. "You see," he continued, "what I told you the other day, you know, about the one-legged great-great-grandfather and all that, is really just the PR version. Of course, the élevage actually has been in the family for generations, but it was never all that big, and the business I inherited from my father was in serious financial trouble. My father had let it run down. I had to improve both the quality and the profit margins."

"Sounds like a tall order," Alexandre said. "Excellence and cost control sound mutually exclusive."

"Loïc is a genius," Marie-Christine said. "He turned the

business around in no time at all." She blew a kiss across the table to her husband. "He can do anything."

"Getting the élevage back on its feet was the easy part. The hard part came when we started to become successful. I had to expand the herd, and then I needed to acquire a fleet of refrigerated trucks to make deliveries. That involved building relations with banks and the financial community. It was a whole new world for the élevage. And without Marie-Christine it never would have happened." Vienneau gave his wife an adoring look and blew her back a kiss.

For a second Capucine thought all this Hallmark gushiness would prompt a comment from Alexandre, but his interest continued apparently unabated. "Weren't you risking your quality by growing too fast?"

"Ah ha! Ever the journalist. That was the challenge, but we had no choice. The other prestigious élevages were growing and were getting big enough to be able to squeeze us out by cutting prices, so we had to grow to remain viable. But, as it happened, we actually improved our quality," Vienneau said proudly, spearing a hefty chunk of Moloch with his fork.

Alexandre smiled. "Your beef is the benchmark, no doubt about that," he said. "There can't be many top restaurants in France that don't buy from you."

"Are you planning on having children?" Marie-Christine asked Capucine.

"I had Chef Jean-Basile Labrousse on the phone from New York just the other day, and he was telling me how much he missed your beef," Alexandre continued.

"Very definitely. Actually, I think the time may not be too far away," Capucine said with a secretive smile. "And you?"

"We still supply Diapason, his old Paris restaurant."

"I'd love to. Particularly now. But we can't. It's very sad."

"How does he like New York? I saw that the *New York Times* gave four stars to Aubade, his new restaurant," Vienneau said.

"He loves everything about it, but he misses Paris enormously. He said he's lost without your beef. Apparently, American beef has excellent flavor, but it lacks—what did he call it?—some ghastly term, oh yes, 'mouthfeel.' "

"Loïc doesn't want any?"

"He does, but he can't. It's his low sperm count."

"I know it sounds like a sexual act, but we use the term in the industry here, too. American beef has poor mouthfeel because it's shot too full of growth hormones. It does wonders for the cattle in small doses, but we can't use it, because it's strictly forbidden by the European Community. Our tenderness comes from Normandy grass, not chemicals."

"Actually, that's a huge secret," Marie-Christine went on. "Loïc doesn't want anyone to know. He thinks it would hurt the élevage. Damage the reputation of the bulls or something. Men can be so funny."

"For once the EC restrictions are rooted in good sense. Those hormones have appalling side effects."

"What about adoption?"

"I'd love to, but Loïc won't commit. He doesn't even listen when I talk about it. Would you like to adopt a child, dear?"

"Of course, my love, anything you want, anything at all. Just have them send me the bill," Vienneau said, without breaking stride in his rebuttal of Alexandre's defense of the European Community's food regulations.

CHAPTER 24

Capucine slapped her napkin on the table in irritation. Breakfast had become frankly impossible. She might just as well eat tablets of chocolate in her room and avoid all the aggravation. Once again Gauvin had sidled up with his conspiratorial whisper, "Madame la Comtesse, it's the police!" This time he had been so melodramatic, she almost believed he might have a blue roadster pulled up at the back of the château for her escape.

She picked up the receiver in the cloakroom, fully expecting to hear a breathless Isabelle. Instead, a crisp male voice asked her if she was Commissaire Le Tellier and, on hearing an affirmative answer, asked with icy politeness if she would be good enough to hold for Commissaire Pelletier. The phone went silent with that leaden deadness that foretells a long wait. It didn't seem that the DCPJ's largesse ran to upbeat little tunes to keep the caller on hold entertained.

Capucine was so sure the call would be bad news that she let the odors of the cloakroom act like a time machine, sucking her back through a vortex into her childhood. The active reagents seemed to be the sweet wax of Barbour jackets, the even sweeter banana smell of the compound

used to jag out shotgun barrels, and an indefinable amal-
gam of wet wool and leaf mold, overlaid with a soupçon
of overripe Camembert, which she traced to a line of venerable wellies standing rigidly at attention against the
wall. She was transported to a time when she must have
been twelve or thirteen and Jacques had chased her into
the cloakroom, screeching, tickling her ribs, pushing her
into the coats, and . . .

"Allô. Allô? Capu. Capu! Can you hear me?"

"Damien. Sorry, I put the phone down."

"No, I apologize for making you wait. I'm having one
of those days. Look, as you insisted, I presented your request to the staffing committee yesterday afternoon. They
reacted exactly as I thought they would with the usual
crap, keep the gendarmerie motivated, no squabbling
among services, blah, blah, blah." He fell silent. She could
hear someone speaking to him in the background.

"Listen, Capu, stay on the line. It's going to take me
only a few seconds to deal with this." The phone fell back
into its tomblike silence.

Well, that was definitely that, Capucine said to herself.
So much for Jacques's influence. She was tempted to hang
up and let Pelletier call her when he had more time, but as
she thought about it, a loden cape she remembered wearing when she was in her teens seized her attention. She had
loved the way it swallowed her up until she cast it back
like a comic book superhero. She slipped it off its hanger
and draped it over her shoulders. She realized that the ar-
chaic oak hanger must have swung from the cast-iron bar
for at least a hundred years and probably a lot more. She
was tempted to spend the rest of her days in the cloakroom. Maybe Gauvin could install a cot.

"Capu, Capu! Are you there! *Merde!* Allô. Allô!"

"Sorry, I'm here."

"Where was I? Yes, right. Well, they decided you have
'special insights,' "—he gave the words heavy ironic em-

phasis—"into the two cases we discussed. So they've been taken away from the gendarmerie and assigned to you. Voilà." He paused. "What else?" She could hear him shuffling papers. "Oh yes, the local gendarmerie is to lend you whatever assistance you need, and an order to that effect is being sent to them. But it's important you 'liaise cooperatively with them,' " he said with more leaden emphasis. "Which means, don't piss the gendarmes off too much, because the DCPJ doesn't want to hear any complaints, okay? What else? Ah yes, your vacation has been canceled effective, effective . . ." Capucine could hear the crackle of papers again. "Effective last Monday. Voilà. That's it."

"What about the first case?" Capucine asked.

"The first case?" Pelletier asked. She heard papers rattling once more. "The guy who got hit with bird shot while shooting birds? There's no way in hell that's not just a plain-vanilla shooting accident. I didn't even put it on the agenda. Now, listen, Capu, completely off the record, I have a bone to pick with you.

"Let me translate what 'special insights' mean in DCPJ jargon. It means you pulled a string. Capu, I don't know how you did it, and I don't want to know, but it doesn't make me proud of you. You used to impress the shit out of me on the commissaire's course because your integrity set the tone for the way real flics were supposed to act. Shit, it wasn't just me. You impressed us all. And then you go and do this. I don't know what you're up to, but you're acting like a corrupt politician, not a cop." He hung up on her. It suddenly felt oppressively hot in the cloakroom. Capucine tore off the cape and bolted into the hallway.

CHAPTER 25

Capucine skidded to a stop on the cool cracked marble tiles of the hall, gulping air like a surfacing diver who had gone too deep. How cruel life's ironies were. Just as her old family was finally beginning to accept her back into the fold, her new one slapped her face. Well, she just wasn't going to be bothered. That was all there was to it. As she stamped her foot in peevish irritation, she noticed that Odile had left a large picnic basket on the hall table. Two long-necked bottles of Touraine emerged from under the twined-down red check napkin like geese ready to be carted off to market. Of course! How could she have forgotten? She had made plans to go mushrooming with Alexandre. Her mood lifted like a bubble of noxious gas rising out of a swamp and escaping in the sunlight. The day was going to be a glorious one, after all. This outing was going to be even more fun than the last one.

But it turned out that you could no more go on the same mushroom jaunt a second time than you could step twice into Heraclitus's proverbial river.

The start was cheerful enough. Alexandre had filled his cane flask with a single-malt whiskey he had unearthed in the darkest recess of Oncle Aymerie's liquor cabinet.

Odile's picnic proved to be up to her usual standard of bountifulness. Still, the joyous mood of the previous expedition was just not there. Even the interruption of leaping stags and horsemen in period costumes would have been welcome.

As they sipped Calvados with their coffee, Alexandre asked, "You're worried about muddying your watering hole, is that it?"

"Who wouldn't be, with all the grief you and Jacques have been giving me?" Capucine said irritably. She could see Alexandre wondering exactly when Jacques had proffered so much advice but, relishing the idea of a spat, made no attempt to sidetrack him. Discharging the tension, Alexandre bounded up, stuffed the detritus of lunch back in the basket, and began an intense scrutiny of the perimeter of the clearing. Lusting after something to sink her teeth into, Capucine joined him in his search with the enthusiasm of a puppy deerhound on a new scent. Wandering off, she came across a small bunch of lovely flat-capped mushrooms topped off exactly in the same hue as the weathered brick red pants yachtsmen so loved.

"Capucine! Stand back!" Alexandre yelled in alarm.

His tone was so sharp that Capucine recoiled, half suspecting Alexandre had seen a viper she had missed. They were too far north for vipers, but anything was possible.

"Whatever you do, don't touch those things." He came up behind her and pinioned her arms. "Those are the arch villains of the mushroom world—*Amanita muscaria*. They're a dangerous and unpredictable hallucinogenic. Normally, they're fire-engine red, but these must have been washed out by the rain."

Fifteen minutes later Capucine discovered some identical-looking specimens and backed off cautiously. The shape was the same and the mushrooms were domed with a dull orange, not too far removed from the faded red of the *muscaria*.

"These are okay," Alexandre said, plucking one up and sniffing it. "*Amanita caesaria,* Caesar's favorite. Or at least I hope they are. What if we have Odile put them in some omelets tomorrow for breakfast? Russian roulette is a game I've always wanted to try."

Naturally, the Pharmacie Homais was the first stop on the way home. It seemed deserted, but they could hear someone puttering around in the workroom in back, presumably Homais filling an urgent prescription. When he did not stick his head out for several minutes, Alexandre called out, "Is anyone back there?"

Homais answered testily, "*Minute!* I'll be out as soon as I'm done." He arrived unhurriedly a good five minutes later.

"Voilà. Voilà! What can I do for you?"

Alexandre proffered his basket of mushrooms for inspection. Homais poked through them incuriously with a forceps. Eventually he came to the *amanitas,* picked one up with the long pincers, and squinted at it. "Clearly not *Amanita muscaria.* They're *Amanita caesaria,* a good find, but you knew that already." He looked ostentatiously at his watch, a heavy gold Rolex, and said, "You must excuse me. I have to close up. I'm expected at the *presbytère* for dinner."

"With the pastor?" Alexandre asked with a sardonic smile.

"Of course with the pastor. Who else? And, madame, I saw you examining my watch," he said aggressively, raising his arm to show Capucine the watch in question. "Don't get your hopes up. It's not the real thing, only a knockoff I bought in Lyon from a Senegalese street vendor last year," he said with a cynical laugh.

When they were out on the street, Capucine asked, "What was that all about? What's with all your questions?

The last time it was about some newspaper, and today it was all this business about the pastor."

Alexandre burst out laughing. "I adore you," he said. "You're becoming the perfect tough street cop. Any day now you're going to be sporting a manly stubble. You've even forgotten your Flaubert. Remember the pharmacist in *Madame Bovary?* The one who plots continuously against the Bovarys because Emma's doctor husband has displaced him as village medico? The puffed-up pseudo-intellectual who writes endless pretentious pieces for a Rouen paper called the *Fanal?* His name was also Homais."

"Of course. I never made the connection. But what about the pastor?"

"Don't tell me you don't remember. Flaubert's Homais was a militant atheist. His archenemy was the village pastor. They couldn't abide each other, much less have dinner together."

"And what about that business about his watch?"

"There I can't help you. It was odd, all right, but I'm pretty sure Flaubert's Homais didn't have a fake gold Rolex."

Their second errand was to pick up fresh-baked rolls for dinner at the *boulangerie*. Even though the bread of choice in the country was a gigantic loaf of *pain de campagne,* which the paysans put on their chests to slice with their pocketknives, the Saint-Nicolas baker also made delicious glazed rolls, delightfully doughy and yeasty.

The baker and his wife observed the classic division of labor of the métier: Madame looked after the shop while Monsieur, who had been up all night tending his oven, slept. It was rumored that this arrangement suited the baker perfectly as he couldn't abide his spouse, a spindly, flinty woman, as haughty and unyielding as her outrageous hairdo, a coif made so rigid by an excess of lacquer that it looked like a snug bronze battle helmet. She presided imperiously over her cash register while a terrified village girl picked out the customers' selections with tongs and placed them timorously in a white paper bag, which she clutched tightly until her mistress had been paid.

Capucine gave her order for a dozen rolls and, with a politely expectant smile, stepped up to the baker's wife to pay. The baker, who had clearly just woken up, opened the door behind the counter, scratched, and peered sleepily at the shop and at the street beyond the plate-glass window. "*Bonjour, m'sieu'dame,*" he muttered, bobbing his head and disappearing back into his apartment, leaving the door open, their living room plainly visible. Capucine was surprised to see that in addition to the inevitable oversized television and browning reproductions of stags at bay, there was also a substantial mahogany bookcase surmounted with family pictures in inexpensive plastic frames. Intrigued, Capucine leaned forward in an attempt to make out some of the titles. Outraged, the baker's wife slammed the door violently and glared at Capucine.

"Madame," the baker's wife said tartly, "it's inadmissible for you to gape like that. You may well have the right to investigate, but please have the consideration not to disrupt my business. If you want to take an inventory of my possessions, show the courtesy of making an appointment first."

From behind, Capucine heard a mumble from the couple that had just entered the shop that sounded very much like a murmur of assent.

CHAPTER 26

Capucine slathered the thick slice of toasted *pain de campagne* with salty farm butter and then covered it with large dollops of Odile's bittersweet cherry preserve. She gave a satisfied little sigh and looked around furtively to make sure there would be no interruption.

Just as she licked the dripping preserve from the side of the toast, preparing for her first big bite, she heard the dreaded words, "Madame la Comtesse *est demandée au téléphone*."

"Who is it, Gauvin?"

"Monsieur Vienneau, and, if Madame la Comtesse will permit, he seems very upset."

"Capucine, it's Loïc. Something terrible has happened. Can I come and see you?" He sounded close to the threshold of hysteria.

"Of course. I'll be here all morning, or would you like to come to lunch?"

"Not lunch. I'll be there as soon as I can." A short pause, then, "Thank you," awkwardly.

As she went back to her breakfast, she heard the ponderous knocker thump against the front door and Gauvin rush down the hallway to open it. Vienneau stood shyly on the threshold. He was unshaven and smelled of alcohol. It was obvious he had been standing in the driveway and had called on his cell phone.

In the petit salon he refused coffee and sheepishly asked if he could have some Calvados instead. Gauvin brought a small crystal decanter filled with the dark brown liquid and a thimble-sized stemmed glass on a silver tray. Vienneau frowned at the size of the glass and downed two shots in rapid succession. He took a deep breath, shuddered, filled the glass again, and held it between thumb and index.

"Capucine, I'm desperate. Marie-Christine has left."

Capucine looked at him, waiting.

Vienneau downed two more measures of Calvados.

"She had been even more affectionate than usual for the past few days. I thought things were getting better. You see, after Gerlier's death I had to spend much more time at the élevage and so often I would come home late. Sometimes I even missed dinner altogether. That upset Marie-Christine. It would upset anyone! And she became a little—how can I describe it?—a little distant. But this week that changed and she was very loving and attentive, clinging almost."

He gave Capucine a look of almost childish expectancy. She nodded with a small smile.

"Then last night, when I came home, she was in tears. She had been drinking. At first she was inconsolable. I tried to soothe her. We talked for hours. About everything. About nothing. Us. Her parents. The fact that we couldn't have children. That made her sob hysterically." He paused, visibly racked with guilt. "Then she seemed to calm down. The storm had passed. I made a cup of tisane tea for her and found some sleeping pills that Homais had given me last year. She took one and went to bed. I stayed with her

until she fell asleep. But I could see that she was still rest-
less, changing position and moaning constantly." He
tossed off another tiny glass of Calvados.

Capucine still said nothing.

"I had a bit to drink myself after she went to sleep. I
was very upset. Very late I went to bed."

He stared at Capucine. This was the part he didn't want
to talk about.

"When I woke up, she was gone. She'd left this note on
her pillow." He handed Capucine a sheet of very thick letter paper with the name of their house printed at the top
from a hand-engraved plate. In the French manner, the
paper had been folded in four with the writing on the outside.

> *Dearest,*
> *It's not out of cowardice but out of love that I
> tell you this on paper and not to your face. If
> you were in front of me now, I would not have
> the strength to do what I know I must do.*
> *I am moving to Paris. I will stay with my sis-
> ter for the first few days, and then I will have to
> find someplace to live on my own. I do this not
> because I want to leave you but because I know
> I will drag you down. With me clutching your
> waist, even your very powerful wings are not
> strong enough to lift us both off the ground.*
> *Please forgive me and think of me fondly.*
> *I will love you forever.*
> *Yours,*
> *Marie-Christine*

"What do you think?" Vienneau asked.

"You called your sister-in-law?"

"Of course. Right after I woke up. Marie-Christine's

there, but she wouldn't speak to me. My sister-in-law said she was asleep. I think she must have spat out the sleeping pill and waited for me to come to bed and then driven to Paris. What really amazed me is that a lot of her clothes are gone. She must have packed her bags and put them in her car before I came home. She had planned it all out. Right?"

"That's possible."

"Capucine, listen, I'm asking this of you, a police officer. I need the police to bring her back, and I want you to tell me how to get them to do it."

"The police have no authority whatsoever in matters like this. I can tell you as a friend—and as a woman—that your best course of action is to let her work through whatever it is that's troubling her all by herself. If you interfere, it will only make it harder for her."

"You don't understand." Vienneau's pitch had gone up a notch. "She's a sick woman. Her letter is almost suicidal. 'With me clutching your waist, even your very powerful wings are not strong enough to lift us both off the ground.' That phrase makes me very afraid."

"Yes, she's clearly highly upset."

"That's why the police need to intervene. Can't you order some officers to take her to be medically examined? She's obviously taken leave of her senses. She needs help. I understand you are very powerful in the police."

"Loïc, the police only get involved if there has been an infraction of the law, which is certainly not the case here. This is not the way to deal with this. Let time do its work."

"No, no, you're not understanding. I need Marie-Christine. I can't function without her. I can't function without her even when things are going well. And they're certainly not going well now. I never realized how much Gerlier actually did at the élevage. I have to spend all day there, and the work is still not done. Listen, Capucine, I tell you this in the strictest confidence. Last month was the first time since I took over from my father that we lost money. Not a lot, thank God, but we were actually in the red."

He put his elbows on the table and ground his eyes with the heels of his hands. "What am I going to do?" he asked the tablecloth. He raised his head to down another thimbleful of Calvados. "Don't you have any bigger glasses?"

CHAPTER 27

Even the exterior of the little house announced that Lisette Bellec was thriving in her widowhood. Her husband, Lucien, had died violently barely two weeks before, but the narrow stucco row house exuded a feeling of well-scrubbed serenity.

Capucine clunked the knocker, an old horseshoe welded onto a cast-iron hinge, and the door opened immediately. There was a moment's fluttering hesitation as the Widow Bellec—as she would be known in the village for the rest of her days—anxiously wrung her hands, drying them in her apron.

"Mademoiselle," she almost sighed, "I was sure you would come." She paused. "Oh, excuse me. I know I'm supposed to call you Madame la Comtesse now, but I always think of you as Mademoiselle. I'm sure you don't remember, but I worked in the kitchen at the château when you were just a little girl."

Capucine hesitated for only a short beat. "Of course I remember you. You used to teach me to bake when you weren't washing dishes. We made all sorts of cakes. How could I ever forget?"

Capucine was led down the long, thin house—clearly built in the lane between two existing houses in the last century—and into a minuscule sitting room where a dining table and six chairs fought for space with a high-backed banquette. A boxy television, so old it had a large circular dial with numbers for the channels, had pride of place at the end of the table. It was easy to imagine the table elbow to elbow with family, one eye on the flickering screen and one ear on the conversation. There was a single window, which looked out over a yard as long and narrow as the house. A large number of rabbits hopped lethargically in a chicken-wire cage raised to shoulder height on stilts. Beyond, a kitchen garden was being diligently wound down for the winter.

"I'm glad to see you're so comfortable," Capucine said.

"Yes, mademoiselle, I did well by the Père Bellec, thanks to the Lord." She made a rapid sign of the cross and glanced at the crucifix hanging on the wall over the television. "He was a hard man but a good provider."

"I've come to ask you some questions about your poor husband. I'm trying to understand about his death."

Lisette snorted. "He wasn't that poor. He got a good wage at the élevage, and he never spent a sou on me or the house, as you can see. There was quite a good bit more in his postal savings account than I expected. And don't feel sorry for me. His death was like a weight lifted from my shoulders. But I don't have to tell you that. You're married, so you know what men are like." She paused. "Would you like some tea? I was just going to make some."

As the tea was poured from a flowery teapot obviously reserved for special occasions, Capucine nudged the conversation gently back to the murdered worker. "It doesn't seem that your marriage was much of a success," Capucine said and immediately regretted using a phrase more appropriate to a Saint-Germain cocktail party.

Lisette looked at her in incomprehension. "I did what women have to do. I married the first man who asked me so I could have a home of my own and no longer needed to work ten hours a day for servant's wages, sleeping in a freezing cubicle under the roof. Even if I had known what it was going to be like, I still would have done it."

"Are you telling me he beat you?"

"No, not really, or at least not when I didn't deserve it." She laughed as if she had said something clever. "You know what marriage is like. He would go to the café after work and come home drunk, yelling and swearing if his dinner wasn't nice and hot on the table, waiting for him. Then he'd sit in front of the TV, drinking beer until he fell asleep. I'd help him to bed and he'd curse at me." She paused, lost in her memories.

"Of course, when we were still young, you know, he would claim his rights as a husband more frequently than I thought a man ever could. He didn't care if I wanted to or not, and he was always very rough. Many times he made me bleed, and if I told him to stop, then he really would hit me, and not just a *gifle*—a little slap—like when I had done something wrong. I was very glad when he grew too old for that, believe me." She crossed herself, glancing at the crucifix, and then laughed, but this time with a note of heavy irony.

"What about his friends, the people he saw, his life when he wasn't here?"

"Mademoiselle, you know men. He only saw his friends at the café. How could I know them? Decent women don't go to cafés. Of course, nowadays they seem to be filled with these young hussies all tarted up with makeup. What's the world coming to? And, of course, he went hunting in the winter and fishing in the summer, like all men do. It's not a woman's place to know her man's friends. I suppose they all worked with him at the élevage. They must have. Half the men in the village work there."

"Do you know if he had any enemies or if anyone wanted to see him dead?"

"I'm sure he had enemies. All men do. As to seeing him dead, I don't know about that, other than me, of course." She laughed an almost carefree chuckle but suddenly became serious, as if an unpleasant thought had occurred to her.

"So it wasn't true, what Capitaine Dallemagne said about you and the taxes?"

"Capitaine Dallemagne came to see you?"

"Just the other day. He asked me almost the same questions you did about Lucien. And as he was leaving, he told me you worked for the *fisc,* the tax agency, and you were going to try to take my inheritance away. But I knew that couldn't be true. He's a jealous one, he is, that Capitaine Dallemagne. These flics, they're all the same. Oh, pardon, mademoiselle. They say you're a flic, too. Can that be true? I don't know what to believe anymore." She crossed herself again, darting an even more reverent glance at the crucifix.

"My dear Bebette. I'm now a commissaire in the Police Judiciaire in Paris. I have nothing at all to do with taxes, thank God." Capucine started to cross herself and nipped the gesture in the bud. The habit was infectious. *Get a grip,* she told herself.

CHAPTER 28

As subtly as a face aging, the cloakroom had morphed. If before it had been merely the stage for a comic interlude, with perhaps a secondary role as a portal into Capucine's childhood and early adolescence, it had progressively revealed its own genius loci and become a vital sanctuary from the present time.

Behind the closed door, now a universally recognized sign at Maulévrier that she was not to be disturbed under any circumstances, Capucine picked up the receiver of the telephone, ancient even in the world of rotary dial models, and laboriously dialed Loïc Vienneau's home number.

"Allô," Vienneau answered anxiously.

"Allô, Loïc. It's me, Capucine. Good morning," Capucine said, trying hard to project a warm smile down the line.

"Do you have any news?" Vienneau's voice was just a shade below a shout.

"No, I'm sorry, I don't. I was calling you about something else."

"I got through to her," Vienneau said. "It took some doing, but I did it! I tried all yesterday and kept getting her sister, who wouldn't put me through and who wound up becoming sharp with me. So I tried a little trick this morning. I waited until I knew her sister had left for work and borrowed my financial director's cell phone. You know how all the cell phones have the same prefix—oh-six?" He paused, seeming to actually want a confirmation for the obvious truism.

"Yes, I did know that, Loïc."

"Good. So I called her sister's apartment, and she picked up, not knowing who it was." Capucine was astonished at how childlike Vienneau had become.

"And what did Marie-Christine have to say?" Capucine asked.

"That's just it. She didn't want to talk to me. She says she needs time to herself. Can you imagine!"

"So then what did you do?" Capucine had a sinking feeling as if trying to put a drunk dinner guest into a taxi at three in the morning.

"I called our doctor in Rouen to discuss Marie-Christine's condition. It was a disappointing conversation. He said the same thing you did, to leave her alone and let her come to grips with her problems. I don't understand this. What's wrong with everyone? Why can't they see what's happening to Marie-Christine? She's obviously not well—"

Capucine cut him off. "Loïc, I was calling to ask your advice."

"My advice?"

"Yes, I need to find out who Lucien Bellec's friends were at the élevage."

"Lucien Bellec . . . oh, of course, the poor man who was shot. The person who would know about that is Pierre Martel, one of the foremen. He's the one who showed you around, remember? He knows everyone and everything that's going on. Just go to the front gate and ask for him. I'd go with you, but I have a meeting with the bankers in Rouen this morning. Now, listen, do you think you could call the doctor yourself and—"

Capucine rang off with the strong feeling that Vienneau was probably still blabbing into the phone after it went dead.

Summoned by the security guard, Martel arrived quickly. Recognizing Capucine, he adopted the classic stance of male aggressiveness, legs spread, thumbs hooked into his belt, hands circling his genitalia. He stared hard at her, daring her to speak.

"Monsieur Martel, I wonder if I could ask you a few questions about Lucien Bellec."

"You're not going to ask me squat. I already gave my deposition to the flics, so you can fuck off."

"You already gave your deposition?"

"You deaf or something? That's what I just said. The gendarmes came around the other day, and I said what I had to say, and now I'm done with you guys."

"The gendarmes came here to ask you questions about Lucien Bellec?"

"You got it. Capitaine Dallemagne himself. I told him what he wanted to know and he said I wouldn't have to answer any other questions, no matter who else showed up, 'cuz he was the boss."

"Did Capitaine Dallemagne also ask you about Clément Devere?"

"I'm not going to tell you what he asked me, but I'll tell you what he said. He said you were a Paris cop who had no authority down here. He said you were snooping around, hoping to find someone who was cheating on their tax returns. He said you were looking to make trouble for the élevage. He didn't exactly tell me to shut my trap in front of you, but I ain't that dumb that I don't know which side is up and which side is down." He widened his stance and hooked his thumbs deeper into his belt. "Time for you to get off the property, or I'll call the gendarmes." He sneered, delighted with his perceived ascendency.

With a resounding clunk the penny dropped. Ever efficient, someone from the DCPJ must have notified the gendarmerie about Capucine's assignment to the Saint-Nicolas incidents the minute the staffing committee broke up. And the gendarmerie must have sent some sort of communiqué immediately to Dallemagne. And he had not wasted a second trying to beat her to the punch by a couple of days. Well, at least it had gotten him off his butt and on the move.

CHAPTER 29

Apparently, an uninterrupted breakfast was something that was just not going to happen at Maulévrier. Yet again, just as Capucine had dropped a lump of sugar in her café au lait, Gauvin crept up to tell her in his usual whisper charged with suppressed excitement that the "police were on the line." Maybe the solution was just to have Gauvin serve her breakfast in the cloakroom and be done with it.

It was the receptionist at the commissariat who announced that Isabelle wanted to talk to Capucine and was going into her office with David so they could use her speakerphone. As she waited, she put her legs on the table and tipped the chair back. She missed Isabelle admiring her calves and David her shoes. Of course, there wouldn't have been all that much to check out that morning. She was wearing an old pair of tweed trousers; a long, drooping, belted tan cashmere cardigan; and clunky square-heeled walking shoes. All very un-Paris and un–Police Judiciaire. The cardigan would have made wearing her service pistol impossible.

Isabelle's strident voice burst into her reflections. "Commissaire. Commissaire! Are you there?" Then, "Merde, David, this fucking thing doesn't work."

"Yes, it does, Isabelle. I can hear you perfectly. You don't have to shout. Hi, David! So what's going on?"

"There's been another one."

"Another one, what? A Belle episode?"

"Exactly. This time she ripped off Jean-Marie Lavallé."

"You mean the movie actor? The one who did all those cape and sword films in the sixties and seventies? I didn't think he was still around."

"He is. Totally. He's only in his seventies. Healthy as a horse. Just maybe a little less rich." The two brigadiers' snickering sounded like static on the line.

Capucine ached to be in the room. She missed Paris very much indeed.

"So he has this killer apartment on the quai de Montebello," Isabelle continued. "You know, just across the river from Notre Dame. There's this long terrace, and every single last room looks out over the cathedral—"

"Back up a minute. Where did she pick him up?"

"I told you."

"No, you didn't, Isabelle," David said.

"Okay, asshole. Commissaire, it was at the flower and bird market. On the Ile de la Cité. The place we always used to take our sandwiches when we worked at the Quai. What I didn't know is that they get rid of the flowers on Sundays and just sell birds."

"Everybody in Paris knows that," David said with disdain.

"Anyway," Isabelle continued, "she did her fainting routine just at the end of the market, you know, where they have one of those new municipal bicycle stands, the kind where you rent the bicycle for the day and turn it in anywhere you want."

"That sweetie must have brass balls," David said. "You

can see that spot from the windows of thirty-six fucking quai des fucking Orfèvres. I mean the entire *Crim'* could have been looking down at her. She must know we're hot after her, and she still doesn't give a shit."

"So, anyway," Isabelle continued, "along comes Jean-Marie Lavallé, all slim and spry, you know, with the hair jelled back, and the open collar, and the trendy intellectual glasses with no frames, looking like he's going off to some TV show to be totally suave and ageless—"

"Isabelle, get on with it."

"So he finds La Belle lying on the sidewalk. It seems he's just bought some goddamn bird at the market, something called a Chardonneret Mullet, which he explained is a goldfinch crossed with a canary, and sings more beautifully than any other bird, and just happens to be totally illegal. He wants this bird to put in his kitchen so it can sing to him when he cooks, which he says is just about the thing he likes to do most in life."

"Sure, that's the thing he likes most," interjected David. Capucine could see the daggers Isabelle shot him with her look as clearly as if she had been in the room.

"So he's walking along, swinging his little cage with his little bird chirping away, and finds La Belle napping happily and says to himself, 'Hey, what a poor sweet thing. I'll just take this little bit of cuteness home with me and nurse her back to health. It'll be cool. She can keep my little bird company.'"

Capucine's impatience got the better of her. "And she stays three or four days and then hoofs it, right? What did she take?"

"A small chest made of copper filigree beaten into a tortoise shell. He must have a thing about endangered species," David said.

"It's called Boulle marquetry," Isabelle interjected. "The guy who cooked up the technique was someone by the name of André-Charles Boulle. He worked back in the early seventeen hundreds."

"This wasn't an original Boulle piece, was it? If it was, it would belong in the Louvre. It would be her biggest hit yet," Capucine said.

"Yeah, that's the funny part," David said. Capucine could hear him rattling a piece of paper. "In the original *procès-verbal* taken down by the uniformed officer who received his initial complaint, he said it was worth twenty-five thousand euros. But when we called his insurance company, he had it listed on his policy as a copy valued at three thousand. Our guess is that he jacked up the value because there was something inside the chest and he wants the insurance company to cover that, too."

"Like, say, a big wad of cash he needed to keep handy in case he wanted to score something fun to stick up his nose," Isabelle added.

"But, of course, he's not going to press charges. Oh, no. All he wants is a police statement certifying the burglary so he can hit the insurance company," David said.

"If it really was cash," Capucine said, "it's interesting she took the chest as well. Look, I need you two to interview Lavallé and get a decent deposition. Also, get the best physical description you can. Focus on what she was wearing when he picked her up and if she left anything in his apartment after she left. Find out if she said anything, told any stories or whatever, that might be relevant to the investigation. We've got to get an arrest quickly. The press is going to have a field day with this. She's done two celebrities in a row. We're going to have to move fast, or we're going to start taking major shit."

Isabelle was put out. She obviously took this as a criticism of her performance on the case. " 'Get an arrest quickly!' You've got to be kidding. This girl is like Fantômas. She doesn't leave traces. She vanishes into thin air. Her scam is so perfect, her victims don't even want to press charges."

"There you go," Capucine said. "Why don't you ask Lavallé how to deal with her? His best role was Fantômas. I'm sure he's got all sorts of insights."

The receiver was banged down on the speakerphone. It was Capucine's turn to have gone too far.

CHAPTER 30

Even as a child Capucine had thought the gendarmerie building was an eyesore and an affront to the countryside. The fact that she now knew it was the headquarters of the cantonal brigade didn't do anything to raise it in her esteem. A good-sized tract had been bulldozed out of the forest halfway between Saint-Nicolas and the next village and encircled by a rough-hewn cement wall—in keeping with an architectural vogue that had lasted for all of several minutes back in the seventies. Behind the wall a futuristic glass pillbox-like structure had been erected in the middle of a vast, stark cement lot.

Inside, the gendarmerie hummed like a beehive, looking every bit the military installation it was. Gendarmes strode back and forth in crisp blue uniforms that had visibly passed a rigid inspection that morning. It was the antipode of her own commissariat. Capucine had a fond vision of her moody punk detectives slouching over their chaotic desks and asked herself for the thousandth time what on earth she was doing.

At the reception counter she presented her police card and asked a gendarme brigadier-chef for Capitaine Dallemagne. The man somehow managed to come to attention while still sitting in his seat. "Oui, Madame le Commissaire," he said crisply and spoke inaudibly into a telephone. Within seconds a gendarme brigadier appeared and escorted her, walking so stiffly he was almost marching.

Dallemagne's office seemed to be even more rigidly disciplined than at her last visit. A capitaine's kepi, resplendent with silver bands, had been carefully placed in the upper-right-hand corner of the desk, the brim perfectly aligned with the edge of the desk, next to a pair of carefully smoothed brown kid gloves, also laid perfectly parallel to the edge. A single slim official blue file was set in the exact middle of the otherwise empty surface.

Capucine was reminded of Capitaine Renault's office in *Casablanca,* but she doubted that this was going to be the beginning of a beautiful friendship.

Dallemagne sat stiffly, only five inches of buttock in contact with the government-issue swivel chair. Without rising, he waved Capucine into one of the two metal seats in front of his desk.

"Madame, I believe you owe me an apology."

"I beg your pardon."

"As well you should. I understand you issued a formal complaint about my conduct of the two investigations we discussed. And you did this behind my back. And," he paused and gave her a particularly malevolent look, "I have it on good authority that, having been officially rebuffed, you had the temerity to invoke your family's contacts. And you did all this without the slightest heed to the damage it might cause my career. This is conduct unbecoming to an officer. Madame, if you were a man, I would call you a cad and invite you outside for a physical explanation. But as it is, I am simply speechless."

Which was the last thing he was. Not only had he managed to fire two broadsides before Capucine had even opened her gun ports, but he firmly held the weather gauge. She had underestimated her enemy.

"Capitaine, this is not about careers. It's about seeing that justice is done—"

"Well said, madame, and your interference has seriously undermined the credibility and authority of the gendarmerie in this canton. The negative consequences of that action to the pursuit of justice are impossible to calculate. What do you have to say for yourself?"

"Capitaine, I regret that you have formed this interpretation of the events. However, as it happens, I have received formal instructions from the DCPJ to take charge of these two cases and to avail myself of you and your men for assistance."

Dallemagne looked at her fixedly for several beats, saying nothing, with no change of expression. He was definitely far better at this sort of thing than she had anticipated. Eventually, he picked up the file on the desk, opened it, and riffled the pages against his thumb and crooked forefinger.

Capucine could see that they were official *procès-verbal* forms used for reporting the statements of witnesses.

"These are eleven PVs that my men and I have collected over the past few days. Bellec, Lisette. Martel, Pierre. Seven workers at the Elevage Vienneau. And the parents of Devere, Clément." He closed the file and pushed it across the desk toward Capucine. None of the reports were longer than a paragraph, and each stated, in the bland, passive voice of officialdom, that the person interviewed had nothing to report. They were useless in a police inquiry.

In view of her experience over the past few days, Capucine was sure that Dallemagne had been energetic in spreading his rumor that she was a secret minion of the fisc far beyond the people he had interviewed. She was equally sure that he had sent copies of his PVs through the gendarmerie hierarchy, effectively scoring points for his zeal in cooperating with an arrogant sister service. As political tactics went, it was brilliant. He'd effectively sabotaged Capucine's investigation while making himself look as good as he could under the circumstances. Now all he needed was for her investigation to fall flat on its face. Then he would be entirely vindicated.

Stiffly courteous, Dallemagne walked her to the door of the building. "Madame, it was an honor to have been of service to the Police Judiciaire. If I can be of any further assistance, please don't hesitate to let me know."

As she walked slowly back to the Clio, it was abundantly clear to Capucine that any hope for a solution lay far, far outside the box.

CHAPTER 31

She told herself, and everyone else, that she needed to go to Paris to deal with the mountain of paperwork that must be sitting on her desk and review the progress of her teams on their cases. She said that because she still hadn't quite made up her mind.

It turned out to be a long day. The pile on her desk was far more mountainous than she had imagined, and three of her teams were stymied. There was also a pile of "*dans votre absence*" phone message slips as thick as a deck of cards. It was a very long day. At one in the afternoon a uniformed brigadier brought her a *croque-monsieur* and a quarter-liter carafe of Côtes du Rhône from the café at the corner. She ate half the sandwich and sipped a little of the wine while making changes to the duty roster for the next week. The afternoon wore on. Before she knew it, it was 5:45. Now or never.

She picked up the phone and pushed the speed-dial button labeled MOHAMED BENAROUCHE.

"Do you have a second, Momo?"

"Sure thing, Commissaire."

Of the three brigadiers she had brought with her from the *Crim'*, two, David and Isabelle, had blossomed, gradually becoming more rounded officers. Only Momo, now that he was in a neighborhood commissariat where petty crime and domestic disputes were far more prevalent than serious felonies, had flopped like a fish out of water. He was a force of nature, a huge North African, physically bigger than David and Isabelle put together. He always reminded Capucine of a Sig service pistol, big, heavy, square, and lethal. Of the three brigadiers, she was most attached to Momo. After all, he had carried her through her terrible first case, sometimes literally. He was the one who had no ambition in life other than to "get her back," as he liked to say.

Capucine looked up from her file as Momo's bulk blotted out the light from the hallway. His smile looked out of place in the surly toughness of his pockmarked Moroccan street fighter's face.

" 'Sup?" he asked, somehow managing to sound as respectful as if he had added the required "Madame le Commissaire."

"It's going to take some explaining. Shut the door and let's try some of this Calvados I brought back." The slammed door cracked like a pistol shot as Momo flicked it shut with his foot.

Momo was a practicing Muslim but far from devout enough to renounce alcohol. Quite the contrary. She still kidded him about the time he nearly blew his cover on a stakeout in the Paris Arab ghetto of Barbès by asking for a beer in a café.

Capucine produced a fat bottle marked "Calvados Boulard, Pays d'Auge, Hors d'Age" and two small tumblers from a desk drawer. She poured them both half an inch. Capucine sipped hers. Momo shot his back in one swallow and pursed his lips in an appreciative frown.

"You don't get this kind of stuff in the cafés where I go," he said.

Capucine poured a good two inches in his glass. Now that the niceties were over, it was time for a decent drink.

"I'm working on a funny kind of case. In Normandy. I don't think I should have taken it on in the first place. But I let my pride get the better of me, and now that I'm officially responsible, it turns out I don't have the resources to solve it. Does this make any sense?"

"Sure. I figured it had to be something like that. You were spending a lot of time in Normandy. Nobody likes apple pie that much." Momo helped himself to a third shot of the Calvados. He knew perfectly well the whole bottle was intended for him.

"Look, Momo, I need you to do something dangerous for me. I have no right to even think of asking you, and you can refuse if you're not completely comfortable with the assignment." Capucine caught herself chirping and noticed that Momo was smiling indulgently, restraining himself from asking her to cut the crap and get on with it.

"Okay, okay, let me explain."

"Commissaire, I keep telling you, I'm just here for the heavy lifting. Just point me in the right direction and tell me what to do. You don't have to do no explaining."

But she did explain at length and told him exactly what she wanted and what risks were involved. When she was done, Momo nodded, downed one more shot of Calvados, and stood up.

"You got it."

He picked up the bottle, still almost three-quarters full, slid it in his jacket pocket, and clumped out of the office.

CHAPTER 32

It was like nothing he'd ever seen. The fields were as moist and green as the lettuce in fancy supermarkets after the sprayer had gone off. And the cows! Snowy white with pink noses like in a book for little children. The whole setup looked like some TV ad for yogurt, not a place where you were going to sweat and get dirt under your nails. What the hell had Commissaire Le Tellier dreamed up this time?

The endless swelling emerald hills made him sleepy. He nodded with the swaying of the bus, his head sinking lower and lower. A murmur woke him. There it was. A fancy stone archway with the name of the place—Elevage Vienneau—in big iron letters on the top. But the bus kept on going and turned only after half a mile or so, into a deeply potholed, narrow road running beside a crumbling cement wall that had been stained black over the years by the exhaust of passing cars. It pulled up with a loud air-brake fart at an ugly cement gateway. CITÉ OUVRIÈRE— workers' compound—it said on a faded wooden sign with the paint coming off in chips. Below, black painted iron doors had red rust running down in streaks like drying blood.

Everyone on the bus got off and ducked through a small opening in one of the portals. Inside, the world reverted to the familiar. Two long darkened stucco buildings glared at each other, their tiny windows squinting like gang members squaring off for a street fight. The reedy ululation of popular Arab tunes blaring from multiple boom boxes mingled with the singsongy lilt of high-pitched conversations in French-Arab patois. If it weren't for the desperate feel of a prison yard, it could have been his childhood home in the Paris projects.

He tramped up three flights of stairs to the room they had told him would be his and opened the door. A man, lying on one of the two beds, reading a newspaper in Arabic, jumped up on the defensive. But when he saw it was only another Maghrebian, and not a *blanc* with authority, he relaxed and fell back on the bed.

"*Salaam aleikom,*" Momo greeted him respectfully.

"*Labess,*" Momo's new roommate drawled in reply with studied cool, stretching out to show how laid back he was, while slowly going over Momo from top to bottom. "So, my brother, this is the best job you could find?"

After exchanging names, Momo treated Mustafa to the epic he had prepared, about finding himself out of work in Paris and having a friend who had a cousin who had a brother-in-law who had once worked at the élevage, and who had given him a name to call, who, wonderfully, had hired him over the phone and told him which train to take. It was a lot less than he had been making in Paris when he had been working but a lot more than when he had not. But he was going to have a roof over his head and his belly was going to be full and he'd have some money to send to his *bled* in Algeria, right? Momo hoped he hit just the right note of dumb naïveté and hopefulness.

Mustafa snorted and said, "You'll see what you'll see," assuming the role of older cousin, cynical and protective. He watched Momo closely as he unpacked the few dingy secondhand work clothes he had purchased in a dismal back alley of the Marché aux Puces the day before. "Your hands look like they've never seen a day's work, but there's too much sun in your face for you to have been behind bars in the *cabane*. So what were you doing before the genius brother-in-law of the cousin of the friend told you to come here, *mon frère?*"

Momo launched into the backstory of his epic: he had worked in his cousin's tiny convenience store in the Twentieth Arrondissement. "That job was the best, *mon pote*," Momo said with carefully constructed earnestness. "I got to run the till because I can speak French. So no hard work. Just sitting on a stool all day. I'm sure going to miss that."

"You're not wrong there," the roommate said with a cynical twist of his mouth.

Just as Momo was prepared to embroider his epic, he was cut off by a warbling wail, just like the air-raid sirens in black-and-white World War II war movies.

"*La bouffe*—dinner!" announced the roommate. "It's shit, but you get to eat as much as you want. They'll lose money with you," he laughed admiringly.

During the meal Momo discovered that the workforce consisted of two distinct groups, Maghrebians and Turks. The Turks were in a distinct minority and sat by themselves in a tight enclave in a corner of the long-tabled refectory. A clear sign of the dominance of the Maghrebians, the meal was North African, a thin lamb tagine poured over mounds of couscous. By the time dinner was over, Momo's reintegration into the world of his childhood was complete. He found himself thinking in Arabic and was no longer irritated by the constant touching and prodding. He even bridled at the colonial arrogance of the French, feeding their former subjects mutton, even as they worked on a beef ranch, in the mistaken belief that was all Arabs ate.

After the meal Mustafa, ever the protective big brother, invited Momo to go with his new pals to an Arab café a few streets from the workers' gate. Momo begged off. Mint tea in a seedy bistro was not going to do it for him that night. What it was going to take was a whole lot of cigarettes and booze, two things his fellow workers sure as hell were not going to take kindly to.

Back in the room, he squeezed his shoulders through the narrow window and leaned out, confident that he would be undisturbed for at least a couple of hours and, with the room light out, was invisible from the courtyard. He lit a cigarette and cupped it in his hand, relishing the rush as the smoke went as deep into his lungs as he could get it. The one thing you really learned in the police was how to smoke on a stakeout without being seen. Leaving the cigarette on the sill, he squirmed back in, extracted Commissaire Le Tellier's now half-full bottle of Calvados from his bag, put it on the little ledge, and twisted his torso back out the window. Who else would have given him a bottle of really good stuff?

It was hard to think of her as a bigwig commissaire. What the hell was she up to this time? He didn't mind long nights, he didn't mind getting shot at, but he really minded not having a friend to talk to. He pulled the cork, lifted the bottle, swallowed twice, grimaced, and waited for the alcohol to join the nicotine in a sinuous belly dance. The cool air felt good. The world took a quarter turn. He felt good too. He was doing something he should be doing. Something worthwhile. A sense of peace descended over him like a warm blanket.

He knew he was going to be able to sleep.

Of course, sleep raised another little problem. Commissaire Le Tellier had told him he couldn't take his tricolor police card with him. That made sense. It was likely enough that someone would go through his stuff. But she also told him not to take a piece. Sure. Why not just leave his dick at home, too? He took the last swig of Calvados in the bottle and jiggled his left foot, relishing the feel of the gun holstered to his ankle. He had paid for the Smith and Wesson 340PD out of his own pocket, and the damn thing had cost close to a month's salary. And then he had shelled out another bucketful of cash for the rubber grip with the laser aimer. All he had to do was squeeze the grip a little and a red laser dot would tell him where the bullet would hit. Good thing, too, because one shot was all he was going to get. It was a real bastard of a gun. It fired a .357 Magnum, and the scandium alloy frame and titanium barrel were so light, the recoil felt like a truck had slammed into your hand.

He'd had enough to drink to find the thought of him kneeling next to Mustafa for morning prayer, heads on the floor, unshod, as the Qur'an required, with his 340PD strapped to his ankle, hugely funny.

Momo flopped on the bed belly down, pulled the holster off his ankle with a loud Velcro scratch, put it under his pillow, clunked the empty bottle of Calvados in his bag, shot it under the bed, and passed out.

CHAPTER 33

Mercifully, even though it was essentially a Maghrebian meal, coffee figured prominently in the refectory breakfast. Momo passed on everything else—the mint tea, the white yogurt with puddles of acidy whey, the sliced country bread, the slightly rancid butter, the runny red jam—and concentrated on getting as much coffee, black and very sugary, into his system as quickly as he could. It didn't help much with his headache. If he had been in his apartment, a shot of Cognac and a couple of cigarettes would have done the trick, but as things were, he had to make do with the coffee.

Just as he thought he might be beginning to feel better, a big *blanc* came into the refectory, moving a lot of air, as they said. He was not as big as Momo, but almost. He looked around, singled out Momo, and strode up to the table.

"Benarouche," he boomed with the false friendliness of a small-town politician canvassing for votes in a supermarket. "All rested up? Your bed as soft as could be? Ready for some hard work? You bet you are," he said, clapping Momo on the back.

He pulled out a chair with his foot, spun it around, and sat with his arms crossed over the back. Conversations ceased in a radius of twenty feet.

"My name is Martel. I'm your foreman."

Momo mumbled, "Oui, monsieur," with all the subservience the situation seemed to require.

Martel nodded, eying Momo in cold appraisal.

"I'm going to put you on the kill floor. Big guy like you can be useful there. You're going to back up your roommate for the first week, until you get the hang of it, and then you're going to be on your own. Think you can handle that?"

Just as Momo muttered another "Oui, monsieur," Martel barked out an earsplitting "Mustafa!" Momo's headache shot up several notches and began to throb aggressively.

Mustafa trotted up eagerly, his cool-guy demeanor of the previous night volatilized.

"Mustafa, Mohamed here is going to be on your detail. Show him the ropes. I want him to learn fast. Someone his size is just what we need to deal with the skittery ones that hold up the line. You come see me on Friday and report on how he's doing. Got it?"

Before the "Oui, monsieur" was half said, Martel marched out purposefully, looking neither left nor right.

Ten minutes later Mustafa led Momo toward a large iron-fenced corral. The morning's encounter had made him chatty. "I learned the work of the abattoir in a much smaller place than this. Every day there was a fuckup. The corral was too small and the chute was a piece of crap. The steers were always bucking and trying to get out. Here you could fall asleep doing the job. You'll like it, if you have a strong stomach."

About a hundred brilliant white steers stood with the massive placidity of bovines, half dozing in the early morning sunshine, flicking at flies with their ears. Two workers leaned against the railing, chatting quietly. As Momo and Mustafa came up, they exchanged a lack-adaisical "*Labess.*"

"This all there is today?" Mustafa asked.

"Not too many made the weight for slaughter. It's going to be a day at the beach." The hand laughed happily.

"Let's get going. They want Momo to see how the corral works before he goes inside," Mustafa said.

One of the men walked over to a circular pen at a corner of the corral. With its two partitions attached to a post in the center, it looked like a giant revolving door. He pushed one of the partitions through a quarter turn, creating an opening to the corral. The other man, still at the rail at the opposite end, produced a two-foot length of broomstick with some shreds of a white plastic garbage bag tied to the end. He climbed up on the fence and waved his makeshift flag back and forth slowly. Without showing any real fear, the steers edged slowly away. In a few seconds, ten of them had eased into the pie-shaped open section in the circular pen. The first man pushed the partition slowly back, shutting the steers in, and rotated the other partition, revealing the entrance into a long, funnel-shaped cement walled walkway.

Very quietly, in a coaxing tone, the hand encouraged the steers. "*Allez, allez,*" he said in French, making encouraging flapping gestures with his hands.

Mustafa laughed. "Don't let the *blanc* catch you talking to the cattle in Arabic. They don't like that. It makes the meat taste rotten." They all laughed uproariously.

The steers complacently walked around the semicircle and entered the walkway. The hand pushed a gate shut behind them.

"See?" said Mustafa. "They're happy. They think they've turned around and are going back where they came from. In that other place I was, we'd have the bull prods out already and we'd all be yelling and banging the rails. We'd have a good fuckup in the making."

The steers shuffled down the walkway—which became progressively narrower, until the sides almost touched their flanks, gently forcing them to walk single file—and stopped in front of a closed steel door in the wall of the abattoir.

"Time for you and me to get to work," Mustafa said. He led Momo through a door in the abattoir building and around to the other side of the steel door that held back the steers.

"This is the kill floor." He pulled a lever and the door slowly pivoted open. When the first steer walked in, he shut it again. "We'll do just one so you see how it works. Then we'll open the gate and let the rest of them through."

Encouraged by Mustafa, who shook another white garbage bag on a stick, the steer ambled slowly through the extension of the chute. A center divider had been built into the floor, inclining gently upward so after a few feet it reached the animal's brisket. A motorized rubber conveyor belt on the top of the divider lifted the steer a few inches off the ground and moved it forward. When the steer first noticed that it was no longer advancing under its own steam, it glanced around nervously but, looking down, saw the floor just beneath its hooves and calmed immediately, to all appearances enjoying the ride.

Twenty feet down the line another gate opened, admitted the steer, and closed with a quiet click. The conveyor stopped.

"Now we move fast," Mustafa said.

He pushed a big yellow button on a console, and with a violent hiss of compressed air, two stainless-steel panels closed around the steer's neck and a third pushed its head up. Mustafa grabbed a round yellow cylinder about the size of a large flashlight hanging on a chain from the ceiling and pressed it against the crown of the steer's head. There was a sickening thunk and the steer went limp, its head resting on the plate and its body held up by the center divider. The whole thing had taken less than two seconds.

"Is it dead?" Momo asked.

Mustafa shook his head, reached down, found a chain, looped it twice around the animal's hind leg, snapped on a catch, and pushed another button. The steer was lifted into the air and began traversing the room, twitching and writhing slightly, until it went through a door of curtained plastic strips and disappeared.

Mustafa held up the yellow cylinder in front of Momo's face and pushed a button. The device jumped and a black tube around the chain writhed. "The stunner. Works with compressed air. A six-inch bolt jumps out and goes into the steer's head." He pushed the button again for effect. "Too fast for you to see. Do it right, the steer's knocked out but still alive. Do it wrong, it's dead and the blood won't drain out, or it's conscious and you get to see a belly dance on a chain." He laughed cynically.

"What happens in the next room?" Momo asked.

"The steer gets turned into steaks. There are a lot of *frères* in there, bleeding, skinning, and butchering. Those are the guys who make the big money. You have to be here a long time before they let you do that work."

Momo felt slightly nauseous. He blamed the Calvados.

"We need to get started. You work the stunner and put the leg chain on. I'll work the entry gate and the head restraints. I'll help you if you get in trouble." Mustafa pushed the button for the trap to the outside chute, and the steers began ambling in, unsuspecting, at their tranquil bovine pace.

The day was endless. Momo made a number of mistakes, the consequences of which were unthinkable. Halfway through, the foreman came by and said in his politician's bellow that Momo was learning all right but would have to work faster. It took almost the whole shift to get through the small herd in the corral. At first Momo thought he would never be able to stomach it and longed for a drink. He bitterly regretted having finished Commissaire Le Tellier's Calvados the night before. After a while he found he could escape the kill floor by locking his mind on the challenge of sneaking out of the compound to get his hands on a decent bottle of Scotch. That made it almost bearable.

CHAPTER 34

Even after a week at the commissariat, Capucine felt she had made only an insignificant dent in the paperwork on her desk. Important things were not getting done because they were still buried six inches deep in the pile. The imperative of getting to the bottom of the stack announced itself with the urgency of a genuine catastrophe. As she worked, the phone rang. She made no effort to pick it up and continued her review of one of her lieutenants' reports on a claimed wife beating, a particularly brutal one, requiring several stitches. The case was challenging. The woman in question was promiscuous enough to be termed an "amateur prostitute." The oxymoron irritated Capucine, but she couldn't think of a better way to put it. The woman had explained that her husband beat her every time he learned of one of her trysts. She'd pointed out that he wasn't all that quick on the uptake or she would be beaten daily. The lieutenant believed one of the woman's many lovers was responsible for the assault, not her husband, who had never inflicted serious damage in the past. Still, unless an investigation unearthed evidence to the contrary, it was highly likely a judge would put him behind bars for a few months and he would emerge to the administrative difficulties of a convicted felon. The lieutenant wanted a wiretap installed.

Capucine uncapped a dented gold Waterman, a present from her grandfather when she had passed her *bac* at the age of seventeen, which ever since her university days had been kept filled with Waterman *Bleu Floride* ink in the unshakable belief that it had been the invariable choice of Sartre and Simone de Beauvoir. She made the occasional tick mark against the telling points that emerged from the cesspool of sordidness of the report and at the bottom noted that she would seek the approval of the *juge d'instruction* for the wiretap, which seemed entirely warranted.

The phone had stopped ringing but began again immediately. Capucine muttered an irritated "*Oh, là là*" and picked it up.

"I knew you were there, Commissaire," the brigadier at the front desk said, his smile as fulsome as if he had been in the room. "There's a woman here—a lady," he quickly corrected himself, "who wants to see you but doesn't have an appointment. Should I send her away?"

"What's her name?"

"Madame Vienneau."

"Tell her I'll be right out to get her."

Despite herself, Capucine felt awkward seeing Marie-Christine in the commissariat. She had never had a social visitor in her office, not even Alexandre, and she found it difficult to throw off her professional mantle. Her first reflex was to invite Marie-Christine down to the café around the corner for a coffee, which was what she would have done if one of her staff had come to her with a personal problem, but under the circumstances that wouldn't do at all. Nor could she take her into one of the interrogation rooms for a flimsy cup of vending machine espresso, de rigueur for entertaining informants and other "friends" of the police. Capucine decided there was nothing else for it but to hear out Marie-Christine across her desk.

Marie-Christine seemed just as ill at ease as Capucine. "I feel terrible about barging in here like this. I know your time is hugely valuable, but I felt awkward asking you to lunch." She paused and giggled girlishly. "Actually, I wanted to see you running a real police station, wearing your big gun."

Obligingly, Capucine stood up and performed a little pirouette, showing off the Sig Sauer in its speed holster in the small of her back and the pair of handcuffs looped over the waistband of her skirt next to it. Capucine said, "I told you when we were driving to Honfleur, it has an appealing S and M look, but it's pure torture when you have to sit in a car." They both laughed and the awkward moment was gone.

"The real reason I wanted to see you was to explain why I did what I did," Marie-Christine said. "I'm sure all those people down in Saint-Nicolas think I'm a hysterical harpy with her hormones out of control. I don't care about them. But I *do* care what you think."

Capucine reached across the desk and patted Marie-Christine's hand. The commissariat was definitely not the place for feminine confidences.

"You know, lunch wasn't such a bad idea. I'm actually a bit peckish."

"Do you really have the time?"

Capucine nodded and smiled. She was already on the phone to the front desk.

"Brigadier, would you call Benoît's and see if they can squeeze two more in?"

The real story, as Capucine knew, was going to wait until lunch was winding down.

The restaurant was one of those mythical Paris places that are wrongly believed not to exist any longer, a true neighborhood bistro with cubbyholes for the patrons' napkins—changed once a week—and only a small handful of items on the blackboard menu on the wall, where all the customers, with no exceptions, were well known to the owner. There was only one waitress, a corpulent woman whose apron strings disappeared into the folds of her waist, a far bigger bully than anyone's mother had ever been. As far as the waitress was concerned, there weren't a handful of items on the menu; there were only two: for men *saucisses de Morteau,* thick, smoked sausages with little twigs holding the ends shut, on a creamy bed of *lentilles du Puy,* and for women a fillet of *"flétan"*—the Parisian generic for any flatfish. No discussion would be brooked. Capucine would very much have enjoyed the *saucisses* but knew enough Freud to recognize vicarious dieting when she saw it and accepted the inevitable.

Only when coffee had been reached—cheese was not even offered, and the reluctantly proposed dessert to be shared had been declined—did Marie-Christine unburden her soul.

"I really adore Loïc," Marie-Christine said earnestly. "I love him with all my heart. Our two lives have grown into one. You won't believe it, but we met at Castel. I never thought true romance could be found in a discotheque. He was with someone he didn't like, and I was with a girl-friend because I had just been dumped and was trying to get drunk to forget about it. Somehow we just found our-selves dancing together. When I woke up with him the next morning, I realized how lucky I was. He was older than the boys I had been going out with and was strong and gave direction and purpose to my life, which had gone completely adrift.

"He had just inherited the élevage and it was in a com-plete mess. His father had been senile and had been inter-ested only in his crazy breeding theories. Sales had fallen way off, and the élevage was losing money hand over fist. It was a nightmare for Loïc. He was working so hard, he needed to spend his weekends in Paris, getting away and blowing off steam.

"Of course, we fell in love right away and developed a routine. He would come to Paris every weekend and stay at my apartment. I couldn't go to Saint-Nicolas, because there's no hotel and it would have been completely out of the question for me to sleep at his house. Can you imagine!" Marie-Christine giggled.

"But I would drive down for the day pretty often and came to know the ins and outs of the élevage. Loïc quickly got bored with coming to Paris. His heart was really in the country. He proposed to me and I accepted in a flash."

She stopped and took a deep breath. "Don't take this the wrong way. Remember I told you that I inherited a good bit of money when my father died several years before and I had invested it in the élevage? What that meant was that I bullied my trust officers into investing, but I guess that amounts to the same thing," she said with a giggle.

"It's important you understand that when we started going out, Loïc had no idea I had any money. I really do think he fell in love with me that first night at Castel. Anyway, it all worked out for the best. The élevage took off again. It was really spectacular. I don't know how Loïc did it. He invested in some new bulls—his father's experiments had seriously weakened the herd—expanded some of the buildings, came up with an advertising campaign, and the next thing we knew, we were heralded as one of the leaders of the new generation of French agriculturists and were making buckets of money. . . ." Marie-Christine's voice trailed off.

"So what happened?" Capucine asked. The restaurant was almost empty, and the kitchen staff was setting the tables for the evening service, but she knew they would not be disturbed.

Marie-Christine snapped herself back into the conversation. "I'll tell you about that in a minute, but I want to tell you about the money part first. It's because of that that I'm in the mess I'm in now.

"Lazard Frères has always managed my trust, and they're very strict about it. When we got married, their lawyer insisted that the marriage contract be under the provision for separation of assets, so each partner's property would remain his and only the property acquired after the marriage would be considered joint. Do you know how that works?"

Capucine laughed. "When I started out in the police, I worked in fiscal fraud. I know a whole lot more about that stuff than I'd like to."

"Well, the Lazard man told me that the money I was lending the élevage was probably more than the place was worth. Remember, it was nearly bankrupt at that point. He said that if we ever divorced, I could wind up as the majority owner even if Loïc had paid my trust fund back later. It annoyed me to think they were preparing for my eventual divorce, but I guess that's part of their job.

"That's my problem. I can't control what Lazard does. If I ever divorced Loïc, I'm afraid he would lose the élevage. Is that right? You know all about these things."

"I haven't seen the numbers, but it's certainly possible."

"That would be like cutting his right arm off. You just can't do that to a man. Can you understand that?"

"So you *do* want a divorce."

"I don't know what I want. Loïc is wonderful, kind and understanding, just like the father I always wanted, and I love him. Well, I don't have to tell you. Alexandre is so much older than you are. Being with Loïc is not like having a real husband. The bed part is such a chore." She leaned over, put her hand on top of Capucine's, and said in a rush, "He never wants to do it and then after three or four months he panics because we haven't and then he takes one of those awful blue pills and we have to sit around for an hour trying to think of something to say waiting for it to kick in. Sometimes it winds up working, and sometimes it doesn't. And all the trying, my God. It's just so horrible. Poor you, I'm sure you have to go through the same thing."

Capucine was sorely tempted to tell her that that was not at all the way it happened with Alexandre, quite the contrary in fact. But, diplomatically, she merely nodded encouragingly.

"What are you going to do?" Capucine asked.

"Who knows," she sighed. "I told you all about Philippe when we were in Honfleur. I used to think it was just him. But I've discovered my physical needs are much more important than I ever imagined." She paused and gave Capucine an appraising look, deciding if she could embark on the next stage of confidences.

"I've found someone else, an old school friend. It's platonic—I mean, we're not in love or anything like that—but we spend a lot of time in bed. I feel so much better in my skin. I feel like a woman again and not a daughter. I love all the things he makes me do in bed. He's even more adventuresome than Philippe—"

"What about Loïc?" Capucine asked. She had nothing against sexual confidences but was not about to take time off from her commissariat to listen to them.

"What am I supposed to do? Go back to Loïc and have affairs on the side? I couldn't stand that. Divorce him? I couldn't stand that, either. I thought you'd point me in the right direction." She burst into uncontrollable sobs.

The waitress stared at them unconcernedly. If it had been she crying her eyes out, Capucine hoped the woman would have had the sense to bring a plate heaped with sausages and lentils.

CHAPTER 35

Friday evening found a reluctant Capucine back at Maulévrier. Even though she was in the same village as Momo, abandoning her desk at the commissariat paradoxically felt like a dereliction of her duty to him.

Oncle Aymerie's ebullience aggravated her sense of guilt. He bubbled over with the news of a prodigious ferret shoot planned for the next morning. Ferreting was a pursuit—she couldn't bring herself to consider it a sport—particularly distasteful to Capucine, a highly cruel and unfair manifestation of the paysan's endless, imaginary war against the harmless, endearing rabbit.

The logistics of the thing were simple enough. Ferrets were sent down into a large rabbit warren, and the terrified little bunnies dashed out of the profusion of holes either to find themselves trapped in purse nets or shot in the back by hunters with shotguns. The main virtue of the exercise appeared to be to affirm the reality of social symbiosis in country life. Keeping ferrets was the purview of the laboring classes, while wielding shotguns was presumed to be the domain of the leisured. The partnership was further cemented by the perceived gain to the farmers, who saw a measurable decrease in the ranks of their enemy, while the "nobs" always enjoyed any excuse for a day out with their guns to kill something or other. Both sides of the equation received dividends of burlap bags stuffed with rabbit carcasses, which were duly transformed into endless varieties of stews and pâtés.

This was to be the annual incursion into a particularly infamous warren at the base of a venerable tree known, no one knew why, as *le Chêne de l'Evêque*—the Bishop's Oak. The warren in question was viewed as the Roland Garros of ferreting, as extensive as the Vietcong's tunnels, snaking out in all directions, harboring uncountable legions of furry, legumicidal rodents.

Capucine was dismayed that Alexandre had been infected by Oncle Aymerie's exuberance and the two of them had succeeded in exciting Jacques's normally soaring high spirits to even greater altitudes.

Early the next morning Capucine was awakened by Alexandre, looking for all the world like a Gallic version of a P. G. Wodehouse character in his father's baggy plus fours.

"I brought you your coffee. We have to be there at nine sharp. The little bunnies will have returned from their morning's nefarious sorties but will still be scuttling around their tunnels before they dig in for their daytime naps. Timing is all in ferreting."

"You seem very knowledgeable," Capucine said, sleepily sipping a café au lait from a kitchen bowl.

"Wild rabbit is the forgotten mainstay of French cuisine. The diabolic Disney stole them from us. It's probably the only dish you don't dare serve in Paris today—people look at you as if you were some sort of heartless ogre—and yet it's the king of the white meats. When we get back, Jacques and I are going to spend the afternoon making a selection of pâtés and a *lapin à la moutarde* for dinner. You really need to get moving. I don't want to be a minute late." Capucine asked herself why on earth she had been in such a rush to get back.

An hour later Capucine and Alexandre walked up to *le Chêne de l'Evêque,* their guns crooked on their arms. Alexandre might have been about to pose for a 1920s advertisement for an expensive brand of Scotch, peering about with a luminescent grin as if he were expecting a gaggle of paparazzi to erupt from the wood. Capucine wondered if he realized he had affected the most irritating of Jacques's mannerisms.

A large crowd had already gathered around the old oak tree, which, like everything else at Maulévrier, was steeped in Capucine's memories. Jacques appeared out of nowhere and, without a word of greeting, said, "Ah, this gnarled old oak. Do you remember the time we climbed up in its welcoming branches and hid from everyone all afternoon and—"

Mercifully, the two paysans who had been standing importantly by the tree, nursing wooden boxes with large holes drilled in the covers, came up to Capucine with broad tooth-gapped smiles.

"*Mam'selle, Monsieur le Comte* told us to show you our ferrets before we started," one said, reaching into the box slung from his shoulder and proudly producing a white and brown ferret with a long, slim, almost snakelike body. At first blush it was as cuddly and innocuous as one of Alexandre's detested Disney cartoon characters. "He hasn't eaten since the day before yesterday, and he's dying to get down there," the man said with a broad, ruthless smile, displaying all ten of his teeth. The animal looked dispassionately at her with eyes so black they seemed pupil-less and yawned sensuously, revealing its long, needlelike canines.

Not to be outdone, the second paysan opened his box and proudly showed the six ferrets nestled in partitions inside. One of them shyly poked its head out of the box, blinking myopically, hooking strong claws on the side of the partition—the engaging eager to pursue the defenseless.

Oncle Aymerie—with Emilien as his second in command—began to marshal the crowd. In addition to Vienneau, and his apparently inseparable acolyte Bellanger, there were a dozen of the usual shooting guests and a further dozen paysans. Vienneau looked bleary-eyed and disoriented, as if he had been up all night embracing a bottle. Adrift in the fumes of his hangover, he completely ignored Bellanger.

Oncle Aymerie noisily cleared his throat to attract the collective attention. "All right, everybody. The purse nets are in place," he said loudly. Looking around, Capucine saw that at least forty green nets had been positioned on short stakes over the visible openings to the warren. The outermost nets were at least a hundred and fifty feet from the tree. The perimeter of the warren was a lot bigger than when she had been a child. The rabbits had been industrious. "Now, as we all know," Oncle Aymerie boomed, "the guns have to be particularly vigilant and concentrate on their sectors. The nets will get the rabbits coming out of the holes we know about, but most of them will come out of small holes we haven't discovered. That's why the guns are so important. Emilien is going to place you, and when the ferrets go down, I want you to face away from the tree and look into your sector and nowhere else. Otherwise, you're not going to hit anything. Is that perfectly clear?"

Emilien placed his "guns," about twenty in all, including the handful of paysans who had turned up with rudimentary shotguns, in a circle about fifty feet out from the oak. The two paysans put their ferrets down holes close to the tree with muttered exhortative incantations. The air of expectation and excitement was palpable. The guns peered intently into their sectors with fierce concentration. Absolutely nothing happened. And continued to not happen for several long minutes.

The bubble of excitement floated away. It became obvious to everyone that there was no reason for silence, but they were placed too far apart for conversation. One by one they abandoned their forward-leaning crouches with shotguns at the ready and began to slouch. Long, boring moments passed. Capucine fell into a reverie, imagining the ferrets creeping through the long tunnels as the rabbits stole away in controlled panic, soundlessly ducking into side tunnels and trying whatever tricks there were that rabbits used. Still nothing happened.

Jacques, who was stationed next to Capucine, walked over to her. "I know what you're thinking, you little vixen. You're thinking of those long, thick ferrets squeezing through those tight tunnels, panting to sink their teeth into those furry bunnies' behinds. I'm relieved that it isn't just men who are titillated by the phallic nature of the sport." He giggled his Amadean laugh, but quietly enough so it wasn't heard.

"Jacques, get back to your post. The rabbits are going to come out any second now!" Capucine hissed.

A single shot boomed. Out of the corner of her eye Capucine saw the animal lifted in the air by the impact and then roll when it hit the ground. Bellanger had shot a rabbit two sectors away from his and was lowering his gun with a self-satisfied smirk. He had apparently decided that the gun assigned to the sector was asleep at his post and so the rabbit was his by rights. It had been a brilliant shot, but Capucine could feel the collective waves of hatred seeking Bellanger out like science fiction death rays.

The firing erupted with the brio of a war movie, every gun firing out rounds as fast as he could. An army of rabbits scuttled back and forth in desperation at the perimeter's edge, crossing each other's paths, veering suddenly, and crossing again. Then, as if a conductor had lowered his baton, the firing ceased all at once. Oncle Aymerie called out loudly,. "Congratulations. At least a hundred shot and over fifty in the nets. Well done indeed!"

Everyone moved out to walk the area in front of their stations to collect dead rabbits and drop them in a heap at their positions. Several of the rabbits had big chunks of flesh chewed out of their hindquarters, and many were missing hind limbs.

Naturally, the biggest pile of rabbits was in front of Bellanger. A bit surprisingly, there was only one in front of Vienneau. Even Alexandre had managed to shoot six. Capucine's heart went out to Loïc, who seemed far too preoccupied with Marie-Christine to think about anything else.

Oncle Aymerie, the gamekeeper, and Alexandre busied themselves arranging the rabbits into orderly rows, to be counted, photographed, and distributed. Capucine was astonished at how rapidly Alexandre had melded into life at Maulévrier. She felt the slap of rejection. Just as she should have been congratulating herself on her reconciliation with her family, Alexandre seemed to be usurping her spot.

Alexandre came up to her. "Look at that. We did a total of a hundred and sixty-two of the little rascals. I accounted for six myself." He was as delighted as a child who had successfully spelled *anticonstitutionnellement,* the longest word in the French language, and won a spelling bee.

"If you think this is sport, then I imagine you deserve congratulations," Capucine said, fully intending to hurt. To her dismay, Alexandre was oblivious and sauntered off to continue conferring with Oncle Aymerie, no doubt about the culinary potential of the morning's harvest.

Jacques came up. That was all she needed. "Little cousin, marriage is not easy, is it?" he said with a sneer so attenuated she almost thought he might be sincere. She put her arm through his.

"Thank God," she said, "the Calvados has arrived. About fucking time."

"My thoughts exactly, Commissaire Maigret," Jacques said as he led her off to the Estafette, which had just arrived from the château with lunch for the paysans.

There was the traditional awkward moment as the necktied made every effort to make conversation with the workclothed as they used their time-blackened Opinels and Laguioles to cut into enormous loaves of country bread braced against their chests and sliced *saucisson* and *jambon de Bayonne* into robust slabs. Emilien made a great show of uncorking label-less bottles of red wine the dark color of coagulating blood—the stuff the paysans liked to call "good red wine that stains"—and lining them up next to a half dozen large bottles of Calvados. But well before the alcohol spread the paysans' wings, they were already soaring with the joy of a job very well done.

Tranquil that the bridge across the class divide was as secure as ever, and knowing that it would take some doing to coax the ferrets out of the warren, Oncle Aymerie's guests trooped off to the château for their own lunch, which turned out to be one of Odile's bolder creations, roast chicken stuffed with ground pork on a bed of thinly sliced zucchini. Capucine was relieved when she saw the whole chickens but lost her appetite at the sight of the stuffing.

Lunch was a boisterous affair, the guests' early morning elation exacerbated by healthy doses of Calvados on empty stomachs. Alexandre and Jacques rattled like excited schoolgirls about a recipe for rabbit pâté involving chunks of apple, the very idea of which made Capucine lose what little interest she had left in the chicken. The only jarring note was Bellanger, who tried repeatedly to engage Vienneau in conversation with a conspicuous lack of success. Oncle Aymerie made no pretense of listening to any of the chatter and merely beamed happily at his tribe under his tent, concerned only with ensuring that their glasses were constantly full and that their faces were rosy and smiling.

Vienneau seemed to reach a conclusion of some sort, became agitated, glanced right and left nervously, and finally banged his glass with his spoon. In the startled silence that followed, he announced, "I, well, I, um . . . I would like to invite you all to lunch tomorrow. I know it's a bit sudden and it's not the done thing and all, but I think I can promise you a truly exceptional *rôti de bœuf*. What do you all say?"

Even if it had been the result of too much wine, it would still have been an unforgivable gaffe. One simply did not attempt to force a captive group of people into a social commitment, particularly without reasonable notice. The common knowledge of Vienneau's misfortune did not lessen the sense of embarrassment. There were self-conscious shuffles and averted gazes.

But Vienneau wasn't about to give up. "I apologize for inviting you like this on such short notice," he said. "It's just that I can't stand the thought of bouncing around that empty house on a Sunday. It's too much for me. Please say you'll all come."

Oncle Aymerie's perfect manners saved the situation. "What a funny coincidence, *mon cher* Loïc, that you should invite us just as I was going to suggest it myself. I haven't seen your *élevage* in a donkey's years. And I've been pining away for a Sunday roast *comme il faut*. Of course we'll all come."

CHAPTER 36

If anyone had attempted to describe the lunch as a success, it could only have been because of the food. The Vienneaus' cook—Loïc's cook, now that one thought about it—seemed to have blossomed when released from the yoke of Marie-Christine's hausfrau authority. Despite Vienneau's instructions not to deviate a single iota from the traditional norms of a classic Sunday lunch, she had nonetheless managed to produce the sublime.

The pièce de résistance was a *rosbif* that was the quintessence of all *rosbifs*. It had been presented whole at the table for Vienneau to slice, a darkly charred, lustrous brown cylinder elegantly tied with well-scorched sprigs of thyme trapped under the string. Once carved, the roast revealed its palette, a luminous bronze tan just underneath the crisp, almost black exterior, dissolving into a joyous pink and then into an erotic, moist, almost pulsing vermilion at the core.

Chewing seemed entirely superfluous. At one point Capucine cut out a portion of the carmine heart and held it in her mouth to see if it really would melt. She might even have hummed to herself as she did so, but if she did, it was so quietly that no one could possibly have heard. She was astonished when Alexandre rebuked her silently with pursed lips and crinkled brow. As she fought down an attack of the giggles, she realized that Alexandre was having another of his food epiphanies. It was the potatoes. When the dish arrived, it had looked like yet another Sunday gratin, a pulpy mass of tasteless Gruyère and limp spuds. But this gratin had turned off the marshy road to flaccidity and had taken the straight and narrow toward being a feast for the gods. Transparently thin slices of potatoes had been interspersed with shavings of truffles and parchments of parmesan and delicately covered with a lightly seasoned topping of tart *crème fleurette*—sour cream—before being baked to perfection. No wonder Alexandre wasn't in a mood for levity.

No, the food was hardly the problem. It was the conversation. Topics fizzled like soggy fireworks. No matter how enthusiastically they were launched, they failed to burst into a cascade of interest and fell back to earth with a damp thud. Even though no mention was made of Marie-Christine, her specter dominated the room. If someone brought up politics, the conversation turned to a minister who had been caught in a compromising situation with his mistress; celebrity gossip inevitably brought up the latest mega-actor divorce; even the weather drew the ill-phrased observation that it was time to start thinking about the Caribbean, where everyone at the table knew full well that Marie-Christine was spending the week with her current lover.

Vienneau was frustrated to the point of rudeness. When Bellanger attempted to jump into the breach by commenting that the CAC 40 stock market index had closed nearly one whole percent up on Friday, Vienneau quashed him with an unkind "Henri, there are other things in life than the goddamn stock market."

There was a collective sigh when it was over and Vienneau proposed a walk around the élevage to aid their digestion. Cigars were lit. Deep breaths were taken. Laughter was heard. The mood was that of a class of schoolchildren let out for recess after an interminable lecture.

But the good cheer was short-lived. It wasn't just Vienneau's luncheon table; the entire élevage smacked of depression. The freshly painted white luster of the place seemed to have dimmed. Everywhere one looked, something seemed to need fixing. The workers seemed listless; the steers, morose. Had something changed, or was it just that the day was leadenly overcast?

The group reached a fence enclosing a small herd of chalky white steers, who, in the way of steers, ambled over lackadaisically to investigate. There was much rubbing of rubbery noses and the sort of encouraging commentary one makes to farm animals and toddlers. A worker came up.

"Monsieur Vienneau. I'm glad you're here. There's a problem with this fence. The railings are rotten under the paint." To demonstrate, he yanked the rail they were all leaning against and the end came away from the post. "Last night some steers leaned against the next section and both rails came completely off. I hammered them back in this morning and tied them up with twine, but the field is so close to the road, I'm worried there's going to be an accident if they get loose at night."

Vienneau seemed put out. He made a cursory show of examining the fence and ignored the worker.

"Excuse me for speaking to you personally, monsieur, but this could be a serious problem."

"Yes, yes." Vienneau looked around nervously, visibly attempting to escape. "Thank you for calling this to my attention. I'll bring it up with Monsieur Martel."

"But, mons—"

Vienneau walked away, leading his guests. The worker stared after them, looking frustrated and annoyed.

They continued their walk. Alexandre, Jacques, and

Oncle Aymerie fell behind, chatting in conspiratorial whispers, examining Alexandre's cane. Capucine had second thoughts about her gift.

A little farther on they rounded a corner and came across Pierre Martel haranguing two North African workers. The two men hung their heads, utterly cowed. It was another awkward moment. Vienneau was trapped. He couldn't very well turn the group around and force them to retreat, nor could he lead them into an embarrassing scene.

Vienneau advanced as slowly as he decently could. As they approached Martel, his angry words became clearer. "I'm not putting up with this fucking shit anymore." He grabbed one of the men by the shirt and shook him, raising his other hand threateningly. "All right, you two, get out of my sight. Get back to work before I get really mad." Hangdog, the two workers shuffled off, staring at the ground.

Martel walked up to Vienneau, shaking his head in an exaggerated show of dismay. The two shook hands with the quick pump of business associates. "I tell you, monsieur, getting these shiftless *beurs* to do a day's work is more trouble than it's worth."

"Of course it is. Of course it is. But you're doing an excellent job," Vienneau said, smiling stiffly. Capucine could easily read his mind as he told himself that staying at home after lunch, sipping Calvados around the fire, would have been a far better idea.

"Monsieur, I was just coming to your house to give you these," Martel said, handing Vienneau a thin sheaf of computer printouts.

Vienneau looked a little bewildered.

"It's the week's production statistics."

With obvious lack of interest, Vienneau riffled though the pages and prepared to put the stack under his arm.

"*Pardon,* monsieur, but did you see this?" Martel

pointed to a line at the bottom of the first page. Capucine peered over his shoulder, unnoticed.

"Yes, yes, I see. The average weight of the steers slaughtered this week is down a little bit." Vienneau shrugged his shoulders. "It's seasonal. Happens every year. They know winter is coming. When you've been in the business longer, you'll understand these things. I'll bring the shortfall to the attention of Accounting on Monday. Voilà!" he said in clear dismissal of Martel, whose face flattened in anger as he turned and stamped off.

Jacques, Alexandre, and Oncle Aymerie, who had snuck off without anyone noticing, loped up cheerfully. They had clearly put Alexandre's cane to its intended use.

"We just had a very fulfilling little walk," Jacques said. "We saw the prize bull. Alexandre poked him you know where with his stick, and we were told we couldn't do that." The three chuckled happily.

"And then you discovered what else you could do with that stick, I'm sure," Capucine said.

Just as Alexandre was about to remonstrate, he saw Momo in the distance, walking with two other North Africans. All three seemed dispirited, kicking pebbles on the path, killing time. Alexandre had met Momo on several occasions and was a great fan of his in the way that oil and vinegar have a profound attraction for each other.

Alexandre brightened and inhaled deeply, ready to shout out a greeting. "Say!" he started to articulate before the anomaly of the situation struck him. All he got out was the "S—"

Capucine rejoiced in her reprieve, but her heart went out to Momo. He looked drained and spiritless.

Oncle Aymerie had obviously scored the lion's share of the bounty of Alexandre's walking stick and evidenced a bonhomie exaggerated enough to have qualified him as a stand-in for Maurice Chevalier.

"Come along, you three," he said to Capucine, Alexandre, and Jacques. "Time to go home for tea." He paused and said to Alexandre, "Don't worry. *Tea* is just a synecdoche," struggling valiantly with the final word but getting it right in the end. In a stage aside to Jacques he said, "You have to use words like that with literary types if you want them to understand." The three men laughed uproariously.

Capucine's stupefaction at Alexandre's growing intimacy with her family did not erase her anxiety at the upcoming explanation to him of exactly how it was that Momo just happened to be strolling along the grounds of the élevage. An explanation that would be all the more tricky when she got to the part about not yet having obtained the examining magistrate's approval for such an unorthodox move.

CHAPTER 37

It was probably due to some subliminal childhood memory; Capucine had always loathed the façade of Rouen's cathedral—France's other Notre Dame. Monet had gotten it right: a prodigiously amorphous pile oozing with formless baubles, as meaningless a shape as one of his haystacks, whose only usefulness had been to reflect the changing colors of the day's light. The monolith loomed oppressively, casting a chilly shadow over the empty café terrace in the middle of the place de la Calende. Capucine shivered and felt ridiculous.

Momo and Capucine had agreed to meet at the Brasserie La Flèche at the corner of the square just in front of the cathedral at two thirty in the afternoon. Momo was to take the bus right after lunch on his day off. Both of them had worried that some of his fellow workers might also be on the bus and prove unshakable. Arriving half an hour early and sitting out in the open, she would see him coming and be able to come up with a Plan B if need be. But she hadn't bargained on the cold and gloom.

Enough was enough. She had left her Barbour open, as police procedure dictated, giving her free access to her Sig. She zipped it up tightly, snapped the collar shut around her neck, and took another turn with her brightly striped scarf. She was still cold. And just as bored.

A man arrived with a large, slow-moving basset hound on a leash and sat down three tables away. A waiter came up, a bottle of beer already on a tray, poured two-thirds of it into a glass and the rest into a bowl, which he placed in front of the basset, who lapped it up enthusiastically. It was obviously a daily ritual.

When there was no beer left, the dog looked up at Capucine, two foaming streams spilling from its jowls. His lower lids fell away from his eyes, incongruously making him appear all knowing and infinitely sad. Capucine was convinced the dog fully understood her predicament. The man stood up, sprinkled a few euro coins on the table, and said, "*Salut,* Jean," more or less in the direction of the waiter, who waved lethargically as they walked off.

Capucine snorted and shook her head. She was overreacting again. It was her need to cover all her bets. The thing that went most against her grain was putting all her chips on a single number. But that was exactly what she'd done. If Momo came up dry, she'd have no case. After all the sound and fury she'd be a laughingstock in her family as well as on the force. And on top of it all, she knew she'd asked too much of Momo. She cringed at the thought of their meeting.

She followed the man and his dog with her eyes. Just as they were about to reach a cute shop that was both tea salon and secondhand bookstore, preciously called the "Thé Majuscule"—Capital Tea—she saw Momo, who bent down to pet the dog, using the gesture to look around the square. He was in the clear. Now she could get out of this goddamn cold.

Capucine stood up, folded a five-euro note under a saucer to pay for her tea, and followed Momo into the brasserie. By the time she arrived at their table, Momo already had a double Scotch in front of him. He downed half of it, the single ice cube tinkling in the tall tumbler. She had seen him look happier.

"Not enjoying country life?" she asked.

"Sure I am. Tending your smoke- and booze-free garden is definitely the way to go. The hell with sitting in a café, puffing on a *clope,* sipping a *ballon* of red, and checking out the waitress's legs. Oh, *pardon,* Commissaire. Don't take that the wrong way, but, jeez, this is some assignment you gave me. I get to share a room with some asshole Arab fundamentalist, so I can't even think about having a drink or a smoke, and then I get to spend nine hours at hard labor with nothing more in my belly than lamb tagine." He shook his head in disgust.

"What kind of work do they have you doing?" Capucine asked.

"I got a great job. I'm on the kill floor. It's fun stuff. What do I do? I torture cows. Remember how you used to get all pissed off about the way they do interrogations at the Quai? Well, you'd really love this." He beckoned the waiter over and pointed at his empty glass to ask for another. Once Capucine had given her order and the waiter had left, Momo resumed his litany of complaints.

"What happens is that the steers are pushed down this chute, see? And then some guy with this pneumatic gizmo pops them on the head so they're knocked out. I did that for a week. That part's okay. But then I tried too hard and got promoted. I even got a raise." Momo snorted. "After they're so-called knocked out, they're chained upside down to this rail that slides them into the next room, where someone slits their throats and skins them. That guy would be me."

"Oh, Momo, I'm sorry."

"Don't feel sorry for me. Feel sorry for the fucking steers." He signaled the waiter for a third Scotch.

"So these un-knocked-out steers really jerk around on the chain when you start to skin them. Some of them even start howling." He paused and smiled slightly. By the third Scotch the alcohol was finally beginning to take effect. "What I do is, when no one is looking, I give the dumbass steer a good hard right hook to the back of the head. If you do it just right, you can hear the neck snap. What's for lunch?" He burst into ironic laughter.

"No steak?" Capucine asked with a smile.

"No, and anything that looks like a tagine or contains lamb is even worse. And if you even say 'mint tea,' I'm outta here."

Capucine picked up the menu. "There's *canard à la Rouennaise*. It's the specialty in Rouen. I'm not sure Alexandre would tell us this is the best place to have it, but—"

"Duck? Great. Go for it."

"Your cover is secure, right?"

"Yeah, bulletproof. But it wasn't easy. I don't know shit about farmwork, so I had to come on even dumber than usual. That worked out pretty well. They figured out I was a retard but real good at using my muscles. Just like at the police." Momo laughed and then looked around to make sure he hadn't been overheard. "At first they'd kid me because I didn't have calloused palms and I was the only guy wearing work gloves. But I don't have that problem anymore." He lifted both his hands and held them out palm first in the classic gesture of surrender. "See?" he said, proudly showing off his brand-new orange calluses. "Of course, I still don't know shit about cattle."

"So they torture the steers. That's it?"

"Don't get me wrong, Commissaire. It turns out that's the way steers are always killed. In fact, it seems these guys are better than most. And before they get to my area, the goddamn things are treated like those white, fluffy dogs in the Sixteenth Arrondissement."

The two plates of duck arrived along with a bottle of Volnay that Capucine had selected. Automatically, the waiter poured an inch into Momo's glass for him to taste. Irritated, he pushed the glass toward Capucine and told the waiter to bring him a fourth Scotch. Capucine had never seen Momo in such a bad mood.

"Did you find out anything else?"

"Nothing major. The joint's sagging, but it's not in free fall or anything like that," Momo said, poking his duck aggressively with his fork.

"Sagging?"

"For one, they can treat those cows like they were living in some Passy apartment all they want, but the fuckers aren't growing the way they used to. For two, nobody's really driving the bus anymore." Momo decided the duck was edible and attacked it with gusto.

Capucine let him chew noisily until she could stand it no more.

"Come on, Momo, out with it!"

"All right," he said, his mouth full. "That guy that died, Philippe Gerlier, he was so good, they call him Saint Philippe. According to everyone, he was the one running the place. Your pal Vienneau just did a walk around every now and then, like he did with you guys the other day, but he doesn't have a clue what's going on.

"Apparently this Gerlier really *was* a saint. He worked his ass off day in and day out, except when he was visiting his poor mama, who is dying of Alzheimer's in some clinic in the Midwest of the United States. The guy was half American, but he was brought up in France by his French father after his American wife left him."

"I thought Vienneau took over the management after Gerlier died."

"Not that I can see. The guy trying to run the place is this Pierre Martel, one of the foremen. The problem is that he doesn't really know what to do, either. All he does is yell and bully the hands."

Capucine looked at Momo, waiting for more.

He took a mammoth bite of the duck and swallowed a third of his whiskey. "The big problem is that the cattle aren't growing fast enough. They post the weekly stats in the abattoir, and you can see that they are killing more and more head to make the weekly weight."

"Does anyone know why?"

"Sure. It's because Saint Philippe isn't there to bless the steers anymore." Momo laughed and downed the Scotch, signaling the waiter for another one with his free hand.

"No one has a clue. The place is like a Chinese fire drill. Martel makes everyone run around in circles doing this and doing that. One day they change the feed mix. The next day they dump a new vitamin supplement into the feed. The day after that they change the antibiotics. Then they stop it all and run all the cattle down the chute to get injected with a new kind of vitamin. Nothing works. They gotta find another saint." Momo laughed happily. The Scotch had finally done its work.

"That roast you had that Sunday—"

"How do you know about that?" Capucine asked in amazement.

"Man, we know everything that goes on in the big house, right down to the last fart. Anyway, that particular hunk of meat was from the last batch before cattle started to pine away for their saint. The last of the good stuff."

The duck reduced to a skeleton, Momo leaned back in his chair with his latest drink. "So what do you want me to do now, Commissaire?"

"You need to get into wherever it is they keep the records. Is there some sort of accounting office?"

"There's an accounting department with three employees. Most of the guys have found an excuse to go in at one point or another. One of the accountants is pretty hot. They lock the office doors at night, but it's not a dead bolt or anything, so a plastic shim will get you in with no trouble. What am I looking for?"

"Anything out of the ordinary. If you find something interesting, let me know and we'll figure out what to do next."

Momo nodded.

"Listen. You're being careful about your cover, right?"

"Yeah, Commissaire, I'm just a big dumb guy who don't know from nuttin'. Speakin' of which, I should be getting back. Some of the guys are going into town for dinner tonight. There's a crappy Maghrebian café they go to, and I wouldn't want to miss out on some more couscous. Also, I gotta buy some hooch to take back."

"Momo, you left your police card at home like I told you? You're sure about that?"

"Calm down, Commissaire. I'm not some kid just out of the academy. It's my fucking neck on the line. I know what I'm doing." Capucine noticed Momo tightening slightly, which she took as a sign of irritation. If she had been a bit more observant, she might have seen that he was squeezing his heels together to reassure himself that the Smith and Wesson was still tightly strapped to his left ankle.

CHAPTER 38

"Where the hell are you?" the harsh voice asked threateningly. Capucine smiled serenely and admired Gauvin's latest improvement to her cloakroom refuge, a chipped onyx pen stand—the old kind that threatened to poke you in the eye if you bent over too quickly—which he must have found in the attic and garnished with two cheap Bic ballpoint pens, one red and the other black.

Contrôleur Général Guy Saccard had been Capucine's mentor ever since they had met when he was a guest lecturer at the commissaire's course at the police training school. Despite his august rank—he was head of half of the Paris Police Judiciaire and her boss's boss—he enjoyed teasing her with his bluster. Capucine assumed he was just checking up on her well-being, something he did frequently.

"A place called Saint-Nicolas, sir. It's in Normandy."

"Château de Maulévrier in Saint-Nicolas-de-Bliquetuit? Is that what you're trying to tell me?" She could hear papers being rustled angrily.

There was something unusual in his tone. Capucine sensed it would be unwise to let herself be tempted by the irony of his rhetorical question.

"What the hell are you doing down there?"

"I was on vacation when a case came up. The DCPJ ordered me to look into it part-time."

"They ordered you, did they? You had nothing to do with it, of course." He paused. Capucine could imagine him frowning and shaking his head. "And you really thought that just by pulling a few of your little strings, the DCPJ would assign you to a case and I'd never hear about it. You must have known that they'd need my approval. Why didn't you just ask me in the first place?"

"Because I thought you'd turn me down, sir," Capucine said meekly.

"And you thank me for my approval by hiding in a closet and ignoring your commissariat while all hell breaks loose? Is that how you show your appreciation?"

Capucine searched frantically for hidden cameras. How could he possibly know? She tried hard to collect herself. "What sort of hell is breaking loose, sir?"

"Have you read the papers this morning, or doesn't the press make it all the way down to Saint-Nicolas-de"—he paused for effect—"Bliquetuit?" He pronounced the word slowly and sarcastically. "Blee . . . kay . . . twee." This was more than bluster; he really did sound furious.

"Sir, they come in the afternoon, around three or four."

"Ah, yes, just in time for the *apéro*. A little white Lillet, nicely chilled? Is that what you drink down there? How nice. You must invite me sometime. I'm sure I'd find château life very relaxing after dealing with all the crap that oozes out of your sector."

"Sir, what are you trying to tell me?"

"Ah ha, I thought that would spark your interest. What's going to spoil the taste of your Lillet today is that *Le Figaro* is running a profile piece on your Belle au Marché. There's a map of where all the victims were located, with little pictures of them. A detailed description of her MO. Also a detailed list of what she's taken. And a physical description of her—entirely fantasized by some reporter, by the way. Like it so far?"

Capucine was stunned. "A couple of reporters did come by the commissariat a few weeks ago, but I thought they'd forgotten all about the case."

"And no doubt they would have if your Belle had stuck to run-of-the-mill bourgeois fat cats. She could even have thrown in the composer—who the hell knows who Hubert Lafontaine is? But when you start dicking around with movie stars, then you're going to get the press in big-time. Still with me, Commissaire?"

"Yes, sir."

"Now, here's the fun part. In this piece, your Belle is portrayed as a modern Arsène Lupin, gentleman burglar. But in this version, Lupin just happens to be a female wearing a thirty-nine D bra and black stockings with a garter belt."

"Oh, God."

"And, of course, there has to be a dumb cop you play for laughs. Just like Inspecteur Ganimard in Leblanc's novels, but this time around the dumb cop is called Commissaire Le Tellier."

Capucine knew the world of journalism well enough to be sure this was exactly the way the story would have been written.

"Now, Capucine," he said, alarming her with the use of her first name. "Here's the punch line. This pisses me off for two reasons. The first is that it just so happens I believe in your career, but if the press succeeds in making you look like a fool, your credibility on the street—and on the force—is going to go right down the crapper. And that's going to make it a whole lot harder for you to get your job done. And the other is that it's not just your cred. The whole of the PJ is going to look like assholes, and that makes the force a little bit less effective."

"So what can we do, sir?"

"Take charge of the situation. I want a press conference. With maps, evidence, psychological profiles, everything we can throw at it. I want to give the very firm impression that we have our hands around this one. I'll kick it off, but I want your team up on the stage looking like they know what the hell they're doing, and I want you out in front so they can take your picture. Boobs sell newspapers."

Capucine gritted her teeth.

"I'm e-mailing you a list of journalists the PR department tells me are well disposed to us. Call them yourself. It sounds more sincere when the PR department doesn't do it. Golly, do you think you could come all the way back to Paris to deal with this? Not right now, of course. I mean, after your Lillet?"

Capucine was astonished how close she actually came to hanging up on an officer as senior as a *contrôleur général*.

Capucine spared no efforts in prepping Isabelle for the press conference. After five sessions in her office she was convinced that Isabelle was going to make an excellent showing, and that her last debacle with the press was effectively shrouded by the mists of time. Thirty minutes into the conference Capucine thought it was going exceptionally well. Saccard's gravitas had conveyed the commitment of the Police Judiciaire. The PR department had done a beautiful job preparing a PowerPoint presentation with far more maps, photos, and information tidbits than the press had ever dreamed of. Capucine had made the first part of the talk while David tapped the key on the laptop to advance the pages on the screen. Sensitive to Saccard's comment, she had worn a slightly tight white silk blouse, of which she was able to strain the top button at will by breathing deeply. Her Sig was very much in evidence in the small of her back, a feature Alexandre continually assured her called attention to her *fesses* in a highly fetching way.

But all this was window dressing. It was the second part of the presentation that had been intended to carry the day with the press, underscoring the skill of the team and giving the impression that the case was firmly in hand and an arrest imminent.

Her section over, Capucine smiled at Isabelle, inviting her to come up to the front of the room. Isabelle rose smartly and walked toward the screen, exuding muscular vitality and animal magnetism. Capucine breathed an inward sigh. But the minute Isabelle stepped in front of the audience, she came undone, held fast in the grips of stage fright. Isabelle stood woodenly, wide-eyed, dry-mouthed, tight-throated. The fruits of her sessions with Capucine withered and fell off the tree. She mumbled, raced through her text, and skipped vital points. When she was done, one of the journalists asked her, "So, Brigadier, you really have no clues and are just hoping the case will solve itself? Is that what you're trying to tell us?"

Fuming, Isabelle took a few steps toward the reporter, who fortunately was sitting in the third row. "Listen, asshole, we have this fucking case completely under control. Trust me on that, you—"

Before she could release the final expletive, David was on his feet, holding a sheaf of papers.

"Before I wrap up," he said, as engagingly as if he was selling a miraculous sponge on a late-night TV infomercial, "I'd like to distribute a printout of our presentation, a press release, and glossies of the photos you saw in case you want to use them. I also have bios of the team and glossies of them, too." David's winning smile warmed the room. In their desire not to miss out on the press kit, the reporters pressed around David, who raised his voice and said, "Thank you all for coming. Remember, I'm your liaison officer and I've put my card with all my numbers in the folder. Feel free to call me day or night."

Saccard was visibly impressed. David really did have an enchanting smile, Capucine thought. He was bound to wind up in politics one day.

When Saccard and the press had finally gone their ways, Capucine and her brigadiers trooped into her office. Isabelle slammed the door and turned on David. "Thanks for nothing, you motherfucker. You made me look like a world-class fool."

David acted as if he hadn't heard, stretched as if he was waking up from a nap, and said pleasantly to Capucine, "That went pretty well, didn't you think, Commissaire?"

"I did, actually. Now all we have to do is find her."

"That's going to be a little more tricky," David said. "We don't have anything that remotely looks like a clue."

"Then you're just going to have to make your own. I want you to do two things. First, go back and interview each victim a second time in the light of the other five occurrences. See if any threads begin to emerge. Things she likes to eat, regional expressions, stories of her past reoccurring from one victim to another, even if disguised, anything that will give us a clue as to who she is and what she does when she's not fleecing people. And don't leave out the composer, Lafontaine. Stick with his story, but get him to tell you what his niece talked about in the few days before she left. At one level he'll know exactly what you're talking about. When you see the two magazine illustrators, ask them if they'll do a sketch. We should have thought of it at the time. Those police Identi-Kit drawings are useless. They all wind up making the perps look like they're mentally retarded. Get the illustrators to do something artistic, something where the Belle is really recognizable."

"Right, we're on it," Isabelle said authoritatively. "What's the other thing?"

"When you get back, I want you to turn one of the interview rooms into a command center, close the door, spread out your notes, and start going over all the points of commonality of these crimes—location, victim typology, items stolen, that sort of stuff—and try to see what patterns emerge. It'll be subtle, so you're going to have to be creative. Let me know what you come up with."

"You're going back to the country?" David asked.

"Yes, but it'll be over soon. I miss you guys too much," she said.

As David left Capucine's office, Isabelle stayed behind.

"Got a minute?"

"Of course, Isabelle." Capucine tightened her stomach muscles. "What is it?"

"It's like I told you the last time. You're pushing the wrong guy for promotion. Look what happened out there. You spend hours teaching me and I still fucked up."

"Right. And it's like I told you the last time. I'm not pushing you for promotion because you have a gift for gab. I'm doing it because you're a damn good cop. You know what you're doing and you instill loyalty. I just saw even more proof of that. Now, please get out of here and get on with your goddamn case. The real message of the day was that we need an arrest and fast."

CHAPTER 39

Capucine's second meeting with Momo was in gray, gray Le Havre. The entire city had the bleak quality of a fifties black-and-white film noir. Completing the scene, the weather was particularly oppressive, Baudelaire's low cast-iron sky bearing heavily down like the weighty lid of a farmhouse casserole.

Capucine had told Momo to walk out of the bus station and follow the direction of traffic down the street. He came through the door five minutes ahead of schedule and shuffled down the sidewalk incuriously, for all the world yet another rootless immigrant laborer. Capucine envied him. She had a long way to go before she acquired his ability to melt into the background.

She inched the Clio along at Momo's pace, oblivious to the cars that came up behind her, flashing their lights in irritation, then roaring by in low gear. After two blocks, when she had fully satisfied herself that none of his fellow workers were following, she pulled up next to Momo and opened her door.

Capucine smiled. "Lunch right away, or a drink first?"

"You know, Commissaire, I think I'm beyond all that shit now. Let's just do whatever you want."

Dismayed by Momo's dejection, Capucine battered the Clio into a too-tight parking space in front of a tired, non-descript café, the sort of place that was vanishing from the French scene as rapidly as the grimy, crepe-thin snow melted from the streets in Paris.

When the waiter came up, Capucine was further dismayed that Momo didn't show his usual interest in downing several whiskeys before tucking into lunch. "Just order, Commissaire. Whatever you want is fine with me."

She ordered *steak-frites* for both of them and a liter carafe of the house red. When the waiter left, Capucine was suddenly aware of her gaffe. "Steak was a bad idea, wasn't it?" she asked softly.

"Commissaire, don't worry about me. And steak is perfect. All I've had is fucking mutton tagine for the last two weeks. And you don't get fries with that." He smiled thinly.

Unconsciously seeking absolution for Momo's hardship, Capucine chatted gaily about the current goings-on at the commissariat: new cases, progress on old ones, who had gone where on vacation, who was sleeping with whom. No matter how hard Capucine nudged the conversation, she was unable to spark Momo's interest. It was as if he was showing only polite interest in people who were in his distant past because he had moved on to another job. It wasn't all that far from the truth, she was forced to concede.

The *steak-frites* came: unhealthy-looking quarter-inch-thick entrecôtes opaque with congealing fat, topped with small disks of frozen *beurre composé* made from industrial dried tarragon flakes and artificially colored institutional butter. The disproportionately large plate of overcrisp French fries was intended to distract from the beef's shortcomings. "If you want more fries," the waiter said, "just let me know. We've got plenty ready to go back in the kitchen."

The butter began to melt, making the meat look even more greasy. Automatically, both Capucine and Momo lifted the nasty little disks with their forks and placed them on their piles of fries, hoping that the butter would melt, drip to the bottom, and just go away. Capucine wondered how many millions of French people would be making the same gestures of disdain over their food during the national lunch hour. The thought did not fill her with joy or confidence in France's gastronomic future.

Capucine was at a loss to find a friendly and sympathetic way to ease Momo into his report. She gave up.

"So?" she asked.

"So, now I'm an expert on steers. I know more about them than I ever thought there was to know. I've worked on all the stations in that goddamn place. I fill in for everyone. In a way I kind of like it. It ain't Paris, but it's got its own rhythm. You just kind of ease into it."

"You're not in the abattoir anymore?"

"That's my main job, but since I just fill in there, they figure I can fill in everywhere." Momo chuckled cynically, finished off the carafe of wine, and signaled the waiter for more. "The funny part is that they love my ass. I'm the only guy down there who'll jump in and do whatever crappy job needs doing without complaining." Momo was amused by his success as a ranch hand. "But don't worry, Commissaire. I'll probably stick it out with the Police Judiciaire for a bit longer." He gave his first real laugh of the day.

"Were you able to get into the accounting office?"

"Yeah, no sweat. A three-year-old could get through that lock. If the three-year-old had a credit card he could use to push the bolt back with. The filing cabinets were also locked, but those were even easier. All you had to do was lift up the cabinet and push the locking bar up from underneath."

"Your basic three-year-old might have had a hard time

with that. Your basic flic probably couldn't have done it, either. Did you find anything?"

"Nothing worth calling in the RAID squad and getting them to rappel out of their helicopters and surround the élevage. But I did find some heavy expense account abuse. Can you do time for that?"

"Expense account abuse?"

"Yeah. I went through the travel agent's files. There's not a lot in there, but Philippe Gerlier, you know, the general manager who got knocked off, used to go to the U.S. every three months or so. A place called Rochester, Minnesota."

"He must have been going to the Mayo Clinic. You said his mother had severe Alzheimer's."

"Why not? But the funny thing is that those trips were fully paid for by the élevage. Our boy also stayed in a suite in a fancy hotel, rented himself the biggest car Avis had, and put in for a lot of pricey dinners for two. And all of it paid for."

"Maybe they just deducted it all from his salary."

"Yeah, you never know. What do you want me to do now?"

"Stick with the accounting office for a little while. If there are any secrets at the élevage, there'll probably be at least an echo of them in there."

"And what am I looking for? Oh wait, I know that one. I'll know it when I find it, right?"

Capucine laughed. "No one's seen you snooping around?"

"No. A lot of the guys sneak out at night for a smoke. The faith is going down the tubes. I ran into the foreman the other day on my way back from the accounting office, but I saw him coming and so I lit up one of my Gauloises and then crushed it out real fast like I was hiding it. I think he bought the act."

"Well, keep at it. I really need you to come up with something."

The waiter came back, was utterly indifferent to their indifference to dessert, brought coffee and the check. Momo left first. Capucine was gratified to see him head for a convenience store across the street, no doubt to buy out their stock of pint bottles of Scotch.

CHAPTER 40

In the end it was Isabelle who came up with the successful tactic. It had been her show right from the beginning. She had liberated the cork bulletin board from the squad room—"who looks at all those stupid notices, anyway!"—and nailed it on the wall of the interrogation room metamorphosed into a crisis center. The board, divided into four quadrants, one for each of the Belle thefts, became the focal point of the case. Each section contained photos of the items stolen, neatly tacked next to printouts of anything relevant that could be dredged from the Internet and the key points from the victims' interviews.

The commissariat wags found the board hilarious. Isabelle was the butt of endless jokes. "If this keeps up, there won't be any point in going home to watch American TV cop shows. We'll just spend our evenings here." "Does this mean we're all going to be issued Ferraris, designer suits, and walkie-talkie watches?"

Naturally, David, since he would have been delighted with the gibes, was spared. And, just as naturally, Isabelle overreacted. Still, when the thunderclouds had cleared, both brigadiers had to admit they were pleased with their results.

For the exhibit of the American professors' stolen manuscript, they hadn't been able to find a picture of the actual page that had been stolen and chose instead a langue d'oïl illumination of the period showing an aristocratic couple inexplicably but serenely admiring a hanged man.

They were also unable to find a photo of the specific Daumier that had been taken from the retired civil servant and, as a substitute, put up a selection of Daumier cartoons they found amusing. Capucine had particularly enjoyed one of two effete bourgeois hunters who propose that, to make up for the complete absence of game, each shoot the other's dog.

In addition to the photo of the stolen Marie Laurencin portrait, Isabelle had also insisted on including several pictures of Natalie Clifford Barney. David had argued these were totally extraneous to the case. Isabelle remained adamant and further demanded they put up her favorite quote from Barney—"why grab possessions like thieves, or divide them like socialists, when you can ignore them like wise men?"—which she argued was unquestionably relevant to the case. When David suggested that it might have more to do with Barney's views on polyamorous relationships than physical property, a particularly fiery altercation resulted.

The dancer's stag had been the easiest, and an entire zoo of Mene creatures was on the board, accompanied by several articles on the nineteenth-century vogue for animalier bronzes.

Berlioz's letters posed the most difficulty as there didn't seem to be any photographic record of any of the originals of the composer's letters. David suggested they use the portraits of Harriet Smithson, particularly the ones that put her curly coifs into relief. Isabelle countered that she wasn't going to allow Smithson if he was going to make comments about Barney, and the noise level escalated until they realized that the squad room was all ears, enjoying the dispute to the utmost.

Jean-Marie Lavallé's Boulle chest gave rise to a dozen

photos of Boulle pieces ranging in size from armoires to small boxes and in color from a brown so pale it was almost a pinkish crimson to one as dark as pitch. David's proposal that the exhibit be rounded off with fifty grams of cocaine in a plastic Ziploc bag was instantly shot down simultaneously by both Capucine and Isabelle.

But even among the embarrassment of riches, the unquestioned pièce de résistance was the portrait of the Belle drawn jointly by the two magazine illustrators. Isabelle had made a point of excluding David from the session and had spent a long dreamy afternoon steering the illustrators through the crafting of an image that reflected their depth of feeling for the Belle while remaining faithful enough to the original to be usable as an ID sketch. The pencil drawing showed a young woman in her late twenties with a thick head of light brown or dark blond hair, high cheekbones, full lips, and a slightly troubled expression as she gazed into the middle distance, as if attempting to fathom the meaning of some problem. When it was finally finished, Isabelle's eyes had filled with tears. The women insisted the portrait was hers to keep and had even drafted a note giving her clear title.

But attractive as the board was, it was slow to bear fruit. It took a good bit of nudging from Capucine for Isabelle to realize that, with the possible exception of Berlioz's letters, all the other thefts were related to the plastic arts.

"So what does that tell us?" Capucine had asked.

"That artsy-craftsy types are more caring people?" David had asked with mock ingenuousness.

"You idiot," Isabelle had said, "that's got nothing to do with it. It's obvious that painters and poets are going to be nicer than bankers." She gritted her teeth in an effort to extract the correct answer from the room's ether.

"Think more about the Belle," Capucine said. "How is it that she always winds up with such arty victims?"

Isabelle got it. "Because she intrigues them with her knowledge of art. Is that it?"

"Yes, I think it must be something like that. She has to get the mark beyond the stage of calling the fire department's emergency medics and to the level that they want to take her home."

"You mean the mark feels he's come across a kindred spirit, someone who only they can understand," Isabelle said.

"So you think that she turns most of her Samaritans away, is that it?" David asked.

"Almost certainly. We haven't heard of any thefts from nonartistic people, have we?"

"A bunch of people come up to her when she's lying on the ground, and she gets rid of the losers and waits for someone she thinks she can boost a hefty score from. Is that what she does?" Isabelle asked.

"It wouldn't be all that difficult for her to stand up, dust herself off, and tell the person she wasn't interested in that she was fine and 'thank you very much' or remain lying on the ground, moaning charmingly, if she thought the Samaritan was a winner," Capucine said.

"And what about the art part?" Isabelle asked.

"Nothing bonds people more than being from the same world, doctors, painters, even flics. But, of course, for that to work, you have to know what you're talking about."

"So," Isabelle asked, "you think she's a painter or something like that?"

"Actually, I have a feeling, given her age, that she might just be an art student."

"So why don't we stake out the Beaux-Arts?" Isabelle asked with enthusiasm. And the idea was born.

For three days Isabelle and David sat side by side uncomfortably in front of the art school, on cheap white plastic seats at a tiny white plastic table on the terrace of the Café La Charrette. It was hardly a terrace, just eight limp supermarket tables on the sidewalk, pushed up against the café's windows, forcing pedestrians into awkward little pirouettes as they squeezed between the chairs and a rack of the now ubiquitous Vélib's rent-a-bicycles.

In an attempt to look the part, Isabelle wore a man's thick wool sweater several sizes too large and torn jeans that allowed one of her knees to peep out at the world. It was clear that she thought the contemporary art world still dressed like characters in a seventies cinéma vérité film. Isabelle had completed her look with a thick pile of sketchbooks and art show catalogs on her lap. Of course, the essential prop was a Xerox of the exquisite pencil sketch of the Belle negligently placed on top of the heap.

For the first hour or so, the two brigadiers had thought the stakeout would lead nowhere, but by the end of the morning they had seen six different girls who could possibly be the Belle, three of whom were dead ringers for the sketch.

The next two days produced another half dozen possible candidates. David and Isabelle could not decide if they were seeing different people or the same women over and over again with different hairdos and outfits. On the third day Isabelle sent David to follow one girl who looked like the best of all the matches they had seen so far. David latched on to her after she left her morning courses at the Beaux-Arts and disappeared for seven hours, until he returned to the commissariat to report to Isabelle that she had spent the day shopping, having lunch with friends, leisurely looking at books in the *bouquiniste* stands on the quais of the Seine, and then returning to an apartment in a chic street not too far from the Beaux-Arts. Forty-three seconds on the computer produced her name and phone number. Another eight minutes on the computer yielded the information that she had a sizable bank account and was accustomed to spending over five thousand euros on her *Carte Bleue* each month, mainly on expensive clothing.

It was clear to Isabelle that she wasn't going to get the job done with just David for support. Capucine was going to have to produce more troops. To this end she whined and complained until Capucine joined her at the stakeout on the fourth day.

The balmy days that made surveillance a joy, sitting in the sun, pretending to read a book at a café table, were long over, and the two detectives had the *soi-disant* terrace to themselves.

Capucine had always found the Ecole des Beaux-Arts the least captivating of Paris's monuments, probably because the structures were so far removed from public view. From where they sat, the open gateway in the graffiti-covered wall allowed only a glimpse of the magnificent sixteenth- and seventeenth-century buildings topped by elegant studio skylights. In fact, from their vantage point the most appealing feature was an enormous and cleverly drawn graffito of a happy cat bursting out of his picture frame, grinning down on the courtyard from his three-story-high perch. Capucine was always amazed that not only did the school's administration allow the graffito to remain over the years, but they actually painted around it when the wall was whitewashed.

Capucine sipped her green tea that tasted like bitter carpet sweepings while Isabelle excitedly stirred her electric-green *menthe à l'eau.*

"See!" said Isabelle. "Here's another one. That could be her, don't you think?"

"No, the shape of the nose is all wrong. But the look is the same. I grant you that."

David had already been sent out to tail a girl that Capucine had agreed could well be La Belle. Right after he had left, they had seen two even more likely candidates. The problem seemed to be the rigid conformity of the art students. There were two basic looks: wacky neo-hippie—horizontally striped rainbow stockings, skirt so short it was no more than a token to propriety, impossibly dyed hair in primary colored stripes—and the more prevalent Dame aux Camélias: flowing black dress, thick long hair, brooding, moody introspection. When dressed as either persona, the students seemed to be clones, as indistinguishable from one another as the army of Chinese terracotta soldiers whose faces take close scrutiny to be seen to be unique.

Capucine had a hunch that since the victims' descriptions of the Belle all fit into the latter stereotype, she might adopt the alternative look when at school, which made linking her to the portrait all the more difficult. One thing was abundantly clear. Isabelle was absolutely right, it was going to take a bigger team than the one she currently had to produce a suspect.

"All right, Isabelle, I'm going to assign you three more officers. They'll report to you here right after lunch."

"Me? I thought you'd be taking charge directly. You want me to handle a team of four all by myself?" Isabelle's eyebrows lifted a good half an inch.

"Isabelle, you can do this *les doigts dans le néz*—with your fingers in your nose—as the guys like to say. You've already got David wrapped around your finger, and he's a handful. Just boot them out tailing people and have them report back to you."

"Does this mean you're going back to the country?"

"Not just yet. But I need you to take charge of this. Trust me, I wouldn't give you an assignment if I didn't know you could handle it."

For once Isabelle was at a loss for a snappy retort. She just looked at Capucine wide-eyed, opening and shutting her lips, hoping something tough and cynical would pop out, doing a perfectly creditable imitation of a cartoon goldfish in a baggy sweater.

CHAPTER 41

It wasn't even a real café, just a little house in a back street where some *frère* from the *bled* and his wife cooked meals and served them with glasses of mint tea.

When it was warm, you sat in the tiny courtyard of earth and gravel that had been mostly pushed into the ground years before. When it got cold, you sat at the same tables, which had been moved into the two back rooms that had been knocked into one.

The food was definitely not a draw. Sure, there was always a *harira* or a *kefta* on the boil in the kitchen and you could get a dish of that, but it wasn't any better than the food at the élevage canteen. Of course, ordering it and paying for it, instead of just having it slopped on your plate, made it a lot more appetizing. If you didn't want food, you sat and drank mint tea, which was pretty good, made with sprigs of real mint—Lord knew where that came from—or coffee from the dented espresso machine that had already seen better days when it had been bought secondhand years ago.

There was also what was supposed to be a tiny bar, really just a two-foot plank and a bunch of bottles of radiant Day-Glo syrups on a shelf in front of a cracked mirror.

Next to the mirror was a *Licence II* plaque, the old kind with chipped enamel and funny script writing, which looked like it had been picked up at a local flea market. If it was real, which no one believed, it gave the place the right to sell wine and beer but nothing hard. There was a refrigerator full of Kronenbourg 1664 in the kitchen, but Momo didn't even hope for one of those. If he was dumb enough to ask for one, the other North Africans in the room would start muttering, "Shame, shame," under their breaths, knocking quietly on the table with their knuckles, until he was forced to leave.

The beer was for the French hands, who came occasionally because the place was so close to the back gate of the élevage. They'd usually go to the café in town, because you could smoke there with no one complaining, and there was a billiard table and a TV, and there were no Arabs, but when it was raining hard, sometimes they came to the café.

Still, the place wasn't all that bad. It had that clean smell to it—no sweat or tobacco smoke—a little pungent from spices that reminded him of home. He had taken to coming almost every night. At first he did it because it was good for his cover, but he had to admit it had become an important part of his day. Skulking in his room all evening wasn't doing him any good, particularly since he had no booze and had decided he had to take it easy going to the supermarket to buy that no-name "Scotch" they sold. He'd just get good and drunk when it was all over and the hell with it.

He sipped his coffee quietly. He was going to go home pretty soon. True, he still didn't have anything worth giving Commissaire Le Tellier, but that was just a question of days. Now that he knew his way around the accounting office, he was sure to find something. If she said there was going to be something there, there would be.

Two Maghrebian workers from the élevage came in and

sat at his table. Momo listened to them, adding a mono-syllabic grunt every now and then. Tripping up was al-ways his big fear. It turned out he knew a lot less about the way guys from the *bled* really lived than he had thought.

Six French hands came in and stood around the bar, drinking beer and smoking and talking too loud. The smoking was a calculated affront. They could do what they wanted because the slightest argument would bring the gendarmes, who would close the place down. The place filled up with the smell of the *blanc:* sweet tobacco and yeasty hops and musky sweat about to turn fetid. The café was no longer peaceful and restful and clean. The men banged their beer glasses on the minuscule bar as loudly as they could without breaking them and stomped out, bump-ing into the seated patrons without apology. When the door closed behind them, there was a collective silent sigh of re-lief.

The problem was that watching them down beers had made Momo ache for a drink himself. He had a quarter of a liter bottle of supermarket Scotch in his bag under his bed. If he left now, he'd probably get back to his room be-fore his roommate came in and have a chance at doing some serious damage to the bottle. And even if his room-mate walked in on him, that wasn't going to be the end of the world, was it?

What would be the end of the world would be getting caught going through the accounting office. That would be bad. He'd get fired from the élevage and Commissaire Le Tellier wouldn't have a case. But that wasn't going to happen. He'd already been in there three times and knew how to get in and out and not get caught. It wasn't that difficult. No one wandered around that part of the élevage at night, so there was almost no chance of being discov-ered. Getting back to his room was where he had to be careful. He'd run into that guy Martel when he was re-turning to the Cité from the wrong direction and had to do his number with the cigarette. Praise be to Allah the Merciful that Martel had bought it. Next time he'd take the long route around behind the dorms so he'd be coming back from the right direction.

No sweat if you planned it right. But he really did need a drink. Time to get going.

He crossed the empty courtyard, eased the rickety wooden gate open, and stepped out into the street. Like all the back streets in Saint-Nicolas, this one was unlighted. The walk back to the élevage was always satisfying, often under a canopy of stars. He was amazed how many shooting stars there were. Something you never saw in Paris. As he turned to pull the gate shut, he heard, rather than felt, an extremely loud thunk that resonated in his head, like a computer sound telling you that something you had done was very wrong, only much, much louder. He felt no pain but was surprised to find he was on his knees. It was the second blow that hurt and knocked him on his side. He was completely conscious but couldn't make his arms or legs work.

"Look at the fucking Beur," someone said with a slap of raucous, sneering laughter. "He's not looking so big and tough now, is he?" He was kicked hard in the stomach. The air exploded from his lungs. His upper body felt like it was clamped in a vice. He panicked, fighting desperately to inhale. And it kept on, every kick a rock thrown into the tide of pain. Each blow was punctuated by a line of invective. "Why do you filthy Arabs think you can get away with stealing our jobs?" Thump. "When are you fuckers going to wise up and get the hell back to your fucking desert?" Thump.

Instinctively, his body convulsed into a tight fetal position. All that seemed to matter was protecting his stomach and fighting for air. He was dimly aware that there were three of them. Two kicking and Pierre Martel leaning down, sneering and doing the talking.

Even though it went on and on, his breath came back partially, intensifying the pain, making it almost unbearable. It would be so easy to make it stop. His right hand was no more than six inches from his gun. All he had to do was reach down and it would jump into his fist and the shot would happen by itself. Right into Martel's fat gut. One shot would end it. The other two would run, but Martel would live long enough to give up their names. He'd make sure of that. And then Martel would die.

But he couldn't use his gun. If he did, Commissaire Le Tellier would have no case, and that was what he was here for, wasn't it?

He couldn't stop thinking of the gun, so right there, so tempting, so small he could almost hide it in his hand. He could almost feel the grip tight in his palm, with the end of his thumb and forefinger against the smoothness of the scandium frame, whatever the fuck scandium was. He almost laughed, but the reflex made his stomach muscles convulse, cutting off his breath. He went into a choking spasm. The last thing he remembered was the searing pain of trying to force out a cough.

CHAPTER 42

Emotional disarray worked for Marie-Christine. Before the drama she had been merely a "handsome woman," a damnation with faint praise that gave Capucine the shivers. But today Marie-Christine had the tragic sensuality of a Racine heroine, Phèdre perhaps, eyes liquid and deep set, wandering off into space each time there was a lull in the conversation, lips slack and full and moist, hair perfectly coiffed yet somehow conveying a strong hint of turbulence. In a word, she was beautiful.

Marie-Christine had called her the day before, sounding desperate. "You're really the only person I can talk to and I'm so confused and I just have to talk to someone." Capucine relented reluctantly but hung on to the closed-end slot of lunch instead of the open-ended dinner that Marie-Christine was after.

As she sat down, Capucine wondered if even a quick lunch had been a mistake. Marie-Christine was as keyed up as if she was on drugs.

L'Ecluse on the quai des Grands-Augustins was the only restaurant in Paris that Capucine genuinely loved and Alexandre refused to set foot in. It had opened way back when, when nitrogen wine dispensers had just become popular and *grands crus* by the glass were a novelty. Alexandre hated it because there were six of them and that made it a chain. Even worse, the food, tasty and simple, came from a central kitchen somewhere or other, and the hot dishes were warmed in a microwave. "Restaurants serve meals, not packaged snacks," Alexandre would say with an exaggerated shudder.

Both Capucine and Marie-Christine ordered the same things: chunky *blocs* of foie gras, which came with a basket of thick, toasted country bread, to be followed by slabs of puddinglike chocolate cake, the recipe for which was the house's most closely guarded secret. Both were well worth the vast number of calories. They also ordered glasses of Loupiac, whose unctuous sweetness would see them through both the foie gras and the cake.

Halfway through the foie gras they ran out of platitudes and gossip.

"I've broken up with him," Marie-Christine announced with drama.

"Who?"

"With Jean-Charles, my boyfriend."

"Why?"

"Because I love him. Well, I love being with him. And it wasn't fair to Loïc."

"Fair?"

"I know I'm not making any sense. It's just that I've decided I have to leave Loïc, and I don't want it to be because of Jean-Charles, since he means too much to me. Anyone would do the same, don't you think?"

Capucine put another forkful of the foie gras on a piece of toast and ate it carefully. It was delightful: creamy, and livery, and with just a hint of bitterness. The unctuousness of the Loupiac was perfect with it. This was so definitely the wrong restaurant for Marie-Christine's revelations.

"Jean-Charles is fabulous in bed. Much better than Philippe. Much. Jean-Charles knows exactly how to respond to a woman's needs. Philippe was like a freight train. It was wonderful, of course, but it was almost as if he didn't care if you were there or not. Do you know what I mean?" she asked, looking at Capucine with alarming intentness.

Capucine stayed the mounting tide of amatory revelations by raising a hand and asking for two more glasses of Loupiac. Happily, the waiter was of the chatty sort, and by the time he left, Marie-Christine's élan to share her bedroom experiences had subsided.

"So, do you think I should divorce him? Tell me the truth. Don't hold back."

"Loïc?"

"Of course Loïc."

Capucine paused. She had run out of foie gras and considered buttering the rest of her toast and eating that.

"And you don't want to try and fix it up?"

"You're right. You're so right. I should try. I will try! I owe him that at the very least."

There was another awkward silence. Mercifully, the waiter returned with the two glasses of Loupiac, but unfortunately he noticed the tension at the table and retreated without a word.

"But what can I do? How do you make yourself love someone? Particularly someone who doesn't want to sleep with you."

"Counseling program?"

Marie-Christine brightened. "I could do that. Definitely I would. Do you really think it could help?"

"If you left Loïc, what would you do about the élevage?"

Marie-Christine sighed with relief. "That's the *one* thing I'm clear about. Loïc will have it no matter what happens. I had a big fight with the man at Lazard. You know, my trust officer. He said we would sue for a majority in the company, but I told him I would never allow that. He told me it was not for me to decide, but I won't allow it. I really won't."

"It sounds like you're moving ahead with your plans for the divorce."

"I'm not. I swear I'm not. Would you hate me if I were? I don't know if I am. What else am I going to do? Loïc is wonderful, but he's just a good friend when you get right down to it. The only thing he's passionate about is the élevage." She leaned forward confidentially. "You know, it's even worse than what I told you when we went to Honfleur. The last time we made love was three years ago. And it didn't even last five minutes. And he fell right asleep. I'm sure Alexandre's not that bad. From the way he looks at you, I can tell how—"

Mercifully, like a high-tech deus ex machina, Capucine's phone buzzed insistently.

It was the brigadier on reception duty at the commissariat. "A gendarmerie capitaine, some guy called Dallemagne, just called. Sounded kinda urgent."

Capucine had Dallemagne's number on her cell phone's speed dial. "Ah, Commissaire, kind of you to return my call so promptly. Normally I wouldn't bother you, but I know you're very keen on liaison."

Dallemagne paused for a response, but Capucine remained silent.

"One of our patrol vehicles picked up a man last night who had been in one of these workers' brawls. An Arab. He was inebriated and stank of beer. He had been badly beaten. They threw him in our drunk tank to give him a rest and let him sleep it off. This morning he still wasn't entirely conscious and the duty officer discovered he had a pistol in an ankle holster. A dangerous sort of weapon, actually. One of those expensive lightweight Smith and Wessons that shoot three-fifty-seven Magnums. Funny thing for a Beur to have, but you never know what they'll do."

The bile rose in Capucine's throat, but she said nothing, knowing that that would only slow the story down.

"The reason I'm calling is that it would appear he claims to be a Police Judiciaire officer and works in the Twentieth Arrondissement. Of course, they like to say things like that and think they're more believable if they talk about arrondissements they know." Dallemagne chuckled. "It's the sort of story I'd disregard in the normal course of events, except that when they inventoried his possessions, the pistol turned out to be loaded with police-issue ballistic-tipped bullets. You wouldn't happen to know anything about this individual, would you, Commissaire?"

CHAPTER 43

The second she got off the phone with Dallemagne, Capucine punched in the speed dial for her commissariat, got through to the duty officer, and instructed him to have Momo picked up at the Saint-Nicolas gendarmerie by a SAMU emergency medical unit and taken to an ER in Rouen. The doctor at the ER was to call her as soon as he had assessed Momo's physical condition. With any luck Momo would be in a hospital within half an hour, forty-five minutes at the outside. Far too long, but it was the best that could be done under the circumstances.

That settled, Capucine's adrenaline surge collapsed into a pool of guilt and frustration. Keeping Momo at the élevage after he had already found out the essence had been gilding the lily, and with his blood to boot, as it turned out. She desperately wanted to rush to the scene, but that would have been ridiculous. After all, she was a commissaire of the Police Judiciaire, not a distraught mother, and he was going to be in perfectly good hands.

Her phone buzzed again. This time it was Isabelle. She was out of breath and obviously walking rapidly on a street somewhere. "We've got her! We have *so* goddamn got her! David's watching her do her number right now. I'm going in to make the arrest with him." She could barely contain herself.

Capucine's adrenaline level shot back to its former apex. "Where are you?"

"I'm walking down the rue des Beaux-Arts, heading toward the Marché Maubert, which is where it's happening. David's been staking out one of the art students since early this morning, and he followed her to Maubert, where it turns out *she's the one*. SHE'S THE BELLE!" Isabelle's level of excitement rose, making the sentence sound like some gushy TV presenter announcing the winner of a fabulous prize.

The map of the area popped into Capucine's head. Isabelle was ten streets to her left. David was about ten streets to her right. She enormously wanted to be present at this arrest. Walking all the way to the Marché Maubert was out of the question; maybe if she had been wearing her Prada Skimmers, but definitely not in Zanottis. And the Clio was illegally parked in front of the restaurant, facing west—the wrong way for the market—on the one-way quai des Grands-Augustins, so she had no choice but to head toward Isabelle.

"Turn around and walk back to the quai. Watch for the Clio. I'll pick you up in three minutes."

Marie-Christine was wide-eyed and flushed.

"What's going on? It sounds so exciting."

"We're making an arrest. I'm afraid I have to rush off," Capucine said, shrugging her shoulders, raising her hands palms upward in supplication, while blowing out a puff of air in the Gallic gesture that is intended to signify that we are all but mere slaves to the vagaries of the heavens.

Capucine rooted through her wallet, found a fifty-euro note, put it on the table, squeezed Marie-Christine's shoulder, and said as she dashed out, "I'll call you. We'll finish this conversation later. But listen, like the song, you can't do better than follow your heart." She leaned down and kissed Marie-Christine on both cheeks.

As she ran out the door, she kicked herself mentally. If Alexandre ever caught her mouthing a banality like that, he'd kid her mercilessly for weeks.

Once in the car Capucine almost felt sorry for Marie-Christine. All she had wanted was some sort of sanction for doing what she knew she was going to do anyway, and the poor dear had gotten no more than a piece of chocolate cake. On the other hand, the cake really was exceptional, as even Alexandre reluctantly agreed.

In less than two minutes Capucine picked up Isabelle and maneuvered the car onto the boulevard Saint-Germain, heading toward the market.

Isabelle didn't even wait to slam the door before she gushed with her tale.

"So yesterday we see this girl coming out of the school. I had a really good feeling about her. I had David follow her home and stake her out in the morning. Turns out she lives in the Eleventh. She gets going around noon today. It was just like you said it would be. Yesterday she was all short skirts and lots of colors, but today she was all dark hair and long, flowy dresses. You can bet David gave me the full details of the hair over the phone. Anyway, she takes the metro and gets off at the Maubert station. Right there I knew we had a winner. She walks around the market once or twice, finds a nice spot in a corner, and all of a sudden goes ploof and collapses on the sidewalk. So David calls me and I call you."

"Did anyone rush over to help her?"

"Not at first. But David told me why that was. She didn't faint or anything sudden like that. She just lay down and stretched herself out like she was going to bed. She looked like some sort of kook or something. You know, like maybe she was protesting about how unhappy chickens are. So naturally everyone walks around her trying real hard not to see. But later, every now and then some loser leans over and says something. Most of the time she just lies there, oblivious, with her eyes closed and they go away, but if they don't, David said you could see her say something sharp, like she's telling them to piss off."

Capucine pulled into a bus stop on the avenue Saint-Germain, at the corner of the market, which was thronged with office workers on their lunch hour. It was one o'clock, the frenetic closing hour of the market, when the merchants did everything possible to sell off what they had left. The stalls were alive with the raucous cries of impossible discounts and the excitement of the high-powered forced sell. "One euro! One euro only! Everything I've got, one euro only! Eggs! Eggs! They were in the chicken this very morning. Two dozen for the price of one! Two dozen for the price of one!"

They could make out David in the far corner of the market, wearing a fashionably crumpled off-white linen suit. And fifty feet away they could see the Belle on the sidewalk, curled up with the insouciance of a model in a mattress advertisement, her long, brilliantly dark blond hair artfully fanned out on the ground and her limbs in graceful repose. She definitely had a waiflike appeal that tugged at the heart. The scene was so incongruous, it was electric.

"Isabelle, I want you to duck out of the car as quietly as possible and circle around the perimeter of the market and join David. Then you two make your approach as we planned."

The idea was to get David to pose as a novelist and collector of Limoges porcelain who was out shopping with his sister. In the reality of daylight the setup suddenly seemed utterly ridiculous, but with Isabelle already on the way, they were stuck with it.

Isabelle made her circuit, joined David, put her arm in his, and the two made a great show of peering into the market stalls with fervent interest. Capucine eased out of the car and retreated behind the corner of a building.

When the couple reached the Belle, David turned to Isabelle and said in a high, effeminate falsetto loud enough for Capucine to hear, "Look, Isabelle, that poor girl seems to have fainted. Whatever can have happened to her?"

Capucine cringed and was sure David had blown it right there. She had warned him over and over again to resist his love of amateur theatricals. But amazingly enough, David's patter seemed to work. Isabelle leaned over, her body language expressing both concern and maternal affection lightly seasoned with just a soupçon of sexual interest. Slowly, with fawnlike awkwardness, the Belle rose, steadying herself shakily on David's arm. They chatted for a few minutes. The Belle demurred shyly and then seemed to agree to something reluctantly, almost overcome with embarrassment.

The three walked slowly in the direction of Capucine's car, Isabelle and David supporting the halting Belle. The scene was reminiscent of a couple walking a postoperative patient gingerly around the grounds of a hospital.

When they reached the car, Capucine came up directly behind them and squeezed her electronic key, unlocking the doors with a loud click. Alarmed by the noise, the Belle started and David seized her upper arm and wrist, preparing to immobilize her in a policeman's lock.

The Belle drooped, deflated.

"Mademoiselle," Capucine said, "*je regrette,* but you are under arrest."

CHAPTER 44

The Belle meekly allowed herself to be seated in the back of the car and reclined limply. It was as if she was still persisting in her charade. Isabelle, sitting next to her in the backseat, was tense and keyed up, jiggling her leg violently enough for Capucine to feel it through the floor of the car. It was no secret what she was worried about.

Capucine puttered down the boulevard Saint-Germain at the Clio's relaxed pace. When they reached the quai de la Tournelle and she took the bridge toward the Twentieth and not the quai in the direction of the Ile de la Cité, Isabelle exhaled sharply in relief.

"Hey, we're going back to the commissariat. I figured we'd be going straight to the courthouse."

Isabelle clearly thought that since the Belle had been caught red-handed, it would count as a *flagrant délit* and she would go directly to court for a summary trial and begin her sentence immediately. In that case Isabelle would have received almost no brownie points for the arrest.

"Lying down on the sidewalk doesn't break any law I know of," Capucine said.

They drove on in complete silence.

At the commissariat, Capucine went immediately to her

office to see if she could learn any news of Momo, leaving Isabelle and David to take the Belle to one of the brand-new interrogation rooms. Capucine was well known in the commissariat as a fervent adept of modern interrogation techniques. When she had assumed command, she replaced the classic PJ technique of a Grand Guignol good-cop, bad-cop routine, followed by a sound hammering on the head with a telephone book, with Reid's infinitely more subtle nine steps. She had also redecorated the gulag-style interrogation rooms with the breezy décor of an autoroute motel.

While she waited to be put through to the ER, she realized she was ravenous. The foie gras had been delicious but not even close to substantial enough. She guessed that David and Isabelle hadn't eaten, either, and that the Belle was probably just as hungry. She buzzed the duty brigadier and asked him to get someone to the corner café for an assortment of sandwiches and sodas.

Just as she hung up, the phone buzzed and the ER receptionist came on the line to say that the SAMU had delivered Brigadier Benarouche, but he was still being examined by a doctor, who would call her as soon as he was done.

In the interrogation room Capucine found Isabelle behind the desk and the Belle sitting in the suspect's uncomfortable metal folding chair. The Belle looked as serene as Isabelle was tense. Both were completely silent. David was absent, and Capucine was sure he was in the squad room, propped up in front of the TV monitor that was used for observation. The mirror on the wall was a dummy, its only use to increase the anxiety level of suspects. She looked up at the miniature video camera barely visible in the ceiling tiles.

"David! Come in here. Bring a chair," she yelled, forgetting the efficiency of the very expensive set of microphones she had had installed. "We're going to have some lunch before we get down to our chat." She could feel Isabelle's disapproving frown boring into her back.

David and the sandwiches arrived simultaneously. Everyone stood up. Capucine arranged the chairs around the desk, and the four tucked into their lunch. Somehow Isabelle wound up in the suspect's uncomfortable chair. Despite the potential for awkwardness, it was almost a convivial moment. Capucine pulled rank and grabbed the single duck-rillettes sandwich. Rillettes were one of her favorites, and they were absolutely at their best on a doughy baguette. The effort of chewing the bread partially cleared the nagging thorns of her worry. Momo was in good hands and undoubtedly had enough morphine in his system not to be feeling any pain. Marie-Christine was just a foolish schoolgirl who was always going to find enough support among her boyfriends to be happy, and she could be counted on to do only minimal damage to Loïc. It was the Belle who was the tricky one.

The Belle nibbled at the corner of her sandwich, leaving tiny marks, as if a mouse had been at it. She had a dreamy, reposed look that made Capucine wonder if she really knew where she was.

"Mademoiselle," Capucine said, "before we get started, I have to ask you for your identity papers."

"They're at home. But my name is Miriam Mizrahi, and I live at eleven, rue de la Folie-Regnault in the Eleventh Arrondissement."

"You know in France you're required by law to have your identity papers with you at all times," Isabelle said sharply. Capucine quieted her with a look.

"Mademoiselle Mizrahi," Capucine said and paused. "Is it mademoiselle?"

The Belle nodded.

Capucine went on, "Mademoiselle, you're going to be charged with six separate counts of theft." She looked up at Isabelle for her to read off the names of the victims. Hierarchically, Isabelle prompted David with a jerk of her head. With his ballet dancer's grace, David twisted elegantly, produced a folded piece of square ruled paper from the back pocket of the pants of his linen suit, and read:

"Monsieur et Madame John Admonson, a *langue d'oïl* manuscript page. Monsieur Georges Lafarge, a Daumier caricature. Mademoiselle Thérèse Thibodeau and Mademoiselle Noemie Chesnier, a Marie Laurencin watercolor, small. Monsieur Claude Josse, a Mene animalier bronze statuette of a deer, small. Monsieur Hubert Lafontaine, a collection of manuscript letters by Hector Berlioz. And Monsieur Jean-Marie Lavallé, a Boulle-style *marqueterie* chest, small, possibly containing an important sum in banknotes."

"There were two others," the Belle said, looking down at the table with the guilty expression of a small child caught snatching cookies to give to her friends.

"So you freely and openly admit to your guilt," Isabelle said.

"Calm down, Isabelle," David said.

"Listen, asshole, I'm in charge here." Isabelle caught herself, looked at Capucine out of the corner of her eye, pursed her lips to form the word *pardon*, thought better of it, and remained silent.

"Maybe we should start from the beginning. Are you French, mademoiselle?" Capucine said.

The Belle tore a corner of the bread from her sandwich and shredded it into little pieces. After a while she said, "I'm Syrian. I came here with my mother a year and a half ago. I have a student visa and my mother has a tourist visa. I am a student at the Ecole des Beaux-Arts."

There was a long silence. Little by little the Belle shredded the entire top of her sandwich.

"It would be easier if I could tell you the whole story. Would that be all right?" she asked Capucine.

"Of course. Take your time. There's no rush."

"We are from Halab, what you call Aleppo, in Syria—"

"That's part of the French territory, isn't it?" Isabelle asked of no one in particular.

"It was given its independence in nineteen forty-four," David said quietly. Isabelle shot him a stream of deftly aimed daggers with her eyes.

"We are Jews. My father is a dealer in rare books. I studied art history at the University of Halab and painted under the tutelage of Muhammad Tulaimat, the great Syrian painter, until . . ." She trailed off.

"Well?" said Isabelle. "Come on. Let's hear it."

"Until I fell in love with a wonderful and beautiful young man. An Arab. I was blissfully happy. In heaven. Then one day the rabbi condemned me publicly and forbade me and my parents to go to the synagogue. Our world came to an end. The whole community rose against us. My father could no longer sell his books. They would whistle at us in the streets. We had no money. I had to leave the university. In the end I decided to come to France. My mother came with me."

"And why did you think France would be better?" David asked.

"There is a large community of Syrian Jews in Paris. My mother and I thought we would be welcomed by them."

"And were you?" Isabelle asked, more curious than aggressive.

"No. Not at all. Somehow, they knew of my infidelity to the faith and would have nothing to do with us. We had also hoped that with me gone the rabbi would reintegrate my father, but he didn't, and now my poor papa is obliged to work as a janitor. He can't eat to relieve his hunger, much less send us money."

"So how did you live?" Capucine asked.

"How did we live? We lived in a way that got me here." She looked at Capucine unblinkingly.

Isabelle inhaled, preparing to speak. Capucine raised her

fingers two inches off the desk in admonition. Isabelle released the breath in a sigh.

"At first my mother worked as a cleaning woman. It is easy to find that kind of work in Paris, even if you have no papers, as long as you are prepared to work for very little. I helped her when I could and did babysitting and whatever jobs I could find when I wasn't going to classes at the Beaux-Arts. We lived in a small studio apartment. I can't say we were happy, but it was a life.

"Then my mother became ill. We went to many doctors. It is a form of bone cancer. There is a treatment. But it is very expensive and, of course, we have no social coverage for medicine."

"I begin to understand," Capucine said.

"The first time was an accident. I had gone to the market on the boulevard Raspail, and I wanted to wait until it was time for the market to close. Sometimes you can get food for next to nothing then. The merchants are happy to sell things cheaply instead of throwing them away. We had had nothing for dinner the night before and naturally no breakfast or lunch. I think I fainted. The next thing I knew, I was talking to two Americans. They were extremely kind. I told them I was a student of art. They were professors of philology. They had just purchased a page of a langue d'oïl illuminated manuscript with a representation of an angel forcing a devil to disgorge by playing musical instruments. They told me all about it."

The Belle was visibly moved. She opened a plastic bottle of Evian and in her nervousness dropped the blue cap on the floor. She immediately fell to her knees on the floor to retrieve it.

When she was seated again, she resumed her story. "The iconography was obvious. The angel dominates the devil with her music. It is an illustration of Saint Augustine's dictum that a prayer sung is prayed twice. They did not know that.

"It was an impossible moment. I was fainting from hunger but chatting away about medieval illumination as if I was at a cocktail party back in Halab."

There was a long pause. The Belle began shredding the other side of her sandwich. This time even Isabelle was reluctant to interrupt.

Finally, she began again. "They took me to their house, fed me, and insisted I spend the night. I had told them some absurd story about an abusive boyfriend. The next morning they went out to the *boulangerie* for croissants. I called my mother. She was distraught. And starving. She had had nothing to eat for a day and a half. I felt terrible, but I knew what I had to do. I took the page and ran. I knew just the dealer who would buy it. I bought two big bags of groceries and went home with what seemed like enough money in my pocket to live forever."

She paused again and resumed work on the destruction of her sandwich.

"The whole thing seemed preordained. I had never set out to rob anyone. The opportunity was just given. At one point I even thought it was the Higher Being offering me salvation."

She laughed cynically. "Of course, the money that was going to last forever only lasted a few weeks. The doctors and pharmacies took care of that. After, it became easy. I bought the right clothes for it. I became skilled. I tried to steal only things I knew people didn't really want. Some of them seemed to like me so much, they would have given me what I took if I had just asked. I suppose that's why two of them didn't report my thefts." She paused once again. There was no more sandwich to shred.

"I am going to go to jail now, am I not?" she asked Capucine.

"That's for damn sure," Isabelle said. The Belle ignored her.

"I'm afraid that's for the magistrate to decide, but there are definitely extenuating circumstances."

"I don't care about me. It is my mother I worry about. In a month she will no longer have any money for her medications. Then what will she do?"

The door opened a crack, and the uniformed duty brigadier poked his head in, searched for Capucine with his eyes, found her, and made a gesture with his thumb against his ear and his little finger up to his mouth to signify that she had a telephone call. If he interrupted an interrogation, it was bound to be urgent. And from his expression it looked like it was bad news. Capucine bolted out of the room.

CHAPTER 45

The call was from the ER doctor. Actually, the news wasn't bad at all.

"Commissaire, your man will be back on the job in a few weeks, maybe less. He has three broken ribs and multiple contusions on his torso, some of them severe enough. It looked to me as if he had been repeatedly kicked by someone wearing boots. What worried us most was that he had two blunt traumas on the back of his head—"

"Blunt traumas, Doctor?" Capucine asked.

"From either a blow or from falling. Given their closeness, it seems likely he was hit on the back of the head twice with something heavy. That's always dangerous because it often results in an epidural hematoma, which is often fatal if not surgically treated immediately. I wasn't overly concerned, because from the coloration of the contusions, we knew he had received them about fifteen hours prior to reaching us and the symptoms of an epidural hematoma almost invariably peak within six to eight hours. Other than a severe headache, he showed none of the signs. Nevertheless, I had him sent in for a CT scan, which turned out to be perfectly normal."

"He'll really be back up and around in a week or two?"

"It's hard holding him down right now," the doctor said with a laugh. "He's a remarkably strong and vigorous individual, but I'm going to keep him here for a night just to be on the safe side. He's very keen to talk to you, but there are two points I would like to call to your attention first."

Capucine said nothing, and there was an awkward silence on the line.

"Your officer smelled strongly of beer when he arrived. The initial physical assessment was consistent with alcoholism or very heavy drinking. But there was absolutely no alcohol in his blood. He had not had even one drink the night before. Someone must have poured the beer over his clothes to make it look like he was drunk."

"That's useful to know, Doctor. What was the other thing?"

"The SAMU unit that picked him up found him propped up against the wall of a holding cell at the Saint-Nicolas gendarmerie with water pumping across the floor at regular intervals. As you can imagine, we deal with the gendarmes very frequently and they are normally extremely conscientious. I was surprised that your man had not been brought here directly, particularly since one of the traumas in his head had a deep laceration that required four stitches. The fact that he was denied medical attention is an egregious breach that merits a complaint. He could easily have died in the cell."

Capucine wondered at what point in the evening Capitaine Dallemagne realized Momo was one of her men.

"Anyway, here he is. Remember that the shot of morphine he received when he was admitted is still far from metabolized."

"Commissaire, I'm sorry. I fucked up," Momo said in a voice far more quiet and gentle than usual.

"Don't be stupid. How are you feeling?"

"Not too bad. They gave me a shot that actually makes me feel great. If I could get a drink of something, I'd be feeling perfect." Momo attempted a laugh but cut it off so sharply, Capucine guessed his head still hurt considerably.

"How did it happen?"

"I took a night off. I'd been back twice to the accounting office and thought it would do my cover some good to be seen out with the buds, sucking up mint tea at the local *rebeu* hangout. On my way out some fucker hit me on the back of the head. Then two of them kicked the shit out of me. It was the last goddamn thing I was expecting."

"Do you have any idea who did it?"

"Yeah, you kind of take notice when guys are kicking the crap out of you. The master of ceremonies was Martel, the foreman who acts like he's in charge of the élevage. Remember him? The other two, I don't know their names, but I could pick them out. Count on that."

"And you had an ankle gun, it seems, even though I told you not to."

"Yeah, but did I use it? You try that sometime, lying there doing nothing, letting some assholes use you as a football, when you can blow them away easy as spitting."

Capucine was abashed. "You did an exemplary job, Momo."

"I didn't. I fucked up."

"Why do you say that?"

"Because I did. I went back through the accounting office twice and didn't find anything worthwhile. The problem is that they just keep too much stuff. They have records of everything. It 'ud take years to comb through all that crap."

Just then the duty officer came in with a thin file labeled "Mizrahi, Miriam," containing the order to transfer the Belle to Paris's central holding cells pending a hearing with the *juge d'instruction*. There was a yellow sticky note stuck on the blue dun cover in Isabelle's spiky hand, saying that she was typing out the Belle's confession and would get her to sign it before she was sent off.

"Allô, allô, Commissaire?"

"Sorry, Momo. I was just signing something."

"So I was saying we're not going to find nothing in that accounting office. What I want to do is get ahold of my little playmates from last night and have a cozy chat with them. They tried hard to make it look like your basic *blancs* beating up an immigrant for stealing their jobs, but it sure felt like there was something else behind it. I want to find out what."

"Out of the question. You're going to spend the night in the hospital, and then you're going to come back to Paris and take two weeks' medical leave."

"But what about the case?"

Momo's desire to get right back to work astonished Capucine and deepened her feeling of guilt. There had been no need to keep him undercover so long. The one lesson she could never seem to learn was that *le mieux est l'ennemi du bien*—better is the enemy of good.

"Allô, Commissaire. Are you there? What are we going to do about the case?"

"Don't worry about that. Thanks to you, it's completely buttoned up."

CHAPTER 46

When it was all over, the one thing Capucine had learned was that street-savvy cops need streets to be savvy.

The problems started almost immediately. Early in the morning Capucine sent two plainclothes brigadiers, held to be peerless at stakeout work, to cover the suspect in the village.

At noon they called to say the job was impossible. The suspect's house stood isolated on a dirt road in the outskirts of the village. The first time they drove by and slowed down to take a look, someone peeped out from behind a curtain. There was so little traffic on the road, the suspect's wife must have thought she had a visitor. They were sure that if they drove by a second time, she would become seriously suspicious. Then they had attempted approaching the house from an abandoned field across the street but decided the brambles were impenetrable.

Irritated, Capucine ordered one of the brigadiers to post himself on the terrace of the café in the village square and spot the suspect on his way home. The other brigadier was to take up a position behind a tree on the edge of the field—even if it meant ripping his jeans—and observe the house.

Her confidence still high, Capucine set out. The watchword for Police Judiciaire operations was overkill: always take two or three times as many troops as you think you could possibly need. She rode in the first car—a large white police-modified Citroën C8 hatchback—along with a uniformed brigadier-major, her right-hand man in directing the operation, a driver, and another brigadier. Two patrol cars followed, one with four brigadiers and the other with three. In all, ten police officers decked out in body armor. "That should do it," she had said to herself as they left. Still, if she included herself and the two already in the village, that made thirteen, hopefully not an unlucky number.

In a few minutes the cortège left Paris and began the steep climb at Mantes-la-Jolie, with its magnificent vista of the Seine snaking off into the distance. The view loosened the driver's tongue.

"Say, Commissaire, I didn't know we could do this."

"Do what?"

"Drive out of Paris and go arrest someone."

The brigadier-major was not to be excluded. "We sure as hell can. The Police Judiciaire has jurisdiction throughout France. Right, Commissaire?"

"Definitely." Capucine loved chatting with her men but for once was unwilling to be drawn out of her thoughts. The two officers in the front seat fell silent and watched the dark of the night rise from the valley and blacken the sky, no doubt thinking about the action that lay ahead or maybe the dinners they were missing at home.

During the hour's ride, the brigadier-major received frequent cell phone calls from the two officers in the village. The suspect had been seen crossing the village square at 7:39, heading in the direction of his house. The officer in the thicket did not pick him up and thought there might be a shortcut that led directly to his back door. At 7:53 he reported seeing the blue light of the TV appear in the front window of the house. The officer was sure the suspect had arrived home and was sitting in his socks in front of the tube. Everything seemed to be going according to plan. Still, Capucine was uneasy.

An hour later the little motorcade turned off the autoroute at the La-Trinité-de-Thouberville exit onto the D913 departmental road and proceeded north. In fifteen minutes they saw a white rectangular sign announcing that they were in the village limits of Saint-Nicolas-de-Bliquetuit. It was exactly 9:02.

The three vehicles slowly crossed the village square. Two of them pulled over in a side street while the tail car continued on.

In four minutes the radio crackled and announced, "*En place.*" The brigadier-major replied with a crisp "*Bien reçu.*" The three men in the last car had taken up their position behind the suspect's house.

Capucine's C8 and the patrol car squeezed through the tortuous, too-tight streets, then raced through the outlying roads and stopped in front of a small, ugly one-story house that had been built against a hillock. The front of the unfinished cinder-block basement was above ground—contrasting sharply with the carefully painted white façade of the main floor—as if the architect hoped that one day the hillock would somehow ooze forward to cover it. Clones of the same eyesore had been progressively desecrating the French countryside since the 1950s.

The brigadier-major turned in his seat and looked inquiringly at Capucine, who nodded. He squeezed the microphone and said, "*On y va.*" The occupants of both cars slipped silently out into the night. Capucine and the brigadier-major mounted the steps to the front door, drew their weapons, and took positions at either side. The six uniformed officers formed a semicircle in the little front yard, their Sigs drawn. Capucine was embarrassed by the ridiculous display of force just to arrest one man, but that was what regulations called for.

The brigadier-major hammered loudly on the front door and called out a stentorian "Police!"

A loud, flinty clang, as if a heavy sledgehammer had struck rock, punctuated the interjection, and a hole appeared in the door above their heads. The second shot hit while the echo of the first was still ringing, ripping a large wooden shard from the central panel. A switch flicked and time slowed almost to a standstill.

Even though it was obvious the shots were coming from an assault weapon or a high-powered hunting rifle in the field across the road, both Capucine and the brigadier-major were seized with the instinctive illusion that they came from inside, and moved away from the door.

The third shot hit the thigh of an officer standing in the front yard, throwing him backward, as if his legs had been kicked out from under him. He writhed wordlessly in the gravel, clutching his wound. In the intense quiet after the detonations, his scrabbling seemed unnaturally loud. Bright red arterial blood spurted through his fingers, making a large stain in the fresh white pebbles. It had all been blindingly fast, three seconds at most.

The switch flicked again and time went into fast-forward. Everyone moved at once, dropping to the ground, diving for cover, swiveling around to face the thicket, holding pistols rigidly in both hands in the textbook prone position.

Capucine ran over at a crouch to the downed man and took up a kneeling position, protecting him with her body, her Sig held straight out. She barked out a series of orders to the brigadier-major and punched 15 into her cell phone, the quickest way to get the SAMU, who promised to be there in under ten minutes. The brigadier-major began directing the operation in a majestically clear, resonant voice, compelling enough to induce the most timid mortal to follow him over a cliff.

The five men ran to the C8 while Capucine and the brigadier-major emptied clip after clip into the thicket, laying down covering fire for them. Three took cover behind the C8 and two continued on, flanking the wooded lot to take up positions at the far side to prevent the shooter from escaping in that direction.

One man ran back in a crouch with the embarrassed hobbled haste of a ball boy at a tennis match, carrying a large white medical kit, dove down behind Capucine, and applied a compress to the downed man's leg, leaning into it as if he were about to do a push-up. The two others ducked into the side door of the C8 and reappeared holding evil-looking Beretta Model 12 machine pistols and hefty bags of ammunition hooked over their necks.

Two shots crashed into the C8, one into the body of the van and the other straight through the windows, continuing on to shatter an upper window of the house, giving a good line toward the shooter. The brigadier-major indicated the direction to the two men with automatic weapons with a chopping motion of his right hand and then held both arms out in a Christlike position, directing them to fan out.

They separated at a run, emptying their clips with an enormous rending noise like a giant sheet tearing, threw themselves on their knees at the edge of the thicket, and got down to business, firing methodical half-second bursts, aiming low, trying for a kill. The effect on the flora was devastating. Branches and bits of vegetation flew into the air as if an unseen ogre hacked with a machete. The last thing Capucine wanted was a dead suspect. She bit her tongue to keep herself from calling them off.

She took a deep breath. Things seemed under control. Only two worries: the officer down—death could come astonishingly fast from arterial wounds—and the officer stationed in the thicket, who had not been heard from since his last call to the brigadier-major.

There was a yell from the thicket. "*Je me rends!*—I give up!" The men stopped firing. But the suspect did not show himself and the yell had a muffled quality, as if he had been lying facedown on the ground. One more thing to worry about. He could easily be attempting a decoy so he could cut down another officer or two.

The switch flicked again and time went back to normal speed. The brigadier-major began a new stream of orders in his magnificent voice.

The two men who had gone to the back of the lot came forward along the flanks at a crouch. The missing stakeout man popped out from behind a tree and moved up with one of them.

"Drop your gun and stand up with your arms outstretched." The brigadier-major orated loudly.

Nothing happened.

"Prepare to resume fire!" he ordered.

"No, no, wait! I'm going to stand up. *Ne tirez pas!*—don't shoot!"

Pierre Martel's head appeared from the brush and then his torso, arms up in the air at forty-five-degree angles. Four officers crashed through the brush and handcuffed his arms behind him.

Despite herself, Capucine couldn't help but think that a little pumping adrenaline was really all it took to get them to deal with undergrowth.

With an earsplitting *pan-pom-pam,* the SAMU ambulance arrived and disgorged three paramedics—completely indifferent to the bevy of flics brandishing weapons—who ran up to the victim, carrying a furled stretcher. One of the medics took over from the officer, applying even more pressure on the wound, while the other two lifted the man onto the stretcher. All three dashed back to the ambulance, which screeched off immediately, wheels spinning on the dirt road.

Two men led Martel up to Capucine. He seemed a bit pale but otherwise unchanged from the last time she had seen him, his bull-like truculence intact.

"I showed you, didn't I? It was stupid to have your men drive in front of my house. Even my simple wife knew what you were up to. It was even dumber to put one of them in the café. The whole village knew the police were up to something. But I gotta say, I missed the guy in the covert. Where I screwed up was that I wasted my first shots trying to take you out instead of going for the easy hits." He laughed cynically.

"You'll have plenty of time to tell me all about it in Paris," Capucine said, indicating with her head that Martel be taken to a car. Two officers, with a policeman's profound loathing of a cop shooter, virtually lifted him off his feet in their zeal.

The motorcade moved off, not without a number of discreetly parted curtains in the village. Capucine could easily imagine the comments. "Did you see? It was that woman from the château. All this shooting and dragging people off at night. It's as bad as when the *Boche* were here during the war. And that woman was such a sweet little child, too."

When they reached the A13 autoroute, Capucine's cell phone rang.

"Commissaire, this is Docteur Blanchard from the ER at the Hôpital La Pitié in Rouen." Capucine recognized the voice of the doctor who had attended to Momo. "Once again I was asked to call you as soon as I had a prognosis on your man. He just came out of the OR. The bullet opened the femoral artery but did not sever it. It was successfully sutured shut. He should recover with no ill effects, but it was a close call with the amount of blood he lost." He paused.

"Yes, Docteur?"

"I have to say I'm very glad I don't work for you." He rang off.

Capucine knew he had intended it as a friendly joke, but it still felt like a slap. She brooded over her two mistakes. The first one was that she should have been more decisive once Momo gave her the incriminating information, sparing him what he went through. The second was, well, whatever it was she had done, or not done, to make the arrest go off so badly. She had made a mistake in there somewhere, but she was damned if she knew what it was.

Capucine was on the edge of tears. She resorted to the most powerful solace in her armory, imagining she was in Alexandre's arms, stroking his tummy as she fell off to sleep, but she knew that was not going to happen for a while, maybe even not at all that night. But even so, the thought rocked her in its cradle and she dozed off.

In the front seat, the driver, who had been observing her in the rearview mirror, turned to the brigadier-major. "Did you ever see such sangfroid? The boss has ice water running through her veins."

CHAPTER 47

They were met at the door of the commissariat by one of Capucine's lieutenants—a man as unassuming and diffident as an insurance adjuster. Even though it was one in the morning and he was ending his shift, Durand looked like he was just starting, not a trace of five o'clock shadow, nondescript brown necktie still tight against his collar. The lieutenant led the way to the interrogation room, followed by Martel—held by two uniformed brigadiers, backs of wrists hard up against each other in too-tight handcuffs—with Capucine in the rear guard.

Capucine had no illusions about how much was at stake. She didn't have the slightest shred of proof that Martel had committed the two murders. If he was hardheaded and denied any involvement, she could still take him to court for shooting at the arresting officers and wounding a brigadier, but a good defense attorney would make much of why the arrest had occurred in the first place. Even if he was convicted, the press would give the police a very hard time indeed. Indicting him for the beating of Momo was even less promising. It could easily be passed off as a workers' brawl. And there would be the awkward question of why an armed police officer had not announced who he was and had allowed himself to be beaten. Obtaining a signed, witnessed confession to the two murders was absolutely essential. There was no way around that.

In the interrogation room the uniformed officers removed Martel's handcuffs, seated him in the hard metal suspect's folding chair, and left without a word. Martel swiveled his arms and massaged his wrists, grimacing at the pain of the returning circulation.

Durand took his seat behind the desk, symbolically removing himself from the conversation to come. His role was to remain silent and act as a counterweight in the interrogation.

Capucine smiled apologetically at Martel. "I'd like to get this over quickly so we can all get to bed. I'll bet you're exhausted, too."

As he was supposed to, Martel looked a little confused by her friendly tone.

"You probably worked a hard day, too. What time did you get going this morning?"

Martel relaxed slightly. "Five thirty. We moved fifty head into the feed shed yesterday. Sometimes they have a hard time going from grass to grain, and I wanted to make sure they were settling in okay."

"You showed us that shed when you took us around the élevage. I think it's amazing the way you finish them off on grain to get them to grow faster. But I never understood why they weren't fed on grain from the beginning."

Martel launched into a detailed technical explanation. As he spoke, his comfort level rose visibly and he seemed to forget how threatening his situation was: a man observed him coldly from across the desk, other observers undoubtedly peered at him from behind the large one-way mirror, and he had been demoted to *tu* but still was required to address the officers by the respectful *vous*.

They chatted for a full half hour. Martel became more

and more at ease. Eventually, he stretched back in his uncomfortable chair and started to cross one leg over the other. Capucine put her hand on his knee to stop him.

"You know you're here to explain your multiple crimes. Two murders, the assault and battery of Mohamed Benarouche, a police officer, your armed assault of a contingent of police officers with intent of homicide, and the consequent grave wounding of one of them. Do you understand that?"

"That's complete bullshit!" Martel half rose from the chair, the muscles of his body bunched, ready for a fight.

"Sit down," Capucine said like a whip crack.

Martel sat but with some of his weight still on his legs, poised to jump up again.

Capucine stood up, looming over Martel. "You shot a police officer in front of a dozen witnesses. Right there you're good for life without parole. I want you to tell me about the rest of it."

Martel looked up insolently at Capucine, his feet still under him, ready for action, but his eyes darted right and left, assessing his options.

"Look, that's a bunch of crap. How was I supposed to know he was a cop? All I knew was that he was a lazy fucking Beur who slacked off all day and drank all night. I caught him breaking into the accounting office, thinking he could pick up some cash, probably to buy more booze. He got a friendly little warning, that's all. And taking a few potshots at you guys, well, what do you expect? Strangers drive by my house. I figure my wife is being threatened. So I protect my home. That's what people do. I fired some shots in the air, and yeah, someone got hit in the leg by accident. Big fucking deal. But murdering people, I don't know nothing about that." He crossed his arms, a portrait of righteous indignation.

On the face of it Martel's pugnacious self-assurance seemed unassailable. It was easy to understand why at least half a dozen of Capucine's officers had no faith in psychological pressure and relished the interrogations based on "physical incentives" for which the Police Judici-aire was infamous.

Capucine dug a sheet of paper folded in four from her pants pocket and shook it open.

"We have the ballistics report on the rifle you were fir-ing at us this evening. A Czech CZ five-fifty chambered for three hundred Winchester Magnums. That's yours, right?" Martel nodded.

"It would appear that the bullets it fires are a perfect match for the one found in the body of Lucien Bellec. We need to talk about that." This, of course, was pure fabri-cation. The bullet in Bellec's body had been filed away to perdition in some gendarmerie warehouse, and no ballistic examination had ever been performed.

Martel blanched slightly but said nothing. He remained just as truculent but a little shadow of worry could be seen in the corners of his eyes and his forehead had three slight creases in the middle.

"I don't know nothin' about th—"

Capucine stopped him with her hand on his knee.

"Pierre, right now you need to listen to me. We've got all the proof we need. What I'm doing here is trying to see your point of view so we can work something out. But you've got to help me. I could see when you were telling me about feeding the steers how much you love your work and the élevage. You do, don't you?"

"Yeah, I guess so."

"And you did it so the élevage could survive, didn't you? There were people trying to destroy the élevage, weren't there?"

Martel looked a little confused. The theme wasn't strik-ing a cord with him, yet.

"I didn't do any of that stuff," he said belligerently. "I—"

Capucine cut him off. "You'll get your chance to talk in

a while," Capucine said. "Right now I want you to listen to me."

Capucine took a risk. "It's all about the hormones, isn't it?"

Martel nodded. Inwardly Capucine breathed a sigh of relief. She had succeeded in the decisive pass. All that was left was capework. But it still had to be done just right.

"I want to start with the intern, Clément Devere. Tell me why it was important to remove him." Martel looked anxiously around the room as if someone might come to his help. Durand met his gaze but remained silent, his expression impassive.

"Hey, I'm not a murderer. I'm really not. I—"

Capucine cut him off again with her hand on his knee. She inched her chair closer. "I'm going to want to hear everything you have to say in a minute. You'll get your chance, believe me. I know you're the kind of guy who'd only kill someone unless you really had to."

Martel ran his hands through his hair and licked his lips.

Capucine pushed her chair a little closer. "I want to help you. We're going to sort this out. We really are. Let's do the easy part first. Tell me about Devere. He was threatening the élevage, wasn't he? I need to know exactly what he was doing."

Martel leaned forward and put his head in his hands, the textbook gesture of submission. Capucine had no difficulty reading his mind. He was at a crossroads. His anxiety level had reached the point where he wanted to be anywhere but in this room—even a jail cell would be better—but he could not quite bring himself to confess.

Capucine reached forward and put her hand on his shoulder. "Trust me. We'll make it work. I want everyone to understand you were acting to save the élevage and you're not some thug who can't control his anger. You were just trying to do the right thing, weren't you?"

His head still in his hands, Martel nodded.

Very quietly she asked, "He found out about the hormones, didn't he?"

"I don't want them to think I'm just a dumb bruiser."

"Of course you don't. And you're not. How did Devere figure it out?"

Martel sat up and laughed. "I'm not even sure he did. But he was so anxious to meet that guy Jean Bouvard, you know, the one who bulldozed the fast-food place, that I figured he was going to spill the beans. I just couldn't take the risk, could I?"

"Of course not. But how could Devere have known?"

"He was interested in growth rates of beef cattle. He spent hours reading the charts. He was writing a paper on it for his school. He must have figured out the only way our cattle were going to grow that fast was because they were on hormones."

"And what about Lucien Bellec?"

"That fucker? He had it coming, believe me. His problem was that he got dangerous. He was the guy who helped me inject the cattle. When we had to stop 'cuz Gerlier wasn't around to give us the hormones anymore, Bellec made me keep paying him out of my own pocket. Then, one night when we got drunk together, I blabbed about Devere and he started blackmailing me for that. He was out of control. I mean, the guy could have brought the élevage down all by himself. I had to stop that, right?"

Capucine was astonished how quickly Martel had internalized the interpretation of his crimes he had been offered only a few minutes before. She pushed a small button hidden under the seat of her chair. In a few seconds the door opened and a man came halfway in, leaning on the doorknob, relaxed and smiling. He was in his fifties, slightly paunchy, with a smoker's raspy voice. He wore the infectious smile of someone who really wants to buy you a drink. It was Capucine's other lieutenant, who had just received a plaque for thirty years' service with the force.

"Hey, guys. How's it going?" he said cheerfully, as if he was going to send out for pizza and had popped in to see if his colleagues wanted some.

"Hi, Jean-Luc," Capucine said. "Come on in. Pierre here has just been telling us about the two deaths. We're working hard to make it clear to everyone that he did it for the good of the élevage. We don't want people to think he's some sort of vicious killer."

Yeah! Martel's eyes beseeched. He leaned forward in supplication.

The lieutenant slid in, shutting the door with his foot in an easy gesture, and sat on the edge of the desk, still very much the coworker who had just dropped in for a little gossip. "Listen, Pierre, I'm not assigned to this case, so I don't know the story. Can you take it from the top for me?"

Martel turned forty-five degrees in his chair, completely focused on the new arrival. Convincing the newcomer of the nobility of his actions had become Martel's paramount concern.

"See, I work for this élevage that raises the best beef in France, right?"

"I know that part," the lieutenant said with a laugh.

"So when I get hired a bunch of years ago, the general manager, a guy called Gerlier, comes up to me and says I look like a guy he could trust and that I could double my salary without working extra time. So I find myself in charge of shooting steers with hormones. It's no big deal. You just pop an implant into their ears with a little hypodermic gismo, and they're good for three months. That's how the beef got so good. Get me?"

The lieutenant smiled, took out a pack of Marlboro reds, flipped it open, and offered them to Martel, who looked at Capucine for approval. Capucine nodded and he took one. The two smokers went through the bonding of lighting their cigarettes and relishing the rush of the first drag.

"What's the big deal with these hormones?"

"The big deal? They're illegal. That's the big deal. The European Community has outlawed them, just like they tried to make our cheese illegal. The stuff makes the beef way better, more tender and flavorful, you know, and since the steers grow faster, it costs lots less money. The Americans can use hormones, but we can't. How dumb is that?"

"Got it. So then what?"

"So, one day my man Gerlier gets shot when he's out hunting partridge with the nobs."

"Did he die?"

"For sure. No more Gerlier. No more hormones. That gig was done and gone."

"What about Vienneau? Why didn't you go to him for more hormones?" Capucine asked.

"Vienneau! He doesn't have a clue what's going on. All he did was walk around once a week, trying real hard not to get dirty, letting Gerlier show him what was happening. That guy couldn't find the ear on a steer. How was he going to know about hormones?"

The lieutenant stood up and looked at his watch. Martel became agitated.

"Hang on, hang on. I gotta tell you this."

"Sure."

"So, the next thing I know, we have a smart-ass intern from the agricultural school who's there for the summer. One cute tree-hugging asshole. You know the type?"

"Sure do." The lieutenant took a drag on his cigarette and nodded in ironic sympathy.

"Well, this kid's always out poking at the cattle and going over the growth records and all that, and I'm beginning to think maybe he's figured something out. And wait. It gets worse. So this guy Bouvard, the one you always see on TV getting arrested for freeing us from crap in supermarkets, he's going to come to town to do a number on this new fast-food restaurant we got. And our little intern goes ballistic. He's got to meet up with this Bouvard. I mean, like it's the most important thing that's ever happened in his little life."

"What was he going to tell him?"

"What do you think?" Martel asked with a sneer. "Stands to reason he'd figured out about the hormones. Shit. If Bouvard had found out about that, he'd have gone to town, even though we'd stopped. It would have been curtains for the élevage."

"But you fixed it, right?"

"Sure did! I slipped a couple of Brennekes in my shotgun and went to the demonstration, like I was just having a look before going out to shoot a rabbit or two for my dinner. I pretty much knew what would happen. The flics in that town just can't not push people around. And when everyone was shoving and hollering and the cops were shooting in the air, I just squeezed one off into that intern's chest. Problem solved," he said with satisfaction.

"Tell him about Bellec," Capucine said enthusiastically, as if that had been his crowning achievement.

"Oh yeah, that guy was a real problem. So, like, you need another guy to help inject the hormone implants, right? Someone has to deal with the steer while you do it."

"Sure," the lieutenant said.

"So Bellec was my man. Trouble was that when we shut down the operation, he got pissed off. He had to keep getting paid, even though he wasn't doing nothing no more. And that's where I made my big mistake. I kept paying him. I mean, it wasn't all that much, so why not, really? But then I made my second mistake. I told him about the intern thing. I mean, how dumb can you get? After that he wanted more money, or he was going to spill the beans. And every time I'd pay him, he'd want even more. Then I found my chance one Saturday and took care of him. Not for me, of course. It was because I didn't want him to hurt the élevage." Martel wanted to make absolutely sure that the lieutenant didn't miss the point.

"What do you mean, you took care of him?"

"There was this commotion one Saturday because the hunt had a stag run out on the ice and they were trying to shoot it. Everybody in the village goes down to the lake to look, and I see Bellec in the crowd. I have my car right there, so I get my CZ out of the trunk and pop a three-hundred Winchester Mag into the fucker. Another problem solved."

"Pierre," Capucine said, "you told your story very well. Everyone's going to know that you really had the interest of the élevage at heart. Jean-Luc is going to print it out so you can sign it, and then we can all call it a night and get some sleep."

Martel grinned like a little boy. He was finally going to get out of that horrible room.

Capucine knew it would take less then ten minutes. The microphones had fed the confession into the voice-recognition software of a computer in the staff room. The lieutenant would need a few minutes to make some corrections and add a few commas and would then bring it back to be signed and witnessed by all three officers.

Martel looked tired, but it was the virtuous fatigue of a job well done. Capucine felt depleted, her mind awash with half thoughts of the young Devere, who would never know what it was like to fall really in love or play with his children or have the joy of growing old with someone. She missed the phone book. Martel richly deserved to have his head slumped on the table with a trickle of blood dripping from a ruptured eardrum. The guilty so deserved to suffer like the guilty.

Then she remembered that in half an hour Martel would be on his way to the profoundly depressing La Santé Prison in the Fourteenth Arrondissement, where he would spend every day and every night of the rest of his life, with the sole exception of one morning in court, when he would stare, frightened, at a row of judges perched on a bench like a line of black crows on a branch, confirming his fate. There was at least some order to the universe.

CHAPTER 48

Even though the depths of winter were still distant, there was a mood of finality in the air. It felt as if the credits were about to roll and this was the last trip to Maulévrier, at least for a while. Only Capucine, Alexandre, and Jacques—and, of course, Oncle Aymerie—were in residence for the weekend. The château felt stale and fuggy, as if it needed a thorough airing out.

On Saturday Capucine and Alexandre decided to have a go at the last of the mushrooms. It was too cold for a picnic, but Odile packed a light snack they could nibble while rooting around the browning ferns—two kinds of tiny, glazed, cigar-shaped sandwiches: smoked salmon and Parma ham with Morbier cheese. Naturally, she also included a small flask of the inevitable Calvados.

Alexandre was elated. Either he was delighted to be released from the bonds of Saint-Nicolas or he had drained the dregs of his cane flask before filling it for the day. They held hands. They leaned against each other. They giggled. Capucine finally mastered the art of sipping from the cane flask with grace and elegance, a gesture that ineluctably engendered refined ribaldry from Alexandre. Capucine's thoughts turned to the time they had been frustrated by the hunt. She gripped Alexandre's hand more tightly and then put her arm around his waist. He moaned in ecstasy and dropped to his knees.

"Cèpes! Look at them! A whole basketful. In one spot. Dinner is saved."

As he leaned forward to cut the first of the mushrooms from its stem, Capucine booted his bottom as hard as she could. Undeterred, Alexandre collected cèpes until his basket was filled to overflowing. He rose, smirking slightly, and took Capucine in his arms. "Where were we?"

Capucine kicked him in the shins. "You cad. Do you really think I'm going to play second fiddle to a pile of fungal growths?" Alexandre kissed her. Capucine kicked him again. And once again. But finally, ne'er consenting, she consented.

Later, walking back to town, Alexandre said, "You know, I think we should stop off and see our friend Homais. The stems of these cèpes are a little darker than they should be. I want to make doubly sure they're not one of the poisonous varieties."

Capucine didn't reply but twisted around in that uniquely feminine gesture to check her posterior and make sure no leaves had stuck to her tweed skirt.

Homais's welcome had warmed up a little but had not quite regained its former effusiveness. He invited them to come into his office at the back of the pharmacy—"my sanctum sanctorum"—and place the mushrooms on his worktable. As Alexandre spread them out delicately, Homais sat down at his desk and finished making some sort of note in dark green ink with an extravagant-looking gold Caran d'Ache fountain pen. Capucine wondered where he had learned to ape this classic and highly irritating affectation of Paris doctors.

After a minute or two he reread his note, added a comma or two with an exasperated sigh, carefully capped his pen, and said, "*Très bien,* let's have a look at your trove.

"Ah," Homais said with his insufferably knowledgeable air. "These are not common *cèpes, Boletus edulis.* These are the prince of *cèpes, Boletus aereus,* what they call, even in this enlightened age, *têtes de nègre.* Monsieur, you have the luck of your wife."

"Am I that lucky?" Capucine asked.

"The paysans think it's either pure luck or witchcraft the way you produced a murderer out of thin air, but they understand nothing about modern forensic science. I wrote a piece on your brilliant arrest for the *Paris-Normandie.* It was very well received. I, at least, was happy to have had you sojourn in our little village. Now I am going to write a piece about the recrudescence of *têtes de nègre* so late in the year."

Capucine couldn't help notice both the "I, at least" and that her stay had been consigned to the past tense.

Later that afternoon it was Alexandre's turn to be miffed when he was vigorously shooed from the kitchen by Odile, who seemed almost put out by his contribution of têtes de nègre. Compounding his irritation, the tremolos of Odile's giggles, punctuated by Jacques's Amadean cackle, echoed loudly on the ground floor until the evening *apéro* was served.

Dinner that night had a decidedly valedictorian flavor. The conversation started off as tepidly as the *potimarron* soup, a standard at the château, whose nutlike roundness invited one to curl up in a chaise longue with a book rather than fence across the table with rapier-like wit. Once Gauvin had cleared the soup plates, Odile herself arrived with the main course, blushing like a little girl. It struck Capucine that Odile was the only resident of the château who genuinely enjoyed life without reservation. She held a beautifully chased silver platter that held eight partridges, carefully arranged in two rows of four, covered in a nubbly, attractive brown coating. Conversation skidded to a halt. Partridges were not served breaded. Even more alarming was the aroma. Pleasant for sure, but definitely very un-French.

Oncle Aymerie broke the silence. With the courtly courtesy dictated by his pronounced sense of noblesse oblige, he asked, "Why, Odile, you seem to have outdone yourself. What new creation have you come up with?"

"Monsieur, this is *perdrix* crusted with peanuts and dried mangos on a bed of curry leaf and quinoa." She could barely contain her pride.

"Quinoa?" Oncle Aymerie asked, nonplussed, carefully imitating Odile's pronunciation, "KEEN-wah."

"It's a seed grown on the west coast of Latin America. The conquistadores didn't think much of it, so it never made its way to Europe, but think of it as a sort of Latin American couscous." Alexander's explanation left his audience unimpressed.

"Exactly, monsieur," Odile said. "And the partridge is roasted in a coating made of Greek yogurt, mango powder, crushed peanuts, chopped coriander stems, chopped green chilies, and, oh yes, just a hint of lemon juice. The quinoa bed is simplicity itself. Just add dried chili, curry leaves, mustard seeds, root ginger, and sugar, with chopped basil, tomato, and onions for volume. Voilà. I'm sure you'll enjoy it."

Oncle Aymerie was visibly making an effort to keep his jaw from dropping. "But, Odile, where did you get all these things? Mango powder? Quinoa? Curry leaves?"

"Monsieur, there's a new gourmet shop on the square. That's where I've been buying the coffee you like so much."

"Oh, yes, yes, of course," Oncle Aymerie said lamely.

They began by picking at the partridge with all the misgivings of a ten-year-old forced to try a new food. It was delicious. Not just delicious, but the antithesis of the oh-not-again feeling that any kind of game evoked once the shooting season was under way. There was no question that Odile had been brilliant. But in being brilliant, she had raised another, profoundly visceral question: was Maulévrier really the place for brilliance?

Capucine could see Oncle Aymerie casting around the table, looking for the culprit. There had to be an *éminence grise*. Odile would never have dared such an initiative on her own. He settled first on Alexandre, who was rooting through his plate apparently admiringly, until it became obvious that he was reassuring himself that his precious *têtes de nègre* had not been drowned in the concoction. It was clearly not him. Oncle Aymerie then focused on Jacques and his eyes turned to flint. There would be words after dinner for sure.

"*Ma petite* Capucine," Oncle Aymerie said in a voice more gravelly than usual, obviously determined to change the subject, "tell us about the case. I still don't know what really happened."

"Mon Oncle, explaining how a case was solved always disappoints people. It's like a magician revealing how his tricks are performed. They always seem so simple and tawdry when you know how they're done."

"Ah ha! So you admit you had the ace of spades in your panties all along," Jacques said. "Out with it. I thought I taught you what happens to coy little girls long ago."

Capucine made a caricature of a pout. "If you insist. It's a sad story that started because Philippe Gerlier was dosing the steers with illegal growth hormones. Actually, Pierre Martel and Lucien Bellec had been doing the work for him. Once every three months they would inject a slow-release capsule of a synthetic hormone into the animals' ears."

"Stop right there," Oncle Aymerie ordered. "What's so bad about these hormones?"

"Papa, these are," Jacques said, ostentatiously looking at the door to make sure none of the servants were listening and lowering his voice to a dramatic whisper, "*sex* hormones. So if one day Odile served you a steak from the élevage and ate one herself, why, you would just spend your evening chasing each other up and down the corridors of the château."

Oncle Aymerie was furious. "I won't put up with that sort of impertinence," he sputtered.

Odile, who had just made an appearance at the door to gauge the reaction to the partridges in the eating, was heard to mutter under her breath, "I wouldn't be running fast enough for there to be all that much chasing." Oncle Aymerie turned bright red.

It was Capucine's turn to apply the proverbial oil.

"From the very beginning I was struck by the fact that the growth rate had fallen off when Gerlier died. There had to be a connection, and it was a good bet that he had been injecting them with hormones. What I couldn't figure out was how he obtained them. It was only when I planted an undercover officer who discovered that Gerlier took frequent trips to visit an ailing mother in the American Midwest that it was obvious what he had been up to. Particularly since police records showed that his mother had never left France and had died ten years ago."

"But how did that lead you to Martel?" Oncle Aymerie asked.

"It was obvious that Gerlier couldn't be doing it alone. He would have needed help to inject the steers. Martel was the logical candidate. He was in charge of the cattle while they were in the feed shed, so it would not attract attention if he ordered them sent down the chute for some kind of treatment. He was also so feared that the hands would stay away from him while he was injecting them."

"It was all just guesswork?" Oncle Aymerie asked, dismayed.

"Not at all. The undercover officer, Momo, recognized him when he was beaten. There had to be something behind that assault. I was sure Martel had caught Momo snooping around and was desperate to get him off the premises. I still lose sleep about how close Momo came to getting shot in the back. But it turned out that Martel thought Momo was only rifling the accounting office for booze money. But it still made him nervous enough to want him gone."

"That's clear enough. But how could you have known he killed those two men?" Oncle Aymerie asked.

"I didn't, but he was the logical choice. That day Martel showed us around the plant, Devere talked a good deal about hormones and was very excited about the upcoming visit of Jean Bouvard. Martel was clearly concerned. And Lucien Bellec, well, that just couldn't have been coincidence. I relied on my intuition."

Alexandre had taken the opportunity of the collective fascination with Capucine's narrative to devour his partridges. "Capucine's intuition is as reliable as a hound's sense of smell," he said, chewing contentedly.

"I was positive that if I arrested Martel, I would be able to make him confess. Of course, it was far more of a gamble than I should have taken, but it paid off."

"Ah, the powers of the telephone book!" Jacques said. "It's so superior to that messy waterboarding they make us use. If you don't wear rubber boots when you do it, you ruin your shoes."

Later that night Capucine and Alexandre leaned over the iron railing of their bedroom window, finishing off the contents of the cane flask as Alexandre smoked his last cigar of the day.

"You know," Alexandre said, "the one person who doesn't make any sense to me in all of this is Gerlier. It seems like he was shooting hares with a howitzer. How on earth did you know he was involved? Why would anyone go through all that trouble just to look a little better with your boss or do a little less work?"

"I never would have figured it out unless Momo had told me about one other little detail he discovered."

Just as Alexandre was going to press her for an explanation, she slid her hand under his silk dressing gown. His response was so immediate and so robust, he committed the unthinkable. He let two-thirds of a perfectly good El Ray del Mundo Choix Supreme fall into the azalea bush below.

CHAPTER 49

"You've done well on this case, Commissaire," Juge d'Instruction August-Marie Parmentier de la Martinière said in a tone suggesting he was addressing a grease-stained garage mechanic and was afraid good breeding might require him to shake the worker's hand.

He was barely out of law school and very junior in the pecking order of *juges*. He had been assigned a tiny office, hardly larger than Capucine's country cloakroom lair, but had tried hard to elevate its grandeur to a level commensurate with his vision of himself by furnishing it with ostentatious antiques from his family home. The room was dominated by an ornate ormolu desk that in a larger version would have been appropriate in a minister's office. On its surface was a venerable, scarred, leather blotter with a hinged, gold-tooled leather cover. Since her childhood, Capucine had always wondered how these blotters were supposed to be used, since there was never enough room for the top flap to be folded back on the desk so the user could actually write something.

The judge lifted up the cover and peeked inside with the suppressed grin of a chemin de fer player tipping up a corner of his cards to reassure himself that he really had an unbeatable hand. Inside there was only one file, suggesting that his work in progress was hardly enough to keep him entertained much beyond morning coffee. He extracted the thin folder and opened it without looking at the contents, eased back in his chair, and negligently crossed one leg over the other. Isabelle sat speechless, catatonic with stage fright.

"Brigadier Lemercier deserves full credit for the case. She's been in charge of the day-to-day work," Capucine said.

"I see you had problems with the press," he said, tapping the file with his index finger.

"Yes, a few weeks ago both *Le Figaro* and the *Nouvel Observateur* ran pieces portraying the Belle as some sort of modern Robin Hood. We had a press conference, and, fortunately, their interest burned out very quickly."

"I'm sure we can remedy that. Maybe another press conference will do the trick. Yes. My office will handle it. I'll present the case, naturally, but I'd like you to be there as well to show what an important role the Police Judiciaire can have if properly directed."

He opened the file and made a note in the margin with an antique gold Parker 51 pen. Homais would have been highly impressed.

"It's a shame you didn't run her in as a *flagrant délit.* I understand why you hesitated, but I would have come right down and made sure a magistrate pushed her straight into prison. It would have given us a marvelous opportunity to show the press how decisive and hard-hitting we *juges* really are. One of my main career objectives is to counter the deplorable current belief that the *juge d'instruction* system has become obsolete. But not to worry. It was an oversight that can be rectified with our press conference."

"Monsieur le Juge," Capucine said, "I hope you had the chance to read the note I sent you. There are extenuating circumstances. In fact, I—and the whole team on the case, too—feel strongly that the charges should be dropped."

Martinière stared at Capucine with wide, disbelieving eyes. His look was simultaneously nervous and aggressive, giving him the demeanor of a rapacious weasel whose prey was making an entirely unexpected move to bolt.

"Drop the charges?"

"Yes. She and her mother are hardship cases. It's quite possible her mother will not survive her cancer. Of course the girl *is* guilty of a number of thefts, but she did make every effort to minimize the damages to her victims. In fact, she succeeded so well that two of them have refused to press charges and two others never even reported the robberies."

Jubilant, Martinière held the pen between crooked forefinger and thumb and stabbed it aggressively at Capucine like a loaded gun.

"The mother. Yes. Of course. There is a mother. I'd completely forgotten. Thank you for reminding me." He flipped through the file to the appropriate section and read it carefully, making tick marks in the margin.

"There are clear grounds for deportation here. As you explain so eloquently in your note, the woman has a lingering and potentially fatal disease. That would cost the nation a great deal of money if, somehow, she managed to obtain social coverage. But since the girl is bound to get at least fifteen years, of which she'll have to serve a minimum of seven and probably more, I could ask for immediate deportation of the mother back to, ah"—he flipped a few pages—"ah, Syria. Yes, Syria." He smiled contentedly. "That's exactly the sort of thing I'll want to announce has already happened when we have our press conference. It will go down extremely well. It will show how decisive we are. I'll call the immigration people before lunch."

He looked at his wafer-thin gold watch, impatient they leave. He had much to do. His morning had suddenly become very full.

CHAPTER 50

"Some husbands are only good for being cuckolded, and even for that their wives have to help them out."

There was a refined ripple of laughter. Alexandre leaned over and whispered in Capucine's ear, "Speaking of which, whatever happened to the delectable Marie-Christine?"

"Shush. I'll tell you after the play."

Capucine's sibilant was taken up by the people around them. There were two "*Chuts!*" from behind and a "*Voyons!*" from the row in front. Alexandre groaned and sunk down in his seat. He hated Feydeau. He leaned toward Capucine again. "All this *fin de siècle* posturing. Wilde I love. Guitry is genuinely funny. But Feydeau is just flatulence. I'm going to the lobby to smoke a cigar. I'll meet you there."

"If you do, you won't get a crumb of gossip from me," Capucine whispered sweetly.

The elderly woman in front turned in her seat. "Voilà. Madame has spoken. Sit quietly and not one more word." She put her index finger to her lips, widening her eyes for emphasis in an exaggerated gesture. She turned to her consort, "*Ah, les hommes!*" He nodded automatically, rapt with the play. In contrast, Alexandre slumped down in his seat and pouted with his arms crossed like a vexed child of eight.

At the restaurant Alexandre revived like a bear rising from a winter's hibernation. It was the latest creation of the chef who had almost single-handedly led French gastronomy out of the aridity of nouvelle-cuisine minimalism back to the lushness of its *cuisine bourgeoise* foundations. After years of inactivity he had suddenly returned to the scene with a restaurant built around a long L-shaped bar overlooking the kitchen, which famously "erased" the barrier between patron and chef. Alexandre had thought it would be perfect for an after-theater meal.

As it happened, the chef was on the premises that night. He had been waiting for Alexandre, who always reserved in his own name, and greeted him extravagantly with hugs, kisses on both cheeks, and loud, joyous whooping. Naturally, everyone in the restaurant stared. This was Alexandre's heaven. The play faded to a dim, distasteful memory.

As the couple sat side by side at the counter, chatting and admiring the precisely choreographed energy of the kitchen, Alexandre rose through the circles of his paradise. He had already downed a dish of crayfish *ravioles* on a bed of green cabbage and was keenly anticipating a duo of duck *magret* and foie gras served with a cherry and almond sauce. And on top of that he was delighted that Capucine, who so often only pecked at her food, had ordered all of four dishes from the tasting menu. She had already dealt with a creamed soft-boiled egg topped with a gobbet of caviar and was just beginning her dissection of a wild quail stuffed with foie gras.

"You're wrong to be so disdainful of Feydeau," Capucine said. "I grant you he's become a bit dusty, but he's a true father of surrealism."

"I seem to recall you promising to earn your supper

with some jaw-dropping gossip." Alexandre caught sight of the chef in the bowels of the kitchen and raised both hands, fingers pinched together, shaking them in the direction of the heavens to indicate his beatific rapture with his meal. The chef beamed in appreciation.

"If I'd wanted proto-surrealism, I'd have gone to a Marx Brothers movie," Alexandre said, pouring her a glass of wine. "Let's get back to Saint-Nicholas. Unbelievable as it seems, I half think I miss the place."

"Actually, I had lunch with Jacques today and he was a cornucopia of gossip." She rubbed Alexandre's leg until his teeth unclenched. There was much to be said for this side-by-side seating.

"He tells me that Oncle Aymerie has been single-minded in tracking down the source of Odile's new recipes. It seems they became the bane of his existence. He finally found a book she'd hidden in her room, something written by a gentleman called Kailash Jaswinder, who turns out to be a chef in Mumbai who pioneered French-Indian fusion. Oncle Aymerie confiscated the book, so he'll be at peace until Christmas, when Jacques is planning a suitable replacement."

"Odile's partridges were actually excellent, though I had been looking forward to my *têtes de nègre*. What about the delectable Marie-Christine? I'm sure Jacques has been keeping his beady little eyes on her."

"His eyes aren't beady at all. And it wasn't Jacques who told me. She called me herself. She's finally decided to divorce Loïc. It was a huge step for her and she agonized over it, but she got him to sign a separation agreement."

"How did they handle the ownership of the élevage?"

"They haven't yet. The law requires that couples be separated for three months before the judge will weigh the merits of a divorce. I suppose that's to keep them from attempting something rash in the heat of the moment. Anyway, for the time being, Loïc will continue to own all of the shares of the company, and Marie-Christine has another three months to figure out how to handle the situation."

"The élevage seems to have survived the scandal unscathed," Alexandre commented after he had swallowed a mouthful of duck.

"I gather that in his devotion he's gone back to spending twelve-hour days on the job and that was what drove Marie-Christine's decision. She felt the only thing that really interests him in life is his élevage," Capucine said.

"He's certainly embraced the hyperbole of the marketing world with open arms. He's taken to bombarding journalists with press release after press release claiming he's completely reorganized the business to make it even more traditional and an even stauncher pillar of French gastronomy. He claims his beef is now identical to the stuff Escoffier used in his famous recipes. It's complete blather, but a number of papers have done pieces on him and I'm sure his sales have improved considerably," Alexandre said.

"Oh, but that's not all," Capucine said, relishing the frisson of gossip. "It seems that the village is so moved at his resolve that the notables have succeeded in getting him awarded the Mérite Agricole."

"I hate to trump you, but I've heard, and this is only a rumor, mind you," Alexandre said quite facetiously, "that he may even be awarded the Légion d'Honneur for his contribution to the French patrimony. I got this from the president of the French Association of Restaurateurs over lunch while you were pinching and giggling with your cousin."

Capucine knew he would not have let the reference to Jacques slide by without comment and had her parry at the ready. But just as she raised her épée to flex it for maximum effect before delivering the coup de grâce, another dish arrived for her, this one a tiny portion of sweetbreads decorated with little nails of rolled-up shards of bay leaves, making them look like baby hedgehogs. She abandoned her retort.

"And I suppose," Alexandre said, "you'll insist we go down to Saint-Nicolas to see him awarded the damn things."

"Absolutely. I have some unfinished business there."

CHAPTER 51

The ceremony took place in Saint Nicolas' *mairie*—its town hall—the ruins of a fifteenth-century *château-fort* that had been converted into a public building. The village was unanimous in its opinion that the conversion had been anything but a success. The architect, obviously highly impressed by Mies van der Rohe and his cronies, had preserved the three standing walls of the original keep and constructed the rest of the building in glass and steel, clearly aiming for dramatic effect at minimal cost. Unfortunately, the walls of the château had lost all their original character and the steel and glass structure was awkwardly proportioned. The sole saving grace of the building was its large, well-lit reception area, suitable for the weddings of those who refused to set foot in the local church and the presentation of trophies for soccer tournaments, bicycle races, and, naturally, civic honors, should such an occasion ever present itself.

The morning press augured ill for Loïc Vienneau's awards. *Les Echos,* one of France's two main business newspapers, announced the acquisition of the Elevage Vienneau by Opportunité S.A., the holding company that owned the chain of Charolais Allô restaurants, as well as a large number of autoroute service centers and a good-sized in-plant factory canteen business. Even though the local *café-tabac* stocked only two copies of *Les Echos*, the news spread like rabbits running through a field of alfalfa and it was speculated that the decorations would be canceled.

The concerns were put to rest when the minister of agriculture himself arrived with a huge din in a helicopter that landed heroically on the postage stamp lawn of the *mairie*. It was immediately obvious that there had been an administrative mishap. The minister clearly thought he was to present the Legion of Honor to some sort of scientist who had achieved a significant breakthrough in genetic engineering. He was also astounded to find one of his cabinet advisers already on the scene, apparently with the intention of awarding the same individual the Mérite Agricole. He confiscated the box that contained the lesser medal and shooed away the adviser, who had the virtue of actually knowing who Vienneau was. The adviser, who seemed well acquainted with this type of confusion, retreated unconcernedly to the bar that had been set up for the reception and contented himself with the champagne, a Veuve Clicquot chosen by the mayor himself.

Consulting his text, the minister spoke at length about the prowess of a certain Dr. Vienne and the victory that might eventually—but not quite yet, of course—free all corn crops from the terrible bane of Diplodia ear rot. Mercifully, the minister mumbled and the public address system had the unfortunate habit of cutting in and out, so the audience applauded at each electronic pause and was none the wiser. After the required fifteen minutes the minister made a vague papal exhortation of approach with the fingers of both hands, placed the red ribbon of the Légion d'Houneur over Vienneau's neck, kissed him on both cheeks, and bolted for his helicopter, leaving the medal of the Mérite Agricole on the table in its box.

The cabinet adviser, unperturbed, downed the remains of a fourth flute of champagne, calmly approached the podium with the rolling gait of a seaman, pushed the microphone aside, made a well-turned and rousing speech in a loud, clear voice about the glories of French beef in the troubled times of the threat of mad cow disease from perfidious Albion across the Channel, placed the second medal around Vienneau's neck to vigorous applause, and beat a retreat to his car.

The bar was instantly transformed into a rugby scrum. For the fifty or so guests, most with hands so work hardened that they were difficult to close into fists, real champagne was a treat so rare it would be experienced only a few times in their lives. They were not going to miss out on this occasion. Vienneau stood awkwardly at one end of the bar, red and green ribbons draped around his neck, looking foolishly at the crush of people, at a complete loss for what to do.

Alexandre had had no difficulty slipping through the crowd and securing three of the plastic flutes of champagne. He and Capucine went up to Vienneau and offered him one.

"Thank God you're here," Vienneau said, downing half of his glass. "I had no idea this would be so awkward."

Capucine and Alexandre offered the standard bromides of congratulations.

"Listen," Vienneau said earnestly. "Opportunité is hosting a dinner at the Rallye Normand tonight," he said, naming an expensive but un-starred restaurant a few miles from the village. "I'd love it if you two could come. It's a bit last minute and all, but I hope you can make it. It would mean a lot to me."

At the dinner Capucine and Alexandre found themselves seated ingloriously in the oubliettes at the end of a very long table, largely ignored by the executives of Opportunité. The order of the day seemed to be the adulation of their chairman, who sat enthroned at the center, smiling tolerantly at the repeated toasts made in homage to the magnificence of his administration. Vienneau was nowhere to be seen. Alexandre occupied himself with detesting his dinner, while Capucine reflected on how she was going to manage to do what she had come to do.

"This is like taking a fresh country maiden, destroying her hair with peroxide, gumming up her pores with makeup, crippling her grace with three-inch heels, and labeling it as sophistication," Alexandre said.

"Oh, it's not all that bad," Capucine said, taking a bite of her pheasant.

"I suppose the food's edible, if you still have a stomach for game, which I—unfortunately—no longer do. I'll grant you that. It's the service that's insufferable. They're trying to con the local rubes into thinking that arrogant, stuck-up personnel and astronomic prices make for gastronomy—not the food. The tragedy is that their cooking, even though it's far from Odile's standard, is honest enough and the staff are probably charming farm children who would be delightful if someone freed them from the muzzle of pretentiousness."

Of course, he was right. He always was about restaurants. The staff had the look and feel of cheerful paysans, but they minced around with their faces locked into the stiff rictuses of croupiers or undertakers. Capucine was tempted to pinch one to see if she could elicit a human reaction.

After dessert, fabulously overpriced after-dinner drinks arrived and the sycophantism shifted into high gear with speeches dripping with praise for the chairman's inexorable and courageous quest for a better world, making no reference at all to the acquisition of the Elevage Vienneau, which, after all—even though it was the object of the dinner—was merely a relatively small financial operation when compared to Opportunité's global aspirations. Alexandre busied himself with the double-barreled delights of spelunking in the telephone-book-thick drinks list for the most expensive Armagnac the restaurant possessed—which he intended to consume copiously at Opportunité's expense—and charming a black-clad waitress, who looked to be nineteen at the most, to see if she could be made to giggle without cracking her makeup. Capucine decided she was extraneous to both pursuits and set off in search of the lady's loo.

It turned out that the restaurant also served as one of the amenities of a hotel three doors down the road, to which it was linked by a long, serpentine corridor that wound its way through the intervening buildings. The road to the indoor plumbing seemed endless, filled with wrong turns and dead ends, an eternal detour in a surrealist movie that was supposed to signify something profound. Eventually, Capucine blundered into a cul-de-sac ending with a frosted-glass-paneled door that opened into a small, gloomy, mahogany-paneled bar. Vienneau sat slumped on a bar stool, moodily sipping amber liquid from an oversized on-the-rocks glass.

He greeted Capucine as if he had known she would arrive. He held up his glass. "It's Yamazaki, a Japanese single-malt whiskey. I'm having a rebellion against things French," he said. "Have one. I owe you at least a drink."

"Loïc, you shot Philippe Gerlier, didn't you?"

"Of course I did. I never met a man who deserved more to die."

"But he was your henchman."

"That he was. But he was also fucking my wife." Vienneau downed his whiskey and tapped his finger on the bar to attract the attention of the barman, who shot him a surly I'll-get-to-you-when-I-get-to-you look that was refreshing after the android responses of the rest of the staff. Eventually, two glasses of Japanese whiskey were produced and Vienneau picked up the thread of his tale.

"You're goddamn right I killed him. It took me a while to find the opportunity. I had to wait until the shooting season started, and then I nudged your uncle into inviting him and then prodded him into posting Gerlier near the center of the line. I knew I'd be placed not too far away. The first drive turned out to be ideal. I waited until the partridge rose at the crest of the hill and then let him have both barrels right in the chest when everyone was looking up. It did me a world of good." He slammed his glass down.

The bartender, who was no longer making the slightest pretense of not listening, came over with the bottle of Yamazaki and added an inch to both glasses.

"You did this because he was having an affair with Marie-Christine."

"No, no. Not at all. Marie-Christine always needed to be having an affair with someone. It was part of her psyche and I don't blame her for it, the way you can't really blame a dog for stealing scraps off the dinner table." He downed half of his drink.

"Merde. If I had gone around shooting all the people she'd slept with, Saint-Nicolas would be a ghost town." He laughed and finished his drink. The bartender, who was now leaning across from them, elbows on the bar, as if he were officially included in the conversation, poured another two inches in Vienneau's glass.

"I killed that fucker because he wasn't even really interested in screwing her. He didn't love her. He didn't have the hots for her. He didn't even like her. He was doing it because she was there for the taking and he just couldn't pass up a freebie." Vienneau pushed a bowl of peanuts toward Capucine to illustrate his point, drunkenly spilling half of them on the bar.

He collected himself. "Look, how do you think I knew he'd be such a willing flunky with the hormones when I interviewed him? It was obvious he didn't have a shred of integrity. I hired that guy when he had been thrown out of some small élevage in the Limousin for petty embezzlement. I needed someone to take over day-to-day operations, and that included dosing the cattle on the sly. Gerlier didn't give a shit. He was happy to do anything. He had no scruples at all. He did exactly the job I wanted him to do. But I wasn't going to let him get away with treating my wife like some scullery maid you fuck because there's nothing on TV, now was I?"

"Why did you need an assistant all of a sudden?"

"So you know I'd been using hormones since the day I took over the élevage, do you? Well, I was. You're right. I took over a dying business and moved it to the top. And when I'd done it, I just didn't want to get my hands dirty anymore. I wanted to do statesmanlike stuff, like running the breeders' association and things like that. I wanted to act like the company chairman I was. And Gerlier was my man. He was perfect. In a way it was Marie-Christine who screwed everything up, but it wasn't even really her fault."

Capucine looked at him as he swallowed the last gulp of his whiskey.

"And you really had to use the hormones?"

"Of course I did. How else are you going to get beef of that quality and still put a few euros in your wallet? Shit, why do you think I sold out to those clowns?" He laughed cynically. "No hormones and they'll be producing supermarket quality at best. But they know that. All they want is the brand." He shook his head, overwhelmed by the strength of his logic.

There was a long pause as Vienneau chewed an ice cube

and spat the bits back in the glass. The vulgarity of the gesture so irritated the bartender, he snatched it up and returned with a fresh one, devoid of ice, filled nearly to the brim with whiskey.

"So tell me," Vienneau asked, "how did you know?"

"How did I know that you killed Gerlier? I suspected from the beginning it wasn't accidental. The shot pattern was too tight and the angle was wrong for it to have been someone from down the hill. It had to have been someone right next to him, and that meant the person had shot him on purpose. But when my officer discovered you had been signing the expense chits for Gerlier's trips to America while you let the accountant sign all his other vouchers, then I knew for sure."

Vienneau, now the drunken sage, nodded wisely.

"What's still not clear to me is if you were involved with Devere's and Bellec's deaths," Capucine said.

"Nope, I had nothing at all to do with either of them. Martel was entirely my good friend Gerlier's creation. You see, one of Gerlier's roles was to be a *cordon sanitaire,* my security buffer, if anything went sour. He was the fall guy. I didn't want to know what he was up to. To tell you the truth, I had no idea Martel was working for Gerlier. Of course, when Devere and Bellec were shot, I had a hunch Martel might be behind it, the same way you did, but, hey, it wasn't my problem, was it? All I can say is that I'm glad that's all over and I can get on to something else," he said in a tone of someone who has just finished an irksome task like washing his car or doing his taxes.

"So tell me, Commissaire"—he drew the word out to extract the maximum irony—"how many times have you had the murderer confess over a friendly drink and not been able to do one single goddamn thing about it?"

Capucine decided it was high time to get back to Alexandre and began the long trek to the restaurant. For a few seconds she toyed with the idea of acting on Vienneau's confession and then chided herself for her rookie's reaction. Even signed confessions witnessed by two officers of the law were ridiculously easy to overturn in court, and this had just been drunken boasting witnessed only by a bartender who was certain to swear he hadn't heard a word. It was always the same: no evidence, no case. And there never was any evidence in hunting accidents.

At one point in her lengthy odyssey Capucine remembered she had yet to find the little lady detective's room and began exploring passageways she had ignored on the way out. In a narrow side hallway she almost collided with Henri Bellanger, who achieved the impossible by looking even more pleased with himself than usual, sporting a deep apricot tan of the sort obtainable only in the Caribbean and apparently genuinely delighted at the encounter.

"Actually," he said, "I came looking for you. I saw you leave the restaurant and thought I'd find you out here somewhere. I'd hoped to be able to buy you a drink. I owe you a considerable debt."

"How so, Monsieur Bellanger?"

"Thanks to you I just collected a very healthy fee. If you hadn't solved the case, I don't think Monsieur Vienneau would have sold his business. That psychopath Martel would have eased into Gerlier's job, and it would have been business as usual. Vienneau would never have divested."

Capucine, who from her days in the fiscal branch of the Police Judiciaire was fully conversant with the structure of investment bankers' fees, was perplexed. "Surely, the sale of the Elevage Vienneau couldn't have been that important to you."

"Oh, but it was. You see, it was necessary to structure a very complex financial montage. In addition to the usual tax issues, there was a tricky divorce in the works. Of course, I charged a good deal for that."

"Financial montage?"

"Yes, just between you and me, the bulk of the transaction was offshore. So, not only did I map out the transaction, but I portaged the shares for a little while and brokered the transfer of funds from one holding company to another until they wound up, well, wherever they wound up. And, naturally, my fee reflected all that activity."

"Are you trying to tell me the funds are all hidden in some fiscal paradise like the Isle of Jersey?"

"Oh, my dear, how you date yourself. No one but the sort of people who want to buy cashmere twinsets goes to Jersey anymore. Nowadays it's all done with puts and calls and anonymous escrows in faraway places." His toothy smile was made all the whiter by his deep tan.

Back at the restaurant Capucine found that the Opportunité executives had all left and Alexandre had lit a cigar, pulled back his chair, and was telling a long story to the waitress, now sitting on the edge of the table, fully reverted to her gangly teenage persona. As Capucine walked up, she was wrinkling her nose and attempting to take a sip from a comically large snifter while giggling uncontrollably. She caught sight of Capucine through the enormous glass, blushed deeply, and darted off.

"I see you had a lot more fun than I did." She picked up the huge snifter and took a deep draft. "What is this stuff?"

"Something that was allegedly put in a bottle in eighteen ninety-three. Its most impressive attribute is its price."

Capucine drained the glass. "Order me another one."

"I'll do even better. There's one on the list that claims to have been bottled in eighteen fifty-four. Your trip to the ladies' seems to have been eventful."

"I ran into both the bad guys."

"Was it who and what you thought it was?"

"Almost exactly. Except I did learn that the Channel Isles are no longer in vogue."

Alexandre demanded little of his wife except the privilege of having the last word, something she was always happy to grant him. "So," he said, "tradition still prevails and the two national pastimes—tax evasion and eliminating one's enemies with bird shot—continue unabated. As Alphonse Karr, that good boss of *Le Figaro,* liked to say, '*Plus ça change, plus c'est la même chose*'—the more it changes, the more it's the same. Continuity is so reassuring."